MW01171847

TERRAN FOUNDATIONS

BOOK 2 OF
THE TERRAN SPACE PROJECT

Alex Rath

Theogony Books
Coinjock, NC

Chris Kennedy/Theogony Books
1097 Waterlily Rd.
Coinjock, NC 27923
https://chriskennedypublishing.com/

Publisher's Note: This is a work of fiction. Names, characters, places, and incidents are a product of the author's imagination. Locales and public names are sometimes used for atmospheric purposes. Any resemblance to actual people, living or dead, or to businesses, companies, events, institutions, or locales is completely coincidental.

Cover Design by J Caleb Design.

Ordering Information:
Quantity sales. Special discounts are available on quantity purchases by corporations, associations, and others. For details, contact the "Special Sales Department" at the address above.

Terran Foundations/Alex Rath -- 1st ed.
ISBN: 978-1648554223

For my Mom, who has been waiting for the next book. Here it is!

Chapter One

Captain Maxwell Reeves, leader of the Wormhole Traversal Project, a division of the Terran Space Project, had faced many challenges over his life, but it seemed each day looked to break the record. Nearly two months ago, the TSP *Traveler*, Earth's first extra-solar manned mission, had left Earth. There had been many who thought sending so many people through the wormhole was insanity. Many small crew or solo missions were proposed, but the TSP was determined to go through with its effort, and Max had volunteered and been chosen to lead it. The TSP was the only organization with the technology for it, so no other group—or nation—had decided to even try.

The Terran Space Project, a non-profit organization headquartered in Switzerland, had drawn massive economic backing from some of the wealthiest men and women on Earth, and with that power, had hired the brightest minds humanity had to offer. There were already colonies on Earth's moon, as well as Mars, though terraforming was still just a fantasy, and the simple and irrefutable fact was that Earth was dying. Humanity needed a new home, and it was supposed to be *Traveler's* mission to find it.

A probe launched through the wormhole outside the Sol system had arrived in Alpha Centauri, or so everyone had been told, so they'd sent *Traveler* with its complement of four hundred crew and colonists, with Max as its leader. Now, Max knew differently. The probe sighting had been a lie, a creative and impressive fabrication led by Gustav Malmkvist, the CEO of the Terran Space Project. So, instead of receiving more colonists and supplies in fourteen years, it would never come. They were stranded on an alien planet—named Mythos by majority vote—and were making their way.

Max and the brave volunteers had arrived somewhere that matched no star charts they had, so they'd adapted and moved forward. New species were being cataloged every day, to the joy and excitement of the science teams, and all 376 of the team from Earth were keeping busy. Well, 375 really—one had been exiled to the other side of the planet for carrying out an armed insurrection. The other 23 had died either on the journey, because of the hostile alien environment, or during the attempted coup, which Max tried not to think about.

Now, Max knelt in an alien space craft, on an alien planet, looking at the mummified remains of what he could only call an alien being. The light from the helmet-mounted lamp of Colonel Essena Mikhailovna—the MilForce commander—illuminated the compartment that held three humanoid flight suits, and he'd removed the helmet from this one. The head was human-like, but nothing he'd ever seen.

"*You two okay in there?*" Leopold Fischer, the third member of the team at the ship, asked over the radio in his helmet.

"Yeah… You're not going to believe this. We found the flight crew."

"*Crikey!*" Fischer exclaimed, his Australian accent kicking in full force.

"Let's get out of here. I need to figure out how to handle this," Max said as he stood.

Essena led the way out of the ship to join Fischer outside. Fischer was the ship's primary ethologist, and was along because, still much to Max's surprise, they'd ridden honest-to-goodness *griffins* out to the site. They'd come early in the morning, so there was still plenty of daylight from the three stars in the trinary system to work with. There wasn't a clearing anywhere nearby suited for the aircraft they'd brought along. The BN-12 airframe, with its eight ducted and gimbaled fans, would have been perfect for getting in and out via hoist, but they were grounded until they dealt with some mechanical issues.

Max crossed his arms over his chest, as best he could in the environment suit he wore to protect against possible toxins, while he thought. All their communication satellites had been destroyed during Ragnarsson's insurrection, so there was no easy way to get in touch with the city, Eos. It was an hour back to the city by griffin, but that was their only option. At least, that's what he thought, until he heard the engines of an X-94 interplanetary space plane fly over.

"*Eagle to Reeves,*" Colin "Eagle" Shepard transmitted.

"Reeves here, clear copy. What are you doing back up?"

"*Well, I couldn't let you guys have all the fun. What did you find?*"

"Oh, not much. Just an alien spacecraft and the bodies of three aliens," Max said casually.

"*Not funny.*"

"Not joking."

"*No shit? What's the plan, boss?*"

"I don't know yet," Max admitted. "Obviously, we need to do a lot more analysis on the craft, and we're going to want to autopsy the bodies. Leopold, I'd really like to clear cut some of this area so we can land."

"I'm not too sure how they'd like that," Leopold said, referring to the griffins, who disliked it when they cut down anything. They'd found that out the hard way when the griffins had destroyed several of what they'd thought to be indestructible machines.

"Can we explain that we'll get this ship out of here if we can do that?" Max asked. "They don't seem to like the ship."

"Yeah, there's somethin' to that, I reckon. I'll see if I can get it across," he said and walked over toward where the griffins were waiting.

"Eagle, fly back in range of Eos, and let the PCC know we're okay, and what we've found," Max said.

The Planetary Control Center was the nerve center for the entire planetary operation. He knew Kellie Warren would be there, waiting for word on their status. She'd probably sent Eagle out to check on them. That was slightly against protocol, but he and Kellie had begun a sort of relationship on the planet recently.

"*Copy that. Be back in a few.*"

Max watched Leopold communicate with the griffins as the X-94 roared off into the distance. Leopold talked through the speaker in his suit, but also mimed actions. It was odd to watch, but Leopold spent a good bit of time with the griffins, and they'd established a sort of communication. A few of the griffins, these three to be exact, had been spending more time in the city. They were the chosen ambassadors or just the most curious of the griffins in their territory. After a few moments, one griffin turned and flew off.

Leopold returned to Max and Essena and shrugged. "I think he's going to check with the rest of their group."

Max shook his head in wonderment. "That'll never stop being amazing."

"So what're we gonna do?"

"Well, if we can clearcut the area, we'll bring in a mobile analysis unit and set up here. I'm treating this just like we did anything transported back and forth from Mars. There could be potential pathogens we've never heard of or seen that could be deadly. I'm not sure I want anything from this ship back in the city—for now at least. It'll be essential scientific personnel only."

Leopold and Essena both nodded.

Max walked back toward the crash path the ship had made when it came down and looked at the growth. Essena was close by his side, constantly scanning the surroundings. She took her job as the head of the MilForce extremely seriously, and even more so since Max had almost died during Adel Ragnarsson's insurrection while trapped in the PCC with her. He looked at the foliage growth in the crash path, thinking about a crash investigation to consider how long the ship might have been there. The fact that the ship had been covered with vines wasn't really an indicator. On Earth, that would have meant it had been there for a good length of time, but the growth rate of some things on this planet was rapid compared to anything they'd seen back home.

"I wish I knew the growth patterns of these things better. It's hard to tell how long this thing has been here."

"Natural mummification can happen within two or three weeks," Essena stated. Her Russian origin—former Spetsnaz—was clear to anyone who heard her talk, but she never failed to get her point across.

"Really?" Max asked.

"Yes. Have seen it. Space suit is perfect environment. Sealed, no oxygen. Temperature in ship is high."

Max nodded thoughtfully. He hadn't really noticed the temperature, since the suit self-regulated for him, but he wasn't surprised she had.

"Well, I'm pretty sure we would've noticed if it had come in recently, so we can safely say it's been here *at least* a little over a month."

Calling it a month was relative. The length of the day here differed from Earth—only a 20-hour cycle instead of 24, which had been broken into two ten-hour halves—and the year cycle would be different as well. To keep some semblance of familiarity, the standard Earth calendar was still observed so people could celebrate things like birthdays and anniversaries.

Max looked up when he heard a *boom*, assuming it was the sonic boom of Eagle's X-94 returning, but then frowned. Since they'd arrived on the planet, the weather had been what could only be described as perfect. It looked like that was about to change.

"Look," he said and pointed at darkening clouds on the horizon he could see through the crash path.

"That looks like a right nasty storm, mate," Fischer said, concerned.

"Yeah, let's get inside the ship," Max agreed.

As they turned and walked back toward the ship, Leopold proved to be right. The wind picked up from virtually nothing to gusting hard enough for Max to notice in just a few steps. They went from a walk to a run and made it to the ship just as sheets of rain started pelting them.

"Damn, that's fast," Max said, panting a bit. Maybe he wasn't as recovered from his medical issues as he'd thought.

"You are okay?" Essena asked.

He nodded. "I'll be fine," he said and grimaced after he turned away. Max had taken shrapnel to the abdomen during the insurrection, and while it had been repaired, he apparently still wasn't 100 percent.

Thunder clapped so loudly, he felt the reverberations through his suit, and lightning struck nearby. It was so bright, the automatic light filtering on his helmet kicked in to protect his vision. The rain came down hard enough that he could barely see a few meters beyond the hatch.

"Well, might as well poke around a bit more. I'm going to get another look at the cockpit."

Max walked through the ship to the cockpit, with Essena and Leopold close on his heels.

There were two forward-facing seats, narrow and tall, obviously built for the space suits they'd found in the back. A third seat faced the side and another panel of screens. The layout was reminiscent of old aircraft layouts, with a pilot, copilot, and navigator. As much as he wanted to test the systems with the buttons and switches he saw accessible, he resisted temptation and determined to leave that until they could be in a more controlled environment. As a test pilot, he was used to learning new systems quickly, but this time, there was no manual.

He pursed his lips for a moment, then looked beside the seats, under them, and looked for any cabinets or access panels he could open.

"What are you doing?" Essena asked.

Max grinned when he turned a latch and slid open a compartment above what he assumed was the navigator's station. He pointed at four huge bound books.

"Those are very likely at least the emergency procedures for this craft. If our linguists can figure them out, we can probably learn a lot."

"Geez. Just the emergency ones, eh?" Leopold said with a chuckle.

"I'd assume, like ours, they're all electronic, but even in *Traveler*, some of the emergency procedures are in good, old-fashioned books, in case of an electronics failure."

The characters on the binders were utterly foreign, and he didn't know where to start. He knew, though, that among the population, there were several linguists in case of what was considered an incredibly unlikely scenario. First contact.

* * *

Mythos, Eos City, Planetary Control Center

Kellie Warren sat on the raised center platform of the Planetary Control Center in Max's normal seat and waited anxiously to hear back from Eagle. Every station in the PCC was staffed—at least those that were useful at the moment. Some of them, like satellite tracking, were empty, since there were no satellites left to monitor. The main screen at the front of the room was subdivided and showed images from various angles around the city, mostly pointing toward the perimeter, as they were always watching for new wildlife to appear.

She'd sent Eagle to check on Max and the others when they hadn't come back in a few hours. It made sense that it would take a while, but still, she worried. She thought about the previous night, when she'd stayed with Max, and smiled. He certainly didn't deserve what Annica had done to him, and if Kellie was honest with herself, she'd always been a bit jealous of Max and Annica's relationship. She knew Max was special, and hoped last night wasn't just a fluke, or a moment of weakness.

"*Eagle to Center.*"

"Kellie, here. What's going on, Colin?"

"*Captain Reeves and crew are doing fine. They got inside the ship and— well, it's aliens.*"

"You're joking."

"*I said the same thing, but it's for real. I saw a hell of a storm pop up on radar behind me, with no warning at all, but it doesn't seem to be headed this way.*"

"You think they'll be okay?" she asked.

"*Oh, sure. They can get into the ship for cover. They'll be fine, Kellie. Max has survived Mars. This is a cakewalk.*"

"I know. Thanks, Colin. Get back overhead in their range as soon as it's safe."

"*Will do. Now that I know they're good, I'll try to find a point where I can get enough altitude to patch you both in.*"

Kellie nodded, though she knew he couldn't see her. Without communication satellites, the only way to get that kind of range would be for one of their aircraft to rise up over any interference and get in a position where it could pick up signals from both points.

"Have a minute, Kellie?" Azeema el-Mir asked.

Azeema was on the passenger council—*city* council, Kellie corrected herself—and was also in charge of all the construction efforts on the planet.

"A little busy, but I have a few minutes. What's up?"

"I just wanted to let you know, we're taking a rover out to the ore site Eagle found when he was scouting. Hopefully it's something we can use to craft satellite parts at the manufactory, since we're out of the raw materials. Lina's coming, too."

Kellie nodded. Lina Skoog, also on the council, was a survivalist and could climb any rough terrain they encountered.

"Be sure a few folks from MilForce go with you. There are still plenty of unknowns out there. Also, watch the weather. Apparently, a severe storm just popped up over where Max is, with no warning."

"I'm sure they, and we, will be fine. Thank you, Kellie," she said with a reassuring smile, then turned and left.

Kellie hoped the resources Colin had picked up on his scan could be mined and would work. She was finding out just how rough life was before the era of 24/7 satellite coverage, and she didn't like it very much. If they could manufacture them, getting them to orbit would be no problem. One of the X-94s could simply fly it up and insert it right where they wanted it. Communications would be first, but then they'd get weather, navigation, and observation satellites back up.

"*I'm sure they will be fine, Kellie,*" said Annie, *Traveler*'s AI, through the desk's speaker.

"I know. I just worry."

"*Understandable. Perhaps some breathing exercises would help. Your pulse and breathing rates are elevated.*"

"I'll be fine. Any luck with modifying the systems on *Traveler* to enhance communication ranges?"

"Unfortunately, the thick foliage on the planet creates an environment where, no matter what modifications I make, the waves cannot penetrate. I can explain in more detail if you like."

"No, no. That's fine. Thanks for trying."

"Of course, Kellie. I'm here to help."

* * *

Mythos, Crash Site

Max couldn't stop himself from pulling down one of the bulky books. He cradled it in his left arm and flipped it open to a random page.

"Someone's got their work cut out for them."

Based on the spacing, the text flowed vertically, rather than horizontally, as most languages on Earth did. As he turned the pages, he saw a few diagrams he could match to panel configurations, so that was at least a start. He hoped, using that, they'd be able to decipher the language, though he didn't know how long it would take. Annie could probably help there, too.

He closed and hefted the book back into place. Once that was done, he stood still and listened.

"Has the storm passed already?" he asked.

"Will check," Essena said and walked back toward the hatch. "Is sunny again. Is safe."

"We have 'em like that back home," Leopold said. "Just pop up, raise a ruckus, then move on."

"Don't like the weather? Wait a minute," Max mumbled as he and Leopold joined Essena outside the hatch.

Out of curiosity, he looked to where the griffins had been, and they were still there, sitting as if nothing had happened.

"Doesn't seem to have bothered them at all."

Movement caught his eye, and he saw the third griffin swoop down, spread its wings to catch the air and slow his descent, and land beside the others.

"Reckon I'll see what they have to say," Leopold said and walked toward them.

While he checked on that, Max looked around for evidence of damage from the storm, but there was nothing. He'd expected at least a downed tree, but the only evidence that there'd been a storm at all was the vines they'd cut away from the ship had blown away, and everything was soaking wet.

The griffin who'd just arrived walked toward them, with Leopold in tow, and stopped in the crash path. It spread its wings and motioned forward with them until the tips met, pointing down the path. Max figured he knew what that meant, but waited for Leopold.

"If I'm getting this right, which I think I am, it looks like they're okay with us clearing the path the ship made when it came down," Leopold said.

"That was my guess. I think that'll be enough. We'll get a few of the X-94s to load up and drop cutting equipment and crews. We'll have to do it by hand, at least until we clear a landing zone."

"And be careful things cut do not cut back," Essena said.

Max nodded. That was good advice, since one of the first trees they'd encountered on the planet had defensive roots that had actually killed one of their scientists, and Essena had watched it happen. The roots of what they called killer trees could snake up out of the ground, like whips with thorns, and anything it scraped was likely to die. It had taken her a while to get over that, since she'd felt responsible.

"We've got reinforced suits they can wear. I also want them to drop an air sampling package so we can find out if we can get rid of these helmets."

"*Eagle to Reeves. How copy?*"

"Clear copy, Eagle," Max said and looked up, surprised he hadn't heard the plane return.

"*Wait one.*"

Max crossed his arms over his chest and waited. Less than a minute later, the channel clicked again.

"*Center, online?*" Colin said.

"*I'm here,*" Kellie answered.

"Hey, Kellie," Max said with a smile.

"*Thank the Goddess! Are you okay? Colin said there was a bad storm.*"

"It was pretty bad, but yeah, we're fine. We're all fine."

He could hear her sigh of relief. "*Good. What's the plan?*"

"We have permission from our feathered friends to clear the crash path to use as a landing zone. I need cutting equipment and operators, and an air quality package. Make sure the ground team wears reinforced suits. They're not the most comfortable, but we don't know what kind of foliage they'll be cutting through. Once we clear enough area, I'm going to want full teams out here for survey and analysis of the ship. We've got written manuals, and I'll bring one back for Annie to work on, so we'll want linguists on the team as well. Have a mobile decontamination unit there when I land, so it'll be safe to handle. Also, I want at least one aircraft always on station for comms relay. Eagle, set up a rotation for that. I never want the teams we leave out here isolated."

"*Yes, sir,*" Eagle responded.

"*Okay, got it,*" Kellie said. "*I'll get the teams assembled immediately. I'd send Lina, but she went out with Azeema to check out the ore deposit Colin found.*"

"Essena, we'll also want protection for the teams, just in case," Max said.

"Will arrange," she agreed.

"Okay. Once the cutting teams are down, we'll fly back on the griffins."

"*I'll stay on station until you're away,*" Colin said. "*Two more planes are prepping now to drop the teams in. I'm a little worried about that, boss.*"

It was a valid concern. Typically, the BN-12's ducted fans made it perfect for rappelling into an area like this, but using the X-94 was a different animal altogether. It could hover well enough, but it used jets, which meant the person going down had to maintain damn good control of their descent to avoid getting cooked, and they had to go fast in case the wind pushed them the wrong way.

"Kellie, make sure anyone we select for the cutting team has fast rappelling experience. Coming down from an X-94 isn't without risk."

"*Got it,*" she said.

"Okay, Leopold. Let our friends know we've got more planes coming in."

He nodded and walked over to the lead griffin again.

"We've really got to come up with names for them," Max said absently.

* * * * *

Chapter Two

Earth, Terran Space Project Campus, Director's Office

Annica Reeves felt immense satisfaction as the body of Gustav Malmkvist slid to the floor. Gustav—the head of the Terran Space Project, until she'd put a bullet through his head—had done something to her. She wasn't sure what, yet, but she knew he'd done *something* that had made her forget the last month, and he'd somehow been in control of her actions during that time. Her husband, Maxwell, was somewhere in space, and she'd find out where, and get to him, no matter what it took.

First, she needed to prepare herself. She hadn't thought much past killing Gustav once she'd come out of whatever he'd inflicted on her, but now she needed to figure out how to stay out of prison. Thankfully, the TSP was pretty much a set of laws unto itself. Though based in Switzerland, they were privately funded and handled all their own security. There had never been a murder on the campus, so this was new ground. If Gustav had enough influence over people to deceive everyone in the program into thinking the probe had arrived in Alpha Centauri, he'd either had quite a few people brainwashed or had plenty of people loyal to whatever his goal was.

The door burst open, and two members of the TSP's MilForce, their own private security group, entered and cleared the room. Once

19

they saw the situation and knew no one was hiding, they both aimed their weapons at her.

"Put the gun down, Mrs. Reeves," Captain Konda Sanako said.

Annica knew Konda pretty well. Konda had been a candidate for the *Traveler* but had backed out in the last cycle of selection for family reasons. That could work in Annica's favor.

Annica ejected the magazine, pulled the slide to clear the chamber, and set the gun down.

"Weapons down," Konda ordered as she slung her rifle. The other guard, Sergeant Anton Essen, followed suit.

"What happened?" Konda asked and looked down at the obviously deceased Gustav Malmkvist.

Annica considered her answer. The truth would justify her actions, but she had no way of proving it. Unfortunately, she'd never been a very good liar, so that's what she'd have to go with.

"He admitted to me that he'd done something to control me since the day before the probe was sighted. I just came out of it this morning and realized something was very wrong. I have no idea what I've done or said for the past month, but apparently, I left Max—which you know I would never do—and stayed here with... *him*! He also admitted that he faked the probe sighting, and he had no idea where *Traveler* was. He let me out of whatever he'd done because he said he needed me back at full capacity, since whatever he'd done left me, in his words, 'dull-witted.' When he told me, I had access to everything, and... I just couldn't handle it. So I killed him."

Konda and Anton both wore unreadable expressions. She knew from playing poker with Konda that she had an excellent poker face, so there was no telling what was going through her head.

"Do you have any proof of any of this?" Konda asked.

"I don't suppose there are security cameras in here?" Annica asked hopefully.

"No, ma'am," Anton answered.

Annica sighed and thought quickly. "Konda, you know me, and you know Max. I would never leave him. I was supposed to be on *Traveler*. It was a dream come true for both of us! I would never agree to send my husband and four hundred people off to an unknown destination."

"I thought it was odd you didn't go," Konda admitted. "I even asked you about it, remember?"

"No," Annica said and looked down at the ground. "I don't."

"I'm in a tough position here, Annica," she said.

"I know, and I'm sorry. I just... Let me sit at the terminal. Maybe there's something there. He said I'd have access to everything," she said and looked up to meet Konda's eyes, pleading.

Konda shrugged. "Why not?"

They stood back and gave her room to stand and walk around to sit behind Gustav's desk. Annica sat down, activated the terminal, and searched for anything that would prove her story. It wasn't hard. He hadn't lied. She had access to everything. That included email traffic with the people he'd conspired with to fake the probe sighting. She shook her head, wondering what had made him think she wouldn't go public with this information as soon as she saw it. Did he really think she'd fallen for him? It amazed her that Gustav hadn't even tried to hide what he'd done. The emails were there, which established a timeline. She couldn't find anything about how he'd controlled her, but she didn't doubt she'd eventually find it.

"Well, here's proof that he faked the probe sighting. That in itself is a violation of the very spirit of the TSP," she said, and stood so Konda could sit and read what she'd found.

Konda looked at her for a moment, then sat and stared at the terminal. She scrolled through several messages and opened attachments. Annica could still see the screen, and could see that the attachments were various phases and angles of a probe on a screen, just like she'd expect to see in the control center.

"This is... troubling," Konda said.

"Doesn't prove much," Anton said.

"I know Annica and Max, Sergeant. She definitely hasn't been herself lately."

"Still."

She sighed. "I know. Annica, we're going to have to confine you to quarters while we check all this out. If everything you're saying is true, the techs can find it all."

"How do you know you won't end up with techs who were loyal to him and will bury the truth?" Annica asked.

"We could bring in someone from the outside," Anton suggested.

Konda shook her head. "Whoever does this will have access to *everything*. I don't know about bringing in an outsider."

"One of the things we've always prided ourselves on is that our mission is to assist and benefit all of humanity, not just members of the program," Annica said. "We have nothing to hide."

"If all this is true, and it goes public..." Konda said.

"Then we'll probably lose all our funding and never find *Traveler*," Annica finished, dejected.

"I still have friends in the PSIA," Konda mused. "I'm sure I could get one of them in, and they know how to keep their mouths shut."

Annica considered. She didn't know much about the PSIA, other than it was Japan's Public Security Intelligence Agency.

"We need to run this up the chain," Anton said.

"No," Konda said immediately. "I don't know who to trust at this point. Nothing about this leaves this room."

"Captain, we're going to have to log Mr. Malmkvist's death. Someone's going to have to take over the Project."

Konda turned back to the terminal and typed quickly.

"Well. Isn't that something?"

"What's that?" Annica asked.

"Looks like you're in charge now, Mrs. Reeves," she said, and stood, gesturing to the seat.

Annica sat and read the screen. It was a new directive, put in place mere days ago, that assigned her as the successor to his position in the event something happened to him. She wondered if he'd had an idea of what she might do when he'd lifted whatever fog she'd been in.

"What now?" Anton asked.

"See if you can bring in one of your friends, Konda," Annica said. "I want to know what the hell is going on."

"Yes, ma'am. Anton, seal off the office, and get a body bag and take care of Mr. Malmkvist's body. Get help if you need it, but only people you can really trust."

"Am I still confined to quarters?" Annica asked.

Konda considered for a moment. "I think that would be best. I'm sure you can do whatever you need to do from there."

"People are going to ask about Gustav."

"We'll put out word that he's passed, and that you're now in charge. You're secluded while you recover from the loss and assume your new role."

"Okay. That works. Thank you."

"Don't thank me yet. If all this doesn't check out, I'll hand you over to the Swiss authorities."

"I know. But it will. Thank you for at least giving me a chance," she said and stood after she shut down the terminal.

"I'll escort you to your apartment," Konda said. "Anton, the room is yours."

"Yes, ma'am. I'll take care of it."

* * *

Earth, Terran Space Project Campus, Annica's Apartment

Annica sat down on the couch in the living room of their apartment and noticed immediately that all the pictures of them as a couple were gone. She'd held it together as long as she could, and the flood gates finally let go. She closed her eyes, and her heart ached as she thought about Max, wondered where he was, and if he was okay. She sobbed uncontrollably and curled into a ball on the couch as it hit her in a tidal wave of emotion. Max had been gone for over a month, and suddenly she *felt* that month of time, even though she didn't know exactly what had happened. She knew he was gone, and she was here. Alone.

She wasn't sure how long she lay there, but eventually, the well of tears ran dry. With a heavy sigh, she stood and walked to the apartment's kitchen to grab a bottle of red wine, which she'd hidden away in the far back of a rarely used cabinet, and a glass, and she took them to the office. She used an old-fashioned corkscrew to extract the cork and poured some wine into the glass to let it breathe. While she waited, she booted up the terminal and pulled up her message queue. She needed to know what the hell she'd been doing for the past month.

Unfortunately, there was nothing of value there. Either she hadn't been doing much, or her messages had been cleared at some point. Annica hit a dead end there and went to Gustav's account—well, her account now. She looked again at the traffic related to the fake probe arrival in Alpha Centauri, but there was nothing there about why, which was all around when she'd lost time. She kept looking and saw many emails of congratulations from world leaders on the successful launch of the *Traveler*, which put her somewhere between crying again and ripping the terminal from its mount on the desk in anger. She should have been on the ship with Max, but she'd been robbed of that.

Moving on to look at more recent messages, she found communication about monitoring a certain set of frequencies, but no reason given, which was confusing. At the top of the queue, there was only one unread message, and it was a self-sent message, from this account back to itself, with the subject 'In the Event of my Untimely Demise.'

She smirked as she opened the message, which launched a video attachment. The rage that welled up within her made her clench her fists until her knuckles cracked when she saw Gustav's face on the screen.

"*Annica, if you're seeing this, I suppose the lower percentage outcome came to pass, and you're now in charge. I'm sure you're wondering what's happened, and how it happened, but honestly, it doesn't really matter,*" he said, and waved his hand dismissively, which caused her to clench her teeth at his nonchalance at what he had done.

"*What matters is what comes next. We don't know exactly where they are, but I'm quite sure it's not Alpha Centauri. Maxwell has the blueprint for a high speed communication satellite, and when I say high speed, I mean* high speed. *Faster than anything we've ever imagined. It was provided by some... friends from out of town. I'm sure you'll dig and find out all about that, but I'm going to make you work for that one. Let's just say, it's important that the team keeps listening on the frequency I've provided. If they do, hopefully Maxwell will build and put the satellite into space so we can find them. If not...*" he said with a shrug.

"*I'm sorry, Annica, but that's all you get for free. You did kill me, after all, and being dead, I really don't care anymore, though some friends might. So good luck and goodbye.*"

"You *bastard!*" she screamed and slammed her fist on the desk hard enough to send waves across the surface of the wine in her glass.

She picked up the wine and gulped it down, only to pour another glass and drink half of it before she set it down. After she took a deep breath to calm herself, she replayed the message several times, and paid closer attention to the details. *Friends from out of town*, she thought. *That's not a hint at all.*

The way he'd had said it felt odd, so she dove into the file storage folders for the Wormhole Traversal Project. She ignored the general access folders and went into folders marked Secure, which wouldn't even appear in the list for a normal user. For the next few hours, she read through document after document. Some of them were interesting, but none of them pointed to anything out of the ordinary. She went to pour another glass of wine, only to find the bottle empty. She'd finished it without thinking while she was researching.

With a groan, she sighed and shut the terminal down. It would have to wait; she could already feel the wine going to her head. She made her way to the bedroom, only stumbling a few times, and fell into bed without even bothering to get undressed.

"I'll find you, Max. I'll find you," she whispered into the pillow as she closed her eyes and drifted off.

* * *

Earth, Terran Space Project Campus, MilForce Command

Captain Konda Sanako stood at attention before Colonel Shawn Carey, head of the TSP's MilForce.

"So you didn't arrest her?" he asked.

"She's confined to her apartment, sir."

"Would you care to explain why she's not in a cell, and why I had to hear about this through the grapevine?"

"Because she's now the director of the TSP, and the evidence she uncovered immediately appears to point to it being justified. I felt I could handle the situation without bothering you, sir."

"Are you letting your personal relationship with Mrs. Reeves get in the way of your judgment, Captain?"

"Sir, that's come up before, and it seems in that case, I was right. I think I'm right this time, too."

Konda bit her lip as Carey leaned back in his chair and drummed his fingers on his desk. There was a lot more she wanted to say, but she also didn't want Annica in shackles and locked in a cell. Especially if she was right.

"What's your plan?"

"I have a contact in the PSIA I'm going to bring in to do an independent review of the facts. I feel in this case, the facts will lead us where we need to go, rather than relying on opinions about someone's state of mind."

The last was a bit of a poke, and she instantly regretted it. She saw Carey's jaw clench, which was never a good sign, but he took a deep breath, then nodded.

"Okay, Captain. Bring in your expert. But he signs the normal NDA, and this stays quiet. Clear?"

"Crystal, sir."

"Dismissed."

* * * * *

Chapter Three

Landing + 36 Days
Mythos, Crash Site

Max watched anxiously as two X-94s flew in and hovered. The first plane dropped three pallets containing the gear the teams would need for the initial phase of the operation. The pallets had altitude-sensing airbags that deployed to cushion the landing when they were about twenty meters from the ground. Job completed, the plane flew back toward the city to load the next batch of equipment, which would include fully-equipped remote labs. Then came the part Max was dreading. Typically, personnel dropped from the X-94 would parachute in, or use wing suits with parachutes, but the thick canopy ruled out those options for any but expert paratroopers. With a close eye on the wind conditions, the plane dropped a penetrator, then the aircraft lifted until the line was almost taut. After a few moments of minute adjustments, the pilot locked in the auto-control system, and the team members came down one by one.

Max tried not to think of all the things that could go wrong and just hoped everything went right. Even with a perfect descent, the possibility of a broken ankle or leg—or worse—on landing was significant. Each team member would be using an auto-arrester on the line that should read the distance to the ground and slow their descent, but nothing was perfect. One by one, the team came down and cleared the landing zone for the next person. After about an hour, thanks to some delays due to wind conditions, everyone made it down without injury.

Everyone who came down, except for MilForce, who immediately set out to establish a broader perimeter, went to look at the crashed alien ship. Most of the team were cutters, so they weren't so much interested in the science of it, but it was certainly something they'd tell their kids about.

When the last person hit the ground, and the penetrator was reeled back in, two members of MilForce set to cutting away the straps on the pallets. The loadmaster had done a good job, and the air quality sensors were quickly unloaded from the top of the stack and set up. After about ten minutes of analysis, one of the scientists popped his helmet.

"All good. Safe to breathe—until they start cutting, anyway. We'll have to monitor what gets stirred up after that."

Max nodded and removed his own helmet. "Okay. Breathe free until the cutting starts. Might as well enjoy it while you can."

"We should get you back to city," Essena said from beside him.

"Yeah. I suppose so. Ready, Leopold?"

"Sure thing. They don't wanna be around for this anyway," he said as he led them toward the griffins.

"No?"

"Yeah. I don't totally get it yet."

Max nodded and reseated his helmet, both for communication purposes and comfort. He didn't want to think about the wind hitting his face at the speeds the griffins could fly.

"We're taking off, Eagle; the teams will start clearing the area shortly," Max said.

"Copy that. I'll be on station for a bit longer, then I'll be relieved. We have a rotation set up, so the team won't be isolated, per your orders."

"Thanks, Colin."

* * *

Mythos, Eos City

Max barely noticed the view as they flew back to Eos. His mind was racing with possibilities. Where had the ship come from? Why had it crashed? What would his crews find? Was anyone coming to look for the missing ship? Before he knew it, the griffin spread its wings to land, and he almost fell off from the jolt. Because he was so preoccupied, he wasn't holding on tightly enough.

"Dumbass," he said to himself as he climbed down.

As soon as he was down, they walked toward a mobile decontamination unit that had been hastily set up. He placed the book in a small cabinet, then they walked through and removed their suits after they'd been cleaned off.

Once out the other end, the cabinet was waiting for him.

"We've run it through a variable spectrum decontamination routine, so it's clean of anything we're aware of, and *should* be clean of anything we aren't."

"Should be?" Max asked the technician.

"We don't know what we don't know, Captain. I'll put it this way; I'd feel safe handling it. It's been through everything, including complete vacuum. The chances of anything surviving other than the book itself are slim to none."

"Well, I suppose that'll have to do. Thanks," he said, and removed the book from the cabinet.

He tucked the book under his arm and stepped away from the griffins, with Essena at his side. The lead griffin clacked his beak several times at Leopold, who nodded in response after removing his helmet.

"What was that about?" Max asked when Leopold walked over.

"They're going to get a bite to eat. Apparently, carrying the extra weight makes 'em hungry," he answered with a chuckle.

"Makes sense. Thanks, Leopold."

"I will set up guard rotation for site," Essena said and headed off toward *Traveler*, where the MilForce was still based. Barracks and a military headquarters were still being printed by the massive 3-D printer that was responsible for nearly all the structures that were currently in place.

Max headed toward the PCC and shed his helmet and suit in the entryway. While the decontamination lock was now permanently open, there were still hangers for the environmental suits, which he took advantage of. Finally rid of the suit and much more comfortable, he headed into the center and toward his station.

The PCC had become his second home in Eos. It was the only prefabricated structure on the planet, since it had been set up immediately upon planetfall to begin moving operations off *Traveler*. The walls were lined with stations for everything, from communications to security operations. Each station had at least four displays, all linked to the central computing power still on *Traveler*. A server room would be built eventually and the hardware moved, but that was still at least a month in the future. It would require excavation and a lot of raw materials that were meant to be collected from the planet. The front of the room was dominated by a single large display that could be split into as many views as necessary for anything that required more eyes than could gather around a station comfortably.

Before he got to his station, Kellie was on her feet and walked quickly over to him to wrap her arms around him.

"Glad you're back," she said into his shoulder.

He smiled and hugged her with the arm that wasn't holding the book. "Glad to be back. Come on, we have work to do."

She let him go after one more squeeze and walked with him.

"So what have you got there?" she asked when he set the book down on the desk.

"My guess would be, some kind of emergency procedures text or a manual for the ship. It was one of several, but I want Annie to get to work in parallel with the linguists we'll be sending out once the labs can be set down. It'll be a boring job, but get someone to put this in front of one of the high-res cameras, and flip through the pages, so she can record them all and start working on figuring it out."

"*Finally, something interesting to do,*" Annie said. "*I am glad to see your safe return, Max.*"

"Thanks, Annie. I'll also upload the camera footage from our suits, so you have some visuals to relate to the diagrams."

"*That will be helpful.*"

"Kellie, assign someone to this?"

"You got it. See you later," she said, picked up the book, and walked out of the PCC.

Max typed in the commands to pull the camera footage from all three suits and upload them for Annie's use and for the archive. Everyone would be able to access and view it, which should help alleviate the desire many would have to go to the site and see it firsthand. His hope was that, once as much analysis was done as could be done, they could figure out a way to bring the ship to the city. He knew the engineers would want to tear it apart, and he didn't want that done in the field.

They estimated that it would take the rest of the day to clear the crash site. If all went well, they'd have time to set up the portable runway, which would act as both a landing surface for the planes, and a level surface for the labs to set up. Thanks to the planetary rotation in the trinary system, there were only about four hours of total darkness out of the 20-hour day, so they had plenty of time to work. The trick was maintaining circadian rhythm. For that reason, the team also had tents that would go completely dark when sealed. Once the runway was set up, the team would be able to come back to the city after a shift of working.

The rest of the day, he went over the plans for the different types of analysis, and the personnel needed for each, that would occur out at the crash site. Kellie had it all set up, per his request from the site, and he didn't need to make any adjustments. With a nod of satisfaction, he changed gears to the expedition that had gone out with Azeema to check on the ore deposit.

"Any contact from Azeema's team?" he asked.

"They landed about an hour ago, sir," the person manning the comm station reported. "Nothing since then, but we were told to expect a few hours of zero contact. In another hour, they'll at least get airborne to give a report if they're not heading back."

"Sounds good, thanks."

With everything in place, there was nothing to do but sit back and wait.

* * *

Mythos, Crash Site

Captain Eva Snow—formerly a US Navy SEAL team operator, now a part of MilForce in the Terran Space Project—leaned back against the crashed ship and watched the clearing crew as they cut some of the surface layers of foliage away. The first few hours would be easy, according to the cutters, then the work would really start.

Cuttings were being policed up as they went and shoved aside to be collected later and used for whatever it could be used for. That was outside her realm. Her mission was the safety of the crew. To that end, she had five people on a perimeter in full body armor suits. They were a few steps above the reinforced suits being worn by the cutters that were safe against the killer trees they had already encountered. The MilForce version was also protective against bullets and lasers, to an extent.

She was interested in the crashed ship, but that was as far as she'd let it get. While she was on a mission, nothing outside her assigned goals was allowed to get in the way. She stood up and walked over when one, then another, and then another saw being used ground to a halt. The sudden silence was eerie after several hours of non-stop audio assault from the saws.

"Problem?" she asked as she approached.

"Yeah, we got the surface shit gone. All the branches are cut away, but now we're cutting the trunks of these trees. I don't know what they're made of, but it's more than our saws can handle. We're going to have to get out the laser cutters."

"Okay, whatever you need to do. Just try not to cut anything you don't intend to cut."

"Don't worry about it. Captain Reeves wanted the best, so that's who we have."

"Excellent. Do we need to worry about a fire from the heat?" she asked.

"I'd call it a possibility, but not a probability. These cutters are specific for cutting dense, flammable materials. Honestly, I don't know the science behind it all, but I think it's *too* hot to cause a flame, because it just vaporizes whatever it hits."

Eva nodded. She probably knew more about lasers than he did, but there were many types, and it was always good to check for unintended consequences.

"Good enough," she said, and went to make her rounds. She didn't *have* to visually check on each of her team members, but it gave her an excuse to walk around, and she felt it created more of a bond with the team.

She approached the ship just as the cutters were getting back to work. The laser cutters they were using resembled laser rifles, but were more industrial in appearance. They also came with a backpack battery cell, rather than a small, interchangeable battery like military rifles.

The foreman was the first to fire his up. She could see that it projected a low-powered, bright green aiming beam, since the actual laser was outside the visual spectrum. Smoke rose from the trunk of the tree he aimed at, and he was able to slice through it from side to side in less than a minute. The trees were too tough for saws, but even they were no match for a high-powered cutting laser.

"Okay, this should go faster now. To your grids, let's get to work!" the foreman said.

She nodded in appreciation as they spaced out and got to work. They were staggered so that if something shifted ahead of or behind one of them—since they were sometimes standing on the trunks of the trees they were cutting in the crash path—no one would be thrown off balance.

Sure enough, they moved more quickly, and she could see the trunks collapsing to the ground, though she wasn't sure what the plan was to move the massive logs out of the way. When one section was done, they'd coordinate a shift in position, and keep going. She took a moment to chide herself for not giving the professionals—in what she considered a 'safe' field of work—the credit they deserved.

Things went well for several more hours, then something went wrong. An explosion of what looked like a yellow-green gas filled the air around one of the cutters.

"Clear out, pull back to the ship!" she ordered immediately.

The cloud spread quickly and engulfed three of the cutting team before they could retreat. They stumbled toward the ship, but the cloud became so thick, she lost sight of them. She switched the visor of her suit to thermal and charged forward to help them get out.

She was joined quickly by the rest of her team, who escorted the three cutters out of the cloud and back to the ship.

"Can't... breathe," one of them said in a choked voice, grasping for his helmet clasp.

"Get them inside!" she said.

Eva led by example and dragged one of them inside before she helped get the helmet off the stricken cutter.

The female cutter gasped for air and slid down to sit. "Must have clogged up the air intake," she managed to say.

"Cloud is moving off to the east, away from us, and dissipating quickly," one of her men who'd remained outside said.

"Get the decon gear and let's get everyone cleaned off," Eva ordered. "Don't touch your skin. We don't know what this stuff is. See if the atmospheric sensors can get a reading."

Her man outside ran to get the portable decontamination gear, which consisted of a pressure washer with disinfecting chemicals, while someone else moved to the air quality sensors to see what they could find out.

She looked closer at everyone, including herself, and they were all coated with the green stuff to varying degrees. Examining her own suit more closely and dragging her finger across it, she could see that it wasn't a gas, but a fine, powder-like substance.

"You're kidding me," she said to herself.

"Got a reading; you're not going to believe this."

"Let me guess. We've been pollinated?" Eva asked.

"Yeah, how'd you know?"

"I grew up in the South. This used to be a big problem before most of the forests were cut down."

"Well, I'd say this is slightly different. I'll have to get a sample for a better analysis, but I'd say if anyone was exposed to that without a suit, they'd probably be dead, simply due to the concentration of it."

"Yep. That's different. I'll notify Eos. I think we're going to need fresh suits. The intakes and filters on at least these three are probably shot."

* * *

Mythos, Eos City, Planetary Control Center

The day had gone, thankfully, uneventfully for Max. He'd received regular status reports from the crash site and Azeema's expedition. Both were proceeding safely, but Azeema wanted more time on site to get deeper core samples. Max yawned and stood up to head to his apartment to call it a day, when his comm chimed for his attention. He sat back down and accepted it on his terminal.

"Reeves here, go ahead."

"*Captain, it's Eva; we have a situation at the crash site,*" she said. "*The clearing team hit… something that released a thick cloud of, believe it or not, pollen. It's covered everything, and clogged the air filtration systems on the clearing team who were closest to it. We're getting them into the alien craft, and using the portable decontamination gear, but we're done for the night.*"

Max frowned. Eva Snow was MilForce, a former Navy SEAL, so he knew the team was in good hands.

"Is there enough clearance for the plane to land and bring the team home?"

"*Negative. There's still a lot to get done. So far, everyone seems to be okay, but based on what we've seen from this planet so far, obviously, I have concerns.*"

"Understood. Is there anything you need?"

"Fresh environment suits for the cutting team, just in case we can't get these fixed up."

"Copy that, they'll be on the way. Anything else?"

"No, sir."

"The hits just keep on coming," he muttered to himself once the channel closed.

He gave orders to have a drop pallet loaded with new reinforced suits for the cutting crew as well as extra food and water. He put the loadmaster in direct contact with Eva in case she thought of anything else before the plane took off. With that done, he made his way out of the PCC before anything else could come up. It had been a long day.

* * * * *

Chapter Four

Earth, Terran Space Project Campus, Annica's Apartment

Annica woke to the sun burning through her eyelids from the open blinds of her bedroom. She sighed, remembering how much she'd had to drink the night before, but knew she had a lot to do, so she got moving.

After a hypo of an anti-hangover concoction and a quick shower, she was dressed and back in the office. Before she dove back into the research, she saw a high-priority message from Konda to her personal account. An expert from the Public Security Intelligence Agency was already on site and at work to dig up whatever he could. Konda was clear she hadn't given the agent any hint as to what the desired outcome would be, but had posited the scenario and asked him to dig to either prove or disprove it.

That was fair. Konda was a friend, but she was MilForce first. She wouldn't want to plant an idea in the agent's head as to what she *wanted* the result of the investigation to be. Annica just hoped he was good, and fast.

She felt relieved, knowing someone was on the task and that soon she'd be proven right. With that worry out of her mind, she dove back in and resumed the search where she'd left off the night before, looking for answers. She rewatched the video in the most recent message and fumed. The worst part of it all was that even when the evidence was provided to prove she was right, she couldn't go public with it—at least not outside the campus. To do so would be to ruin the reputation of the TSP and likely lose funding and any chance of finding Max.

Suddenly, an idea struck. She went back to the messages she'd found about faking the probe sighting. The initial messages stated that the intent was to keep the funding they had, and not ruin the reputation of the TSP with a failed mission. So he'd led the effort, but the stated purpose was bullshit. The probe not showing up where they'd expected wouldn't have been a huge problem. Annica herself was prepared for that, and had even prepared a release, explaining that they would keep watching the sky and waiting for a ping back from the probe. Wherever it was, they'd be ready to explore. Sure, it would have been a setback, but it wouldn't have ruined the TSP. Not like the news that they'd faked results would.

She went through all the messages and noted the names of those who were involved. They would certainly be the first people she wanted to talk to. Everyone in the TSP was good at keeping secrets, and had signed non-disclosure agreements, but keeping something like this under the covers was remarkable.

* * *

Earth, Terran Space Project Campus, Annica's Apartment

Late in the afternoon, Annica still hadn't come up with anything concrete. She growled under her breath and ran her hand through her hair. She was stuck on Gustav's mention of "friends from out of town," but couldn't figure out who he'd referred to. There was a suspicion, but it was ridiculous.

With a deep sigh, she tried to come up with another context search she could run on the file libraries, when there was a knock on the door. She rose, grateful for the interruption, and walked into the living room.

"Come in," she said, and the door opened to reveal Captain Sanako.

"Annica. You're looking…"

"Rough, I know. Has your friend turned anything up?"

"As a matter of fact," Sanako said, and held up a thumb drive. "You were right. He faked the whole thing, and we have the proof. He was also able to recover some messages that had been deleted from your queue. We know you were under the influence of a mind-control program. My friend said he flagged a bunch of files that were hidden away, which you'll want to look at."

Annica collapsed into a chair and sobbed. She'd known she was right, but hearing it from someone else broke her.

"This is good news, isn't it?" Sanako asked gently.

Annica looked up at her and wiped her eyes. "For me. But we don't know where *Traveler* is. We don't know where Max is. Unless he found something else? What's in those other files?" she asked hopefully.

"He didn't say, but he did say he didn't find anything about the actual location of *Traveler*. At least, nothing that stood out. Space travel really isn't his area of expertise. But now, you can lead the charge to find them. The shooting has been ruled justified, and you're free to handle things as you wish, Director Reeves. Public Relations is already working on a cover story for his death to release to the outside world."

She took a deep breath, then stood. "Okay. I'm going to get a shower and get to work. Is the office cleaned up?"

"Yes, ma'am. It's like nothing ever happened. Even the hole in the wall has been patched."

"Good. Thanks for everything, Konda."

"Just doing my job. Let me know if there's anything else we can do."

* * *

Earth, Terran Space Project Campus, Director's Office

After a longer shower and some fresh clothes, Annica sat behind the desk of the director of the Terran Space Project, her new desk. While she wanted to confront the people she knew had been involved in the faked sighting, she wanted to be armed with as much information as possible first. Plus, she knew it wouldn't make much of a difference in the long run, so she slotted the thumb drive provided by Captain Sanako's friend and reviewed his brief report.

The amount of data he'd come up with in so little time was, to her, impressive. She made a mental note to find out if they could hire him away from the PSIA. He linked to several confidential documents detailing the sort of mind-control program that had been used. She started a to-do list of actionable items that could make a difference, and the first item on it was to task a team to devise a way of hardening the IT infrastructure so nothing like that could ever be done again.

Further in the report, there was the list of files and correspondence that proved the Alpha Centauri probe sighting had been faked. She passed those over, because the how wasn't as important as the why, and there wasn't anything there to answer that question. As far as the majority of the people at TSP were concerned, everything was fine, and they were simply waiting for *Traveler* to appear in Alpha Centauri. For now, that was acceptable.

The last section of the report was a list of files he flagged as 'of interest.' She shifted the list to a secondary display, and located and opened the first file on the list. While she wasn't sure at all what to expect, what she saw was certainly nothing she could have prepared for. It was gibberish. Lines and squiggles covered the screen. She performed an image recognition search, and the system, one of the most powerful and inclusive databases in the solar system, came up with nothing.

She decided not to get stuck on one thing and moved on to the other files. Several of them were similar and she immediately closed them to come back to later. Then she came to personnel files, just like the one on every passenger and crew member of *Traveler*. She scanned through, assuming they must have been discarded applications, since they all listed significant criminal records, but then she came to a name she recognized. Adel Ragnarsson, a member of the passenger council.

Her eyes widened as she read through what must have been the original file. Ragnarsson was dangerous, and he never should have passed the initial screening. Somehow, Malmkvist had managed to erase all traces of his past, from everywhere, to get him on the ship. As she dug, she saw how. Ragnarsson had a list of aliases, and most of his crimes had been documented under them. He was still wanted in several countries for cyberterrorism.

Annica checked on who'd prepared the file, and she swallowed hard when she saw the name. It was one she knew, but she also knew he'd died in a car accident during the selection process. She quickly cross-checked, and found that all three of the suspect files had been prepared by the same person. Her hands fell away from the keyboard as she lowered her head and closed her eyes.

"An accident. Right. Why did you do this, Gustav?"

She wanted to know why, and she felt like it was important, but she also needed to focus on what to do with the information. The conclusion remained the same; if this got out, the reputation of the TSP would be ruined. She had no choice but to keep it under wraps and selectively release what needed to go out in order to find *Traveler*.

To that end, she pulled up the personnel list for the Special Projects Team Gustav had created. They were the people who'd faked the probe sighting, and were monitoring the frequency range Gustav had provided. She checked the frequency range, and it ran between 500 and 550 Terahertz. Communications wasn't her expertise, but she was fairly sure the range of such a wavelength didn't make sense for space communications. It seemed there were more than a few oddities about this whole thing.

As she'd been researching, her to-do list had grown, and she decided it was time to get started. The first item on the list was a meeting with Shao Yating, the CIO for the TSP.

* * * * *

Chapter Five

Landing + 37 Days

Mythos, Eos City, Max's Apartment

Max woke up, and immediately his mind went to the men and women who'd stayed out at the crash site. He quickly got up, got dressed, and went to his office in the apartment. Nothing had gone badly wrong, or Kellie would have woken him up.

With the team stuck out there, Kellie had taken a power nap and then stayed up all night in the PCC to monitor the situation. Even though night was only four hours, everyone was given at least eight hours of downtime to sleep. The day cycle had changed; the needs of the human body hadn't. He'd realized early on that to be an effective leader, he, more than most, needed to make sure he was well rested.

He opened a channel to Kellie while he pulled up the daily status reports.

"*Morning, Max,*" she answered.

"Morning Kellie. How's the team doing out there?"

"*Good. They've been up for a few hours already. They've hit some more of those pollen pods, but now that they know what to look for, they're able to take them out without getting engulfed.*"

"ETA on a landing zone?"

"Current ETA is another four hours or so. They've asked a plane to come in with a hoist in two hours so they can hook the logs up and have them drug out of the way. They're just too dense to grind up like they'd originally planned."

"I wonder if that could be a good thing. If they're that dense, they might be of use to us."

"Way ahead of you. One of the comm guys is an amateur woodworker, and he already asked for some to see if it could be worked. We're also going to get a sample back when we can and have Annie see if it could be broken down to use in the manufactory."

"Sounds good. Anything from Azeema?"

"They got back after dark, and it looks good. We're going to get a mining crew set up and send out the equipment we have to start extraction. The ore isn't anything we know, but it's similar enough to hematite that it can be processed the same way, and it comes out like iron. They've dubbed it 'niron,' near iron, and it's stuck, so I guess that's what it is."

Max chuckled and shook his head. "Well, there you go then."

"Yeah, the geologists aren't amused, but it is what it is. There's a pretty well concentrated vein that they've found so far."

"I'm sure there'll be more they can put their names on. Go ahead and get some rest; I'll be in the PCC after I grab some breakfast."

"Will do. Thanks, Max."

He closed the channel and smiled. They had an ore source, and that satisfied a lot of concerns. Now they'd be able to manufacture spare parts if—when, really—they were needed. The mining equipment they had was minimal, but the manufactory had plans to print everything for a full scale operation. The idea was that they'd taken the equipment to extract enough ore to build the parts for a larger, more permanent mining operation.

The real trick would be doing it in such a way that they weren't blowing huge holes in the landscape, but that's why they had experts. The technology they had would allow them to identify what they wanted, and mine it to be processed, rather than having to strip mine like they had on Earth. It took longer, but they had time, and one of their primary goals was not to destroy the planet while they built on it. They'd seen the results of that already.

* * *

Mythos, Flying Over Mythos

It was a bit after the predicted four hours, due to delays in getting the area cleared of the cut trees, but the portable runway was finally down. Max flew his own X-94 out to the site with the cargo bay loaded with gear and personnel.

He hadn't flown since *Traveler* had departed Earth, and it felt good to be back behind the stick. There'd been a small debate suggesting he shouldn't be piloting himself, since he was the head of the city, but he'd quashed that quickly. To him, maintaining his flight time was important, since he wouldn't always be the leader of the city.

On approach to the crash site, he was pleased to see the results of the cutting team's work. There was an ample clearing to get in and out, and plenty of open area for the science teams to set up. He adjusted the jets and came down vertically to a soft landing before opening the cargo ramp.

After finishing all the power-down procedures, he left the plane and was pleased to see crews already unloading and moving all the gear near the crashed ship to set up. Everyone was mandated to wear full environment suits, just in case, but they were allowed to work without helmets. The air quality sensor had been linked to an audible alarm that would go off if anything was detected that could be dangerous.

Movement caught his eye, and he looked up. They were being watched by at least five griffins. That wasn't a surprise. They were probably as curious about the ship as he was.

He waved, then moved on to where a tent was being set up.

"You ready for this, Doctor Heuser?"

Marc Heuser, a forensic pathologist, nodded. "It's certainly the opportunity of a lifetime. The team is excited but nervous, as you might imagine."

"No doubt. I'm pretty sure that describes the feelings of everyone out here. Full containment protocols. We definitely don't want to expose anyone to anything that could be dangerous."

"Oh, don't worry, Captain. The team is treating this like a viral containment. Full decontamination procedures, in and out. We're going to leave the one in the suit you opened up in the vessel, and bring out one that's still fully sealed once we're ready."

Max nodded approval. "Sounds good. Keep me updated."

He continued around the site, where various teams were setting up their gear. He estimated at least a tenth of the population was here at the site, performing one form of research or another. There was different plant life here, so xenobotanists were cataloging and naming everything they could touch. Besides the botanists, entomologists and ethologists were setting up to study any insects or wildlife they could see.

After making his rounds, satisfied everything was going to go well, he got back into his plane and decided to fly around the planet for a while, just to look around.

* * *

Mythos, Other Side of the Planet

Adel Ragnarsson looked up from his campsite when he heard the distinct sound of an X-94 in the distance. He didn't hold any hope that they'd changed their minds and were coming to get him, but he watched anyway.

He'd been abandoned, two days ago, on the other side of the planet from Eos. He hadn't moved far, except to find a place to set up a base camp to survive while he plotted his next move. His hunting efforts so far had been fruitless, but he'd set some makeshift traps and hoped to at least catch something fresh, and safe, to eat. Those who'd banished him had at least given him rations to survive on, for a while anyway, but those wouldn't last.

Alone with his thoughts, he went through the events that had left him here. He should have acted sooner, and more decisively. He'd underestimated the people's loyalty to Maxwell Reeves. That had been his biggest mistake. He reassured himself with the fact that he was the only person on the planet who knew what was really going on. That made him smile. Reeves had no idea how deep he was or what was coming. Ragnarsson did.

* * *

Mythos, Eos City

After flying a full circuit around the planet, going exo-atmospheric to make the trip faster for the last half, he finally landed at Eos as the first sun was setting. He saw both the BN-12s out of the maintenance hangars and walked over after shutting his plane down.

"How are they looking?" Max asked.

Daniel Russell, one of the head mechanics, walked over and shook Max's hand. "Not too bad. I think we got the problem licked. Put in some new filters around the fans that should hold up. I can go into details if you really—"

"No, that's okay," Max interrupted. He could fly nearly anything, but he left the mechanics to the experts. Basic maintenance was one thing, but they'd had to tear the fans completely apart.

"We're about to send one up for a test flight, unless…"

"Nah, I'm good. Just took a tour of the planet. I need to get some real work done now," Max said.

"I thought flying *was* the real work," Russell joked.

"Yeah, yeah. Great job, and thanks. Let me know how it goes; we could use them at the crash site."

"Will do!"

Max waved to the crew, who were going over the nearest aircraft one last time before it was powered up. He wanted to stick around and watch, but he really did need to get back to the control center. There were parts of him that were ready to hand over the reins, but he'd been convinced the city needed him. For now.

* * * * *

Chapter Six

Earth, Terran Space Project Campus, Director's Office

Annica rose early and went to her office. Sleep hadn't come easily since she'd come out of her trance, as she'd come to think of it. She hadn't even been home yet, though she'd have to soon, even if only to get more clothes.

As much as she wanted to dedicate all her time to her investigation into Malmkvist, there was a lot of work that came with being the director of the TSP. There was a board meeting scheduled in the next week, and that had her nerves on edge. She wasn't sure what she was going to tell them, or what they might already know.

Annica had just gotten started on her message queue when there was a light knock on the door, and Shao Yating stuck her head in.

"Good morning, Director. I'm a bit early, but is this a good time?" she asked.

"Come on in, Shao," Annica said and gestured to a seat.

Yating sat and straightened the pants of her tailored business suit.

"I received your memo, obviously, and already have some of my best people looking over the information provided. Was there something more?" Yating asked.

Annica knew Yating was always direct and to the point, so she took the same approach.

"Yes. I'd like to know how it's possible that the systems within the TSP allowed a program to execute that put me under suggestive mind control."

If Yating was surprised by the direct question, she gave no indication of it.

"It wasn't something that was within the realm of concern, so there was no routine in place to catch or stop such a program from executing."

"Why not?"

"Our role has always been to secure the servers from intrusion from external sources. It was never within our scope to defend from an internal attack such as this."

"A bit naïve, don't you think?" Annica asked.

Yating hesitated. In Annica's experience with the woman, it was a rare display of anything but confidence.

"Well?" Annica prompted.

"Naïve, yes, but not on my part or my team's. May I be blunt?"

"I've never known you to be any other way," Annica said without a hint of humor.

"This is the first organization I've been a part of where internal defenses weren't as strong as external. In my industry, it's well known that the most dangerous access points are inside the system. Internal hardening is almost more important than protecting external access points."

"It sounds like you're admitting you didn't do your job."

"I wasn't *allowed* to do my job," Yating countered.

Annica pursed her lips and nodded slowly. The response didn't surprise her.

"Explain, please."

"Every time I suggested more work to harden the internal systems, something else would come up. There would be a newly revealed external attack vector that took everyone I have to stop or some of my personnel would be reassigned. It was as if former Director Malmkvist didn't *want* there to be internal protections. That makes sense now, based on the information you forwarded. Which reminds me, how *did* you get all that information?"

"I'm afraid I'm going to keep that close to the vest for now. Quite simply, I don't yet know who I can trust, and who I can't. What you say makes sense, but I have to consider that you might have been complicit in what Gustav was doing."

Yating nodded. "Understandable, and I appreciate your straightforwardness. If there's anything I can do to alleviate your concerns, I'll do so. I know my assurances won't mean much right now, but I must say that I knew nothing about what he was doing. If I'd known, I would have stopped it. I've seen first-hand how people in power use programs like that to control people, and I would never soil my hands with such tactics."

It was unlikely that Yating had been involved, and Annica had no evidence at all indicating that Yating had been aware of what Gustav was doing, but she had to be sure. The problem was, Annica wasn't certain how she could *ever* be sure.

"Well, now your directive is to make sure it can never happen again. I'll expect a full report on what I've sent you, and what your plan is, by next week."

"That we can do," Yating stated.

"Good. Let me know if there's anything you need. Otherwise, I'll see you next week," Annica said and stood, indicating an end to the meeting.

"Of course, Director," Yating said as she stood and then walked out of the office.

With that taken care of, Annica dug deeper into the personnel records of the people on the Special Projects Team. Nothing appeared out of the ordinary, but then she started working on a contact tree. It took time, but she felt like she needed to do it herself. Finally, after several hours, she found a link that couldn't be a coincidence. One of the team members, Paula Handley, had lived in the same city, at the same time, as both Gustav and Adel Ragnarsson.

Checking on Paula's specialty, Annica saw she had extensive experience in both linguistics and communications. Alarms blared in Annica's mind. It was a hard connection to find, but it was unavoidable. She set that aside and kept going down the list. After several hours, Paula was the only one with a possible connection—at least one she could discern.

Annica knew she should probably turn this over to MilForce, who had a branch of investigators, and let them lead the investigation, but again, who could she trust? Konda was high on the list, and Anton seemed okay, but beyond that, she just wasn't sure.

Now that was handled, she logged in and checked her messages while she sipped a cup of strong coffee. There was a message from Konda marked urgent, so she read that first. Apparently, her contact had forgotten to flag one of the files he'd found to mark 'of interest,' and she'd sent it over.

Without much hope that it would uncover anything new, she opened the attachment and leaned back to watch. Malmkvist, in this very office, appeared on the screen.

"Captain Reeves, if you're seeing this message, one of the potential outcomes we expected has come to pass, and you haven't arrived in Alpha Centauri. I'm

sorry we couldn't fully brief you on this previously, but it was decided that it was best for the mission.

"The truth is, we felt there was a better than even chance that you wouldn't emerge in Alpha Centauri. A new blueprint for the manufactory has been unlocked in your terminal. You can send it to the manufactory for production, should you so desire. It will produce a new type of long-range signal that might, eventually, reach Earth, so we or our future generations will know where you are.

"I'm afraid there's not much more I can give you, Captain. From here on in, it's up to you. How much of this you reveal to your crew is up to you. Find a planet, start a colony, and survive. Know that we'll be looking for you. Good luck, Captain."

The video stopped on the last frame, and her stomach clenched. She carefully set her mug on the desk and swallowed hard. Her heart felt like it was about to beat through her chest as she manipulated the image to be sure, but there it was. She'd been in the office when he'd recorded the video. He must have already brainwashed her, and she'd known. She'd known Max was likely going off to who knows where.

"Oh, Goddess…"

She closed her eyes and clenched her jaw against the tears that wanted to come. Max must have seen this after the transition through the wormhole, so he knew. He would have seen her in the video and assumed she knew all along.

With a few key presses, she called Konda from her terminal.

"*Yes, Director?*" she answered almost immediately.

"Did you look at the file you sent me?" Annica asked.

"*No, ma'am. Not my business.*"

"Look at it. Watch it. Then come to my office. I may need your help more than ever."

"*Umm. Okay, give me a few to get back to my desk.*"

"Thanks, Konda," Annica said and ended the call.

* * *

A nnica tried to busy herself with her daily load of messages and paperwork while she waited for Konda, but
it was impossible to focus on anything else. She wasn't
even sure what she'd talk about with Konda, she just knew she needed to talk to *someone*, and there was no one else she knew she could
trust.

She let out a sigh of relief when she heard a knock at the door. A
glance at the security panel let her know it was Konda, and she
pressed a button to open the door.

"Konda, come in; have a seat, please."

Konda nodded and walked over to sit in one of the chairs in
front of Annica's desk. It was obvious to Annica that Konda was
shaken by the video.

"So, what do you think?" Annica asked.

"Honestly, ma'am, I don't know what to think."

"I assume you noticed the last few frames…"

The pained look on her face was enough to tell Annica that she
had indeed noticed.

"Yes, ma'am. I can't imagine what must be going through Captain Reeves' mind."

"Oh, I'm pretty sure I know. He thinks I betrayed him, and I'm
pretty sure Kellie was right there to comfort him," Annica said, the
acidic tone of her voice making her opinion on the matter quite clear.

"Do you think she was in on it? Commander Warren?"

Annica sighed and shook her head. "No, probably not. At least, I can't find any *evidence* that she was. But I could tell how she looked at Max. She was jealous."

Konda shifted in her seat, showing uncharacteristic discomfort. "Ma'am, I'm sure you know her better than I do, but she always seemed very professional and dedicated to the mission."

"I'm sorry, you're probably right," Annica said, but she couldn't put any feeling behind it.

She was already a pawn in a conspiracy, the reaches of which she still didn't know. Who else might have been involved? It would have made sense to plant someone like Kellie close to Max. Max and Kellie had known each other for a long time, longer than she herself had known Max.

"No need to be sorry," Konda said. "If you don't mind me saying so, you should focus on what you can do something about here at home. There'll be time to worry about them once you have your own house in order."

"I know, and on that point, there's someone I want you to dig into."

Konda tilted her head. "Who?"

"Paula Handley. She's on the Special Projects Team."

"What's so interesting about her?"

"At one time, she lived in the same city as Malmkvist and Ragnarsson."

Konda looked confused.

"Let me take a step back," Annica said, and explained what she'd found on Ragnarsson and the other two colonists on the mission, and the person who'd cleared them for the mission.

"Well…" was all Konda could say.

"I'm putting in the paperwork today to have you assigned to me fulltime if you don't mind. I'll put in something about being concerned for my safety. I need some help with this, Konda, and I don't know who else I can trust."

She nodded slowly. "Okay."

"I know this is a lot, and it all seems… insane. But it happened, and it's still happening. I have a board meeting coming up, and I need to know if they were in on it."

Konda frowned. "I hadn't even thought of that. Shit. What if they were?"

It hadn't actually occurred to Annica until that morning that the board might actually have knowledge of, and approved, Gustav's plans. She hoped that wasn't the case, but if it was, things could get interesting. At the very least, they could fire her. At the worst… well, she didn't want to think too far down that road.

"I don't know, but I want to go in with both eyes open."

"I'll do everything I can, ma'am, but I'm a soldier, not a tech."

"What do you think the odds are of hiring your friend away from the PSIA?"

"That would be tough. He might be willing, but they're pretty… possessive of their agents."

Annica nodded and sighed internally. Bringing in someone from the outside—especially someone who'd already proven himself—would have been nice, but she'd just have to look internally for someone trustworthy. Best bet would be someone hired recently, if there were any. Someone hired after Malmkvist had cooked up his whole plan. Probably someone without the depth of skill she wanted, but whoever it was would have to learn fast.

"Okay, I'll take some time today to look through personnel records and try to find someone suitable for the work. Thanks, Konda, for everything. I'm afraid it might get a little more complicated before it gets easier."

Konda rose from her chair and adjusted her vest and weapons belt. "A little? Well, if you can't take a joke—"

"You shouldn't have joined," Annica finished. "Max used to say that all the time," she said with a sad smile.

"You'll get this figured out, ma'am," Konda said reassuringly.

"I hope so. Thanks, Konda. I'll let you know once the paperwork is done to reassign you. Until then, business as usual."

"Yes, ma'am," she said, quickly braced to attention, and left the office.

Annica looked at the closed door for a few moments after Konda left. It was the first time she'd shown any sort of military deference to her. Thinking back to Max's days in the military, she knew it was a sign of respect and was grateful. She just hoped it would be enough. Intrigue and shadow operations weren't what she'd joined the TSP for, but she was going to play the hand she was dealt.

* * *

It took several hours of looking at personnel records and running extensive background checks to find the tech she was looking for. The agency had already done background checks, but at this point, she didn't trust them, and ran her own. She finally settled on Sergey Yegorovich, a self-taught programmer and analyst from Moscow. He was young but showed promise, and self-taught was just the kind of person she wanted.

She knew the type. They loved being presented with a challenge and figuring out how to accomplish it. She just hoped he was up to this one.

There was a tap on the door, and Konda opened it. She gestured Sergey through and closed the door behind him from the outside.

Annica rose and smiled. "Mr. Yegorovich. Good to meet you; please have a seat."

He walked slowly toward the chair, looking around the office. She had a feeling it was a show put on for her benefit. He was attempting to look young and naïve, but she knew better, based on his background check.

"Sergey—may I call you Sergey?"

He nodded as he finally sat down.

"Let's drop the act, shall we? I know your background, and I know an office like this certainly isn't impressive to the secret son of an SVR agent."

His expression quickly changed, and he raised a challenging eyebrow.

"Yes, I know your father was a high-ranking agent in the Foreign Intelligence Service. Highly decorated, apparently. Do you think we don't look at everything in your background?" she asked as she sat.

Sergey shrugged. "He was never a big part of my life."

"I know, but you did walk the halls of the Kremlin a few times," Annica said, noting his almost complete lack of Russian accent. "So this office must seem positively spartan."

"Since we're dropping the act, why am I here, Director Reeves?"

"Annica is fine," she said. "Straight to the point. I like that. Very simply, Sergey, I want to bring you in to work directly with me. *For* me. You would report to no one but me, or Captain Sanako if needed. You wouldn't talk to anyone else—I mean anyone—about what we do."

"Why?"

"Because I need people I can trust, and your recent employment marks you among that possible number. Let's just say the TSP isn't as squeaky clean as it presents to the public."

Sergey snorted. "Nothing is."

She grinned at how quickly he'd gotten comfortable being himself. He was exactly what she needed. Someone who could be absolutely honest.

"True. Now, what do you say?"

"Honestly, Annica, it sounds a bit iffy, but it also seems interesting. What would I be doing?"

"I can't really explain that unless and until you agree to join the team."

"And the team consists of… you and Captain Sanako?"

"For now, yes."

He shrugged. "What the hell. Sounds just interesting enough that it might actually test my skills, unlike the drudge work I'm doing now."

"Good," she said, and hit the Send key on the message she'd prepared, transferring him to her staff.

"You now officially work for me, directly, and you have read access to the entire network. Here's where we are."

She spent the next hour revealing everything she'd discovered, sparing no details. He asked questions, and she answered the best she could, but usually her answer was that it was his job to find the answer.

"So, where do I set up?" he asked as he stood.

"For appearances, you'll be joining the Special Projects Team, so you'll work there. So guard your screen carefully."

"Wait, with someone you think is in on this?"

"Exactly. I hope some of your father's skills made it into your genetic strand."

He grinned. "This is going to be *fun*."

Annica drew breath to remind him of the severity of the issue, but he held up a hand.

"Don't worry, I understand what I've gotten into. I just have an odd sense of what's fun."

"I hope so. You start first thing tomorrow morning. Welcome to the team."

Sergey nodded and cracked his knuckles as he stood. "Be in touch," he said as he left her office.

* * * * *

Chapter Seven

Landing + 38 Days

Mythos, Eos City, Planetary Control Center

The next day, after breakfast and a workout—something he needed to get back into the habit of—Max took his seat in the PCC just as his comm went off. He accepted it through the terminal on his desk.

"Doctor Heuser? Is everything okay?"

"Well, yes, and no, and… we finished sequencing the body's genome this morning."

"And?"

"And it's about 99.8 percent identical to ours."

"What?" Max asked. He was no expert in genetics, but that much similarity seemed odd.

"That was my reaction, too. There are some differences in physiology, at least as far as we can tell from these remains, but it's pretty damn close to ours." He shrugged on the screen.

"Any chance someone screwed up?" Max asked.

"Zero. I had the same thought, but after the first result, I had three different sequences run from different parts of the body. Do you realize what this means?"

"Elaborate."

"Okay, so you know that, generally speaking, every human's genetic sequence is about 99.9 percent identical. The extra 0.1 percent is what makes us different."

"I do now," Max said and waved for Heuser to continue.

"The fact that this thing's genome is only .2 percent different is… well, it's nothing we could have anticipated. They're basically human."

"That's impossible," Max said and shook his head.

"I'm afraid it's not," Heuser said. *"Keep in mind, .2 percent is still a pretty big gap. The difference between humans and chimpanzees is only 1 to 2 full percentage points."*

"Still…"

"I know. We're doing chemical analysis now to build a full report, but… let's just say, we're all a little bewildered. We're running every test multiple times, with different personnel when we can, just to confirm everything."

"Good idea. Well, keep at it. Once you have a full report, we'll get the council together."

"Will do. Thanks, boss."

"Oh, one more thing," Max said just before he closed the connection. "Any idea how long they've been here?"

Heuser shook his head. *"None. Could be a few weeks, could be a few years. The plant guys are reviewing the information from the crash path and looking at growth rates, but I've been leaving them to their thing."*

"Got it. Thanks."

After the connection closed, Max did some quick research to fully understand what Doctor Heuser had told him. The similarity was, to his mind, impossible. Humans from Earth had basically the same genetic makeup as these unknown beings—aliens—from a part of the universe they'd never even seen.

He jumped slightly when Kellie walked up behind him and put her hands on his shoulders.

"What's up?" she asked. "You look a bit tense."

"You could say that. Pull up a chair."

She sat, and Max explained his conversation with Doctor Heuser, and what he'd found in his research on the subject.

"That's…"

"Impossible. That's what I thought, but they're sure," Max said. "They're still doing some analysis. Hopefully they'll have a full report for us in a day or two."

"What could this mean?" she asked.

"I got nothing, but this is going to send people's imaginations into overdrive. I know it has mine."

She nodded. "No kidding."

"In other news, looks like the BN-12s are cleared for operations. I got a note that they've got one at the site now to ferry back some of those trees."

"I'm sure they'll be useful for something," she said absently. "Mining operations up and running?"

Max nodded. "Yep. Should have the first container back later today for processing. Hopefully that'll be enough to get the first comm satellite up."

"That'll be nice," she said and looked at him.

"What?" he asked after a few moments of silence.

"You want to be out there, don't you? Doing something."

"Is it that obvious? I've never been much for sitting behind a desk."

"That's true," she said with a smile, "but you're doing good things here, Max. Never doubt that."

"Captain Reeves! There is trouble at mining site!" Essena exclaimed as she bolted up out of her chair at the security station.

"What kind of trouble?" Max asked as he stood and quickly walked over to join her.

"Griffins, but they look different, and are very angry," Essena said as she sat back down. "My team killed three."

"Is everyone okay?" Kellie asked from beside Max.

"Two injured. They managed to get everyone back into plane and up in the air."

"Shit," Max grumbled. "Okay, get everyone back to Eos. We'll have to come up with a plan. Kellie, alert Doctor Chadda that we have wounded incoming. Get out there yourself and keep me updated."

Kellie nodded and ran out of the PCC. Max could hear her shouting into her personal comm to reach out to Doctor Chadda, the city's lead doctor.

Max went back to his desk and commed Leopold Fischer.

"*What's up, Cap?*" Fischer asked.

"The mining crew was attacked by griffins. They said they looked different and were very aggressive. We might need you to take a look."

"*I reckon we can do that. It's outside the territory of the ones we have around here, so it's a different group altogether.*"

"With different rules, probably," Max stated.

"*Yeah, probably so.*"

"Okay, the crew is on the way back with injured. Head out to the airfield and talk to the MilForce team. They'll probably be the best source of intel."

"*On my way!*"

Max clasped his hands behind his head and stretched out his shoulders, which had tightened up. He tried to think of anything else he could do, but right now, it was all a waiting game. New, aggressive griffins and aliens who were eerily similar to humans. What next?

* * *

Mythos, Eos City, Planetary Control Center

Max, Essena, Leopold, Kellie, and Sergeant Pedro Villegas, who'd been out with the mining crew, sat in a conference room in the PCC. They'd just watched the footage from all the cameras that had captured the griffin attack on the mining crew.

"Evaluation?" Max asked.

"Definitely looks territorial," Leopold said. "The feathers and fur are lighter, almost white, so I'd say they live up in the mountains in the area, above the snow line. Did they watch for a while before they came in?"

Villegas nodded. "My team caught sight of a few, but they were always moving. They didn't just hover and watch like the ones we've gotten used to. The attack was an ambush. They came in from a low angle and weren't visible until they were pretty much on us. It's a miracle we didn't lose anyone."

"Not miracle. Good reaction from team, Sergeant," Essena corrected.

"Agreed," Kellie said. "The question now is, how do we proceed? We need those materials."

"Three options," Essena began. "First, try to talk to them, like ones here. Second, track down and eliminate. Third, constant vigilance, and higher presence, with air cover for early warning. Last is most dangerous."

"You're the expert here, Leopold," Max said. "What do you think?"

"I dunno, mate. They seem pretty vicious. I reckon I can try to ask our friends about 'em."

"That's a good start. Do that. Show them the footage, and see what kind of reaction you get. We'll go from there. Until then, the site is off limits. Let's just process what we have," Max concluded.

Everyone rose and left to return to their duties, except Kellie.

"What do *you* think?" Kellie asked.

"I'm not sure, but I have a bad feeling this is going to be a case where we have to eliminate the threat. Unfortunately, there's going to be a solid segment of the citizens who don't like that course of action. I'm all about preserving the planet and its life, but we have to consider our own survival first, and you're right, we need those materials."

"What if we do... have to do that, I mean? How will you handle it?"

Max rubbed his chin and considered for a moment. He'd flown his share of combat missions before he'd switched over to the space program, but none of them had involved eradicating wildlife.

"I'm not sure. Unfortunately, Leopold will probably be our best source of intel there. We know there are different... clans, I guess we'll call them, but maybe they all act similarly, at least as far as their habits. To be sure, we'd basically have to either kill enough for them to get the message not to mess with us, or completely eliminate them all."

"You're talking about making an entire subspecies extinct."

Max frowned. That's exactly what he was talking about, and he didn't like it. One of the mission parameters was that they do as little damage to the planet and its inhabitants as possible. "The alternative is, we give up the site and look for another one."

He shook his head. "I won't make this decision myself. We'll put it to the council."

She tilted her head for a moment then nodded. "Sounds like a good idea."

"Come on. Let's see what Leopold is getting out of the locals."

They walked through the PCC and outside, to see Leopold walking toward them. The three griffins they'd grown accustomed to were laying in the grassy area nearby.

"Well?" Max asked as Leopold approached.

"I'm not sure exactly everything that went on, but I think it's safe to say our friends here aren't friendly with these griffins," he said and tapped his tablet. "I got some very aggressive reactions. Lots of stomping, scratching at the ground, and beak snapping. Scared a few folks walking by, actually."

"So it sounds like our friends don't care what we do as far as they're concerned?" Kellie asked.

"That would be my assessment," Leopold agreed.

Max sighed. "I really don't want to prosecute an attack on an entire subspecies, but we need the materials. What are your thoughts?"

Leopold scratched his head and shrugged. "Lemme think on it. This is a bit of a different kind of predator than I've had to handle before, mate."

"Fair enough. Take the rest of the day, then we'll come together with the council to make a decision on how to proceed. We basically have two options. Do what we have to do to secure the site or find another ore deposit."

"We have another set of mining gear?" Leopold asked.

"Well, as a friend used to tell me, redundancy is good. Redundancy is good. Yes, we have two of almost everything," Max said with a grin.

"Wouldn't saying it once suffice?" Kellie asked.

"He was a nuclear engineer."

"Ahhh. Gotcha."

"Reckon I better get to work on a plan," Leopold said and walked back toward the griffins.

"You think they're actually going to help somehow?" Max asked.

"I think he just likes being around animals more than people," Kellie said.

"Some days…"

Kellie punched him lightly on the arm.

"I didn't mean you," Max said and chuckled.

"Come on, let's grab some lunch. I heard through the grapevine that Bernadette's come up with something new with one of the edible local meats."

"Sounds like a plan. Lead the way."

* * * * *

Chapter Eight

Landing + 39 Days

Mythos, Eos City, Planetary Control Center

First thing in the morning, the city council gathered in the conference room of the Planetary Control Center to go over a few decisions that needed to be made. In addition to the council members, Leopold was present to discuss the griffin situation at the mining site and Doctor Heuser to go over the report that had been prepared on the crashed ship's inhabitants.

Max cleared his throat as Lina Skoog slipped in and sat down—the last to arrive, but still technically early.

"Okay, folks. We have quite a few things to go over this morning, so let's get started," Max said, and the side conversations died down. "As some of you are aware, the mining site was attacked by a group of griffins different from those we have around here. There were no casualties, but several folks are still in the hospital. I brought in Leopold Fischer for obvious reasons. Leopold, what have you come up with?"

"Well, the locals don't seem to care what we do, but they also won't get involved in any way. At least, that's the way I interpret what their reactions were. I want a chance to try to communicate with them."

Essena frowned and shook her head. "I saw footage. Far more vicious than the griffins we see here. There was no warning, just attack."

"As much as I hate to say it, I have to agree with Colonel Mikhailovna," Skoog added. "Can't we just find another site?"

"This site is rich in ore, and we need the ore," Azeema el-Mir said.

"Here we go. The needs of humans outweigh the right to life of anything in our way. That's how it all starts!" Skoog exclaimed.

"Okay, everyone, calm down," Max said with raised hands before an argument could gather steam.

He'd known this would come up, and that was why he was glad he didn't have to make the decision on his own. It was clear Leopold was getting uncomfortable, so Max knew he had to bring things to the point.

"Leopold, I understand your desire, but have you considered that this might be more than even you can handle?" Max asked.

"Oh, trust me, I got a pretty good idea. Remember, I got snatched up by the last griffins I tried to talk to the first time. But I made it back in one piece. I'm not arrogant, mate. I just want a chance to let these fellas live. If it costs me own life, so be it."

The room was silent for a few moments as Leopold's offer sank in.

"I'm going to insist you be accompanied by MilForce," Max said.

"No problem there, mate. I'd prefer not to get eaten, if it's all the same."

"Okay, let's think ahead. If it works, then we're good. We'll figure out a way to make a deal with the griffins to get the ore, if we can. If it doesn't work, and they're aggressive even in attempts at conversation, what then?" Max asked.

"Then it's up to you and MilForce, or find another spot. I don't think there's any structure we can build that would withstand an all-out attack by an organized group of griffins, so you'd either have to set up some sort of defense grid, like we did here, or take 'em all out, and I just can't be a part of that," Leopold said.

Max nodded. "Thanks, Leopold. Anyone have any questions?"

"When do you want to do this? Try to communicate?" Essena asked.

"Middle of the day, I think. When it's obvious we're not trying to be sneaky," Leopold said.

"Today?" she asked with a raised eyebrow.

"Um. Sure. Yeah, why not."

Essena looked to Max.

Max shrugged. "Today it is. Make sure he's safe, Colonel."

"Will put Captain Snow in charge of detail."

"That'll do. You're good to go, Leopold," Max said. He could tell Leopold didn't like being anywhere but outside and briefly wondered how he'd made the trip on *Traveler* without going nuts.

"Thanks," he said, stood, and left the room. He tried to look like he wasn't running but failed.

"Is he okay?" asked Hugh Coghlan, a former police officer from Ireland.

"He prefers being outside with animals more than being inside with people," Kellie explained.

"I can see that," Skoog said.

"Moving on," Max said. "Next order of business is the crashed alien ship. More to the point, the crew of that ship. Doctor Heuser?"

Heuser cleared his throat and tapped on his tablet to bring up what Max recognized as a rudimentary pair of DNA sequences on the screen.

"I've simplified this for the audience—no offense—but in a nutshell, no matter how many times we test it, the DNA of the aliens is only .2 percent different from ours. As I explained to Captain Reeves earlier, that's shocking. They're basically human."

Max looked around the room and saw much the same reaction he'd initially had. Confusion mixed with disbelief. "Perhaps you could elaborate on how significant that is, Doctor?"

"Sure. Between us, each of us at this table has a difference of about 0.1 percent. Keep in mind, that's still millions of differences, but percentage-wise, the gap is small. The gorillas from Africa, before they went extinct, were about 1.6 percent different from humans. Chimpanzees were about 2 percent different. So, a .2 percent difference represents the closest thing to human we've ever seen."

"What does that mean?" Kellie asked what Max thought everyone was thinking.

Heuser shrugged. "It means their DNA is .2 percent different. There's really no other scientific conclusion we can draw. Chemically and biologically, the similarities are so minute that it would take a trained professional to notice them. Visibly, they look human, even on the inside."

"I can confirm that," Doctor Chadda added. "I flew out and took a look, and the anatomy is, well, identical."

"In addition, we handed the suit over to the techies, and they did some analysis on the life support systems," Heuser said. "Based on their analysis of residue, the breathing mix was within parameters that would be survivable for humans. They couldn't really get more specific than that."

The room was silent for a moment as the revelations sank in. Max had had the benefit of knowing some of it ahead of time, so he was prepared with more questions.

"What killed them?" Max asked. "There's no way it was the impact, or the bodies would have been on the flight deck."

"I found no injuries consistent with injuries from an impact that would've been fatal. There was some bruising evident from the seat straps, but nothing major. There were also what appear to be stress fractures on both legs, cause unknown. My best guess, and that's what this is, is that their life support systems failed, and they suffocated," Heuser said. "The mummified state of the body makes it difficult to be much more specific."

"Did the xenobotanists get anywhere on the vine growth?"

"Actually, yes. Based on growth rates, the ship has been there about 50 Earth days."

"So it crashed 11 days before we landed?"

"That's the math, yes sir."

"And their life support couldn't hold out that long. Do we have any idea how long after the crash they survived?"

Heuser shook his head. "Sorry. No."

"Why didn't they just get out of the ship?" Kellie asked.

Heuser shrugged again.

"Maybe something stopped them. Mechanical failure? The presence of a predator?" Max suggested.

"Door worked fine when you got there, didn't it?" Kellie asked.

"Good point. Honestly, it doesn't make sense. Let's assume for a minute that it was one of our ships. It would have backups for the backups for life support. In the end, if we were out of options—assuming whatever air quality testing equipment we had wasn't working—I'd pop the hatch and try anyway."

Essena nodded.

"Is too many failures for ship that looks in good shape," Essena said.

"I tend to agree, Colonel," Max said. "I think we need to get the craft back here and take it apart. Maybe we can find something to give us a hint as to what happened, and more importantly, where they came from, and what they were doing here. Linguists are already going through the manuals I found on the ship. Annie, any progress from your end?"

"I should finish scanning the pages later today. Once done, I will begin my analysis, Max."

"Thanks, Annie. Okay, folks, I know there are probably a million questions, but are there any questions we can actually answer?"

He could tell everyone was in deep thought over all the information that had come out today.

"It's a lot to absorb, and I have a feeling once we get the ship back here, the information flow is going to get overwhelming. All the techs and engineers who've been sitting around waiting for something interesting to do are going to be busy. If there's nothing else, I think we're done."

"Oh, there is one thing," Coghlan said. "I've had more than a few requests from people to be able to arm themselves. Some for hunting, and others are exploring more outside the city, and want to be able to protect themselves from whatever might be out there."

Max frowned and crossed his arms over his chest as he leaned back in his chair. He'd known this would come up eventually, and there was a plan for it, but that had been shelved after the attempt to take over the city by Ragnarsson.

"That's up to the council," Max said.

"I haven't seen much at all that would pose an immediate threat, as long as people remain aware of their surroundings," Skoog said. She'd spent more time beyond the developed area than anyone else at the table.

"Sure, but not everyone is as skilled as you at spotting trouble," Coghlan pointed out.

"Valid point," she conceded.

"What if there's another trigger we don't know about?" Essena asked.

"True, but how long can we use that as an excuse?" Coghlan asked.

"Not excuse. Fact."

"Okay, okay." He raised his arms in surrender. "Still, people want to explore, and some are hesitant to do it without protection."

"No one who was involved in insurrection can have gun," Essena said firmly.

Coghlan pursed his lips, then nodded. "Every weapon available is cataloged and identifiable through various means. Even the laser weapons include tracer elements. So if something is... misused... we'll know who it was."

"Okay, let's put it up for a vote," Max said. "Full weapons release clause activation, with an addendum to prevent possession by those involved in the armed insurrection?"

Everyone's tablet lit up as Annie translated Max's words for the record. Votes were recorded, but the results of each person's vote was only known to Annie.

"*Full weapons release authorized*," Annie said.

"Okay, Hugh. Pass the word. Your team and MilForce will coordinate handing them out and making sure they're all accounted for," Max said.

"Thanks," Coghlan said. "Now they'll quit bugging me about it."

A few people in the room chuckled at the relief in his voice.

Max stood. "I have plenty to do, as I'm sure you all do. Let me know if anything comes up, otherwise I'll be working on the plan to get the alien craft back to the city for analysis."

* * *

Mythos, Eos City, Planetary Control Center

Max sat at his desk in the PCC and stared at his screen, but he wasn't really looking at what was on it. His mind was occupied with trying to decipher why the alien beings had died. There was no circumstance he could think of in which he'd choose to suffocate rather than risking the environment. Even a sudden loss of full power and life support would have given them time to assess the situation and make such a choice, using the remaining air on the ship.

He was drawn from his contemplation when a chime indicating a new message came from his desk. He rubbed his eyes and sat up to open it. The recovery team had come up with a plan to retrieve the craft. It would require both BN-12s operating in tandem. Magnetic clamps would attach to the craft, and they'd have to fly tight formation all the way back to the city. He grimaced, thinking of all the ways the plan could go wrong—and there were many—but he couldn't think of any alternatives. With a few keystrokes, he approved the plan, but added that he wanted the BN-12 pilots to fly the route in formation a few times before they actually hooked up to the craft. They'd be nearly wingtip to wingtip, and that kind of flying wasn't for the average pilot. Though he hadn't brought any average pilots on this mission.

The whole situation bugged him. What were the odds that another species, basically human, would show up on this planet just over a week before his team found it and landed? A feeling he'd been having more frequently lately cropped up. There were things about this mission he hadn't been told, and the answers were an unknown distance away on Earth, in the head of one Gustav Malmkvist, and possibly Annica. His one hope at this point was that they could safely get the craft back to the city and decode their language. Maybe there'd be something of use on their shipboard computers.

Max locked his station and walked outside to get some fresh air. He couldn't help but forget his worries for a moment and smile when he looked out over the still-growing city. The airfield was bustling with activity as Leopold's team prepared for their mission. At the base of *Traveler's* loading ramp, he could see Hugh and his team issuing weapons to those who wanted them. There was a small bit of concern over that, but he tried to put it aside. Weapons were tools; what mattered was who had them. Before the insurrection, he wouldn't have worried at all. Now, he had no idea who might be a ticking time bomb, just waiting to go off at the right moment.

He sighed as his mind started down dark alleys again. To distract himself, he decided to walk over to the airfield to check on Leopold's team in person before they left. As he walked, passersby waved, or smiled, or stopped to shake his hand, or give him a quick hug. It felt good. Even after everything that had happened, these people still trusted that he was leading them in the right direction.

"All set, Leopold?" Max asked as he made it to the waiting X-94.

Leopold shrugged. "I suppose."

"Something wrong?"

"All these guns," Leopold said with a frown.

Max nodded. Along with Captain Snow, who'd lead the detachment, there were three other members of MilForce in full body armor carrying a wide array of weapons.

"I know, but look. They have very specific orders. This isn't going to be another Ascher situation," Max said, referring to the former colonel who'd been killed by a griffin after he'd shot one of them.

"Don't worry, Mr. Fischer," Captain Snow said as she joined them. "We'll keep you safe, but the best outcome of the mission is that we never have to fire a shot. I have no desire for a conflict with those things."

"I think I can safely say you speak for everyone on that point, Captain," Max said. "Having griffins as allies is far better than enemies, but that's up to them."

"No pressure," Leopold said with a grin.

"If you can't take a joke…" Snow said.

"You shouldn't have joined," Max finished.

"Right. Well, ready then?" Leopold asked.

Snow looked over her shoulder, then nodded. "Yep. We're set. Sorry, Captain Reeves, but we need you to clear the field."

Max winced in mock pain. "I'm supposed to say that…" Max walked back to a safe distance to clear the jet blast from the aircraft, then he turned and watched as Snow and Leopold boarded the X-94. When the rest of the aircrew was clear, the pilot powered it up and lifted off vertically, then slowly transitioned to horizontal flight and flew out away from the city.

"Meili keep you safe," he muttered under his breath.

* * *

Mythos, Eos City, *Traveler*

Kellie watched from the ramp leading into *Traveler* as the X-94 lifted off and away. She stayed for a moment to watch Max walk back toward the PCC. He was working constantly, and she could tell it was wearing on him. The only downtime he'd had since the ship left Earth had been due to an injury that had almost cost him his life. The fact was, though, the people looked up to him. They needed him to be there to feel like everything was going to be okay.

Around the visible area before her, she could see people going about their business to one task or another, or—for those who weren't working—relaxing and enjoying themselves. If you ignored the alien flora, it could have been any small, rural town on Earth.

Beyond them, the greenhouses and hydroponic gardens were flourishing, and more were being built in the allotted space. Some of the colonists wanted to start up a ranch, to try to domesticate some of the local wildlife in order to breed them, rather than relying on the hunters. That would open up a whole new issue of where to put it, since the griffins didn't like it when they cleared large swaths of local flora.

She brought her mind back to the task at hand and walked into the ship and toward the manufactory. Then plan was to start printing the parts for the new comm satellite today, and she wanted to check on the progress personally. The satellite would be the key to staying in contact with remote mining and exploration missions so they wouldn't have to keep an aircraft up in the air to relay transmissions.

That was extending the expected flight times and putting more wear and tear on them than Max liked.

She encountered very few people as she walked through the ship. The only people who came on board were MilForce, who still bunked on the ship, and the teams who needed access to the science labs, since an external lab building hadn't yet been constructed. Now, the ship was basically a monument to their travel, as well as Annie's home, and the source of all the power for the city.

Finally, Kellie made it to the manufactory's control room and stood quietly while the operator finished what she was doing.

"One moment, Ms. Warren. Almost done," said Sadie March, the ship's chief engineer.

Kellie nodded and waited.

After a few minutes, Sadie looked up and smiled. "What can I do for you?"

"Just checking on the status of the satellite, and I wanted to take a walk, so I figured I'd come in person."

Sadie nodded. "I think we'll have just enough materials. We're cutting it close, but I made a few small modifications. Since we have a trinary system to work with, I was able to modify the power system and use fewer materials. It'll have more star exposure, so it won't need as many panels and storage batteries."

"Good thinking. Now the big question. How long?"

"Probably a day to get all the parts printed. Then another day to assemble the parts I can't print as a single piece. Call it three or four days before it's ready to send up, for some wiggle room and testing time," Sadie said. Obviously the question had been expected.

"And that's pretty much all we can do until we can mine more metal?"

"I'm afraid so, but there's no shortage of projects to work on. Once this is done, I'm going to break down some of those huge tree trunks they brought back to see what we can do with them."

"Thanks Sadie. I won't bother you anymore," Kellie said with a grin. Sadie was nice, but she also liked to focus on her task without interruptions.

"You know me too well."

"That's my job," Kellie said and left Sadie to her work.

* * * * *

Chapter Nine

Sergey hummed to himself as he walked through the corridors of TSP on the way to the Special Projects work area. It had always been his hope to work his way up through the TSP, but this was faster than he'd expected. He was a black sheep back home, because he actually thought it was a good idea for the world to come together in cooperation to survive.

He'd passed up more opportunities than he could count from organized crime syndicates who'd wanted his experience and probably access to his father. From each of them, he'd gotten information and turned them in to the FSB. Usually, nothing happened, but he'd tried. Even the government had tried to recruit him. The last attempt had been one he would have probably accepted, simply because if he hadn't, he'd feared it might be the last decision he ever made. But then his application to the TSP had been accepted, and here he was.

It was a bit sad to him that, even here, intrigue was at play. He'd hoped the organization was everything it appeared on the surface. A group of like-minded individuals working toward the goal of exploring space to find humankind new homes in the galaxy. In the end, it was inevitable, he supposed. Anytime there were humans involved, something will go sideways. That was why he focused on computers.

They did only what they were told to do. They never disappointed you or came up with self-serving motives. Plus, they kept him from having to deal with people. Computers he knew inside and out; humans were just too much chaos.

Finally, he arrived at Special Projects. He tapped his ID card against the reader, expecting that to be enough, but then a panel in the wall opened, and what looked like goggles slid out of the opening. He recognized it as a dual-retinal scanner. They weren't messing around. He was familiar with the technology. It not only read the retinal pattern, but also the distance between the eyes, and several other factors that someone couldn't fake simply by ripping someone's eyeballs out. Once he put the goggles to his face, he realized it was even better. There was a moving dot you had to follow with your eyes, so the scanner could detect that you were actually there.

Once the scan was complete, he returned the goggles to the stand, which retracted back into the wall, and the door opened. He stepped through, and as soon as both feet were on the other side, it slid closed behind him. It was a man-trap entry. They were serious about no unauthorized personnel getting in here. Looking down, he could see that the floor was one big pressure plate—probably checking his weight to make sure he hadn't carried anyone in on his shoulders. After a few seconds, the door that actually let him into the work area slid open.

"You must be Sergey," an attractive, middle-aged woman said as he stepped in.

"I must," he said and smiled.

"Welcome to Special Projects. I'm Paula," she said and extended a hand.

"Nice to meet you, Paula," he replied, and took the proffered hand.

Sergey wasn't sure whether it was good luck or a bad omen that had him meeting one of the very people he would be investigating. She was certainly sizing him up, that much was obvious.

"You'll be working over here," she said, and led him toward a corner of the room. "Sorry to stick you in a corner, but that's what's available."

"No one puts Baby in a corner," he mumbled.

"Sorry?"

"Oh, nothing. I've always liked being in a corner."

"One of those, huh?"

"I'm sorry? Those what?"

"A tech who would rather be alone with a server cluster than a group of people," she said with a grin.

"Got it in one."

"Welp, there you go. Station will require another retinal scan to log in, and will lock itself if you even look away long enough that it can't detect your eyes for more than sixty seconds. So even if you close your eyes to take a cat nap, it'll lock. Sometimes we work together down here, but mostly, we all have our own individual projects. You don't talk about what you do, no one else talks about what they do. Understand?"

He sat and raised his eyebrows, a bit surprised. "I thought this was an 'all for one, one for all' kind of place."

She smiled. Was that pity he saw in her face?

"Well, it is, mostly—outside this room, at least. You'll get used to it. Or you won't. Time will tell. Good luck, Sergey," she said and walked away.

Well, at least they don't pull punches. They tell you right to your face that you're probably going to be doing something the public shouldn't know about, he thought. *And they're right.*

He sat and took a moment to survey his station. Three screens. That was good, though at home he had six. Of course, at his previous job in the TSP, he'd only had two. So that was something. A green light lit up above the middle monitor, and he looked directly at it. A second later, the monitors lit up, and he was in. The first thing he did was test the security. He held his hand in front of his eyes, and sure enough, sixty seconds later, the monitors went black. As a second test, he did the same thing while typing one-handed into a blank document. The system still locked up, even with activity going on.

Satisfied that the security was up to snuff, he opened his messages and started going through what the director had forwarded to him. He noticed that his old messages weren't in his queue and furrowed his brows. A quick check of the settings told him why. He was on a completely new subnet, and had a selector that gave him access to three subnets, two of which he hadn't even known existed in his previous job. Briefly he wondered why Annica hadn't mentioned that, but the answer occurred to him just as quickly. If he was as good as he'd said he was, finding this would be easy.

With a grin on his face, he cracked his knuckles and considered where to start, then he decided to make sure he was working for the right person first. A quick analysis told him the surface subnet, the one he'd had access to in his previous role, wouldn't hold anything interesting. The second one, the one Annica had sent the messages to, was the command subnet, used for more mission-critical items, so he started there. He wanted to poke around in the third subnet, but treated it like the last present at Yule, and saved it for later.

The system had all the latest fun toys, so he opened a file de-compiler program and put Annica's name in. He sat back and waited while the progress bar moved slowly. The drives on the network were likely huge, not to mention it would also look at any individual computer it had access to. This search could be easily explained if it flagged on anyone's radar. He just wanted to know all about the woman in charge.

While that ran, he opened another window and toggled over to the last subnet, labeled 'SP_XXX.' "Hope it's not the special project's porn collection," he muttered to himself as he browsed around. A few seconds into his exploration, a prompt appeared on the screen.

Authenticate or die.

He rolled his eyes as the retinal scanner lit up again. Someone was a bit dramatic.

Access granted, Sergey. Contents of this subnet are not for dissemination or discussion outside of Special Projects. Have a nice day.

Sergey leaned back in his chair and considered his next moves carefully. Obviously, this part of the system was heavily regulated and probably very well audited. Any search he ran, or document he opened, the system would log it. What he didn't know was who looked at those logs, and why, but he had a pretty good guess. Suddenly he didn't feel as secure as he usually did with his back in a corner.

He was locked in a room full of techs, some of them likely way better than he was. Some of these people had faked the probe sighting and helped brainwash Annica and some of the people on the *Traveler* mission, for unknown reasons.

Well, first things first, let's see what they have on the director, he thought to himself.

He opened another session of the decompiler tool and started an identical search. He could have just used a text search, but the tool would look inside compiled program files, which he often found useful for finding what he wanted. While he waited, he browsed around in the directories. They were all just numbers. Even the file names were purely numeric. Nothing identifiable at all. Smart, but annoying for his purposes.

He shook his head; no, that made little sense. Unless everyone in this room had a perfect memory, there had to be a system, and he wasn't about to ask. Sergey had heard about things like this. In elite circles, sometimes, just figuring out how to use the system was a test of skill. He started looking at every program installed on his system. One of them, he hoped, would be an interpreter that would decode the numbers into something meaningful.

Nothing popped out in his search, so he browsed the directories on the local drives. He grinned when he came across a directory several layers deep that contained a single file that was just a string of numbers. He paused just before he executed it and narrowed his eyes. Too easy? He ran a quick virus scan, and sure enough, it was a virus.

"Nice try," he muttered, but then something unexpected happened.

His screens went black for a second, and then lit back up. Now the background showed a variation of the TSP logo, with a 'Special Projects' rocker added. The window that showed the SP subnet now had names on the directories instead of numbers. Apparently, just being smart enough to scan the file was the trigger. Part of him wanted to dig into that to see exactly how it worked, but that could wait.

As he'd half-expected, the search of the SP subnet finished with no results. The files had probably not only been renamed, but encrypted. He started the search again and moved to the search of the executive net. That search had completed as well, with hundreds of results. That he'd definitely expected. He copied the result set into a new folder on his desktop, and started going through each file, one by one.

* * *

I t took hours, but he finally finished going through the files from the executive net. He learned a good bit about Annica Reeves, and got the feeling he was definitely on the right team. There was a stark contrast in entries before and after *Traveler* departed Earth, and he had no doubt that her story of being mind controlled was accurate. Even the tone of former director Malmkvist's communications to and about her had changed. Some of them had been fairly uncomfortable, as it became clear that Malmkvist had taken serious advantage of his control over Annica, in every way possible.

"Dirtbag," he muttered as he closed the last file.

He felt like he needed a shower, but a break would have to do. One of the benefits of working down here was that he basically set his own hours, but he actually enjoyed his work. He locked his computer, stood up, and wandered toward the restroom after a glance at the time, 7:00 pm. Sergey wasn't the only one working late. Three other people were still working. Two were heads down, hands on keyboard. He knew that mode well. The third was looking directly at him. Paula.

Sergey gave a quick smile and wave and walked into the restroom. He exhaled in relief as the door closed and locked behind him. He splashed some cold water on his face, then leaned on the counter and looked in the mirror.

"Well, you wanted the big time, Sergey. You got it. Now, live through it."

A few minutes later, he left the restroom, to find Paula standing at the counter just outside the door. It was well stocked with snacks, from protein bars to chocolate bars. Everything a tech needed to get through a crunch. Beside it was a refrigerator with a glass door. It was well stocked with water, sodas, and more heavily-caffeinated beverages. There was even a small selection of alcohol. Even techs needed to relax now and then.

"They take care of us down here," she said as she watched him review the selection.

"Yeah, so it seems."

"You doing okay?"

"Yeah, nifty little catch there on the PS subnet."

"Well," she said with a grin, "we can't have just anyone poking around."

He chuckled, though he didn't feel amused at all. Her grin reminded him of a shark considering her prey and deciding whether to attack. Sergey was used to faking social interactions. He generally avoided people as much as possible.

"Work late often?"

She shrugged. "Not so much anymore. Good luck on whatever you're working on," she said, and picked up a bar of Swiss chocolate and grabbed a water from the fridge before going back to her desk.

He opted for a soda and a protein bar and went back to his own station. Sergey narrowed his eyes before he sat. His chair had been moved. He always left his chair out when he intended to come back, so he could just sit back down the way he'd gotten up. It was out of place. Not by much, but he could tell.

Sergey sat down as he normally would, opened his soda, and took a drink and a bite of his protein bar before he unlocked his station. He wasn't looking at anything to be concerned about, yet, but he would have to be more cautious about what he left running. It was possible that other people could unlock his station, and he scolded himself for not thinking of that. Since he hadn't designed the security protocols, he didn't know what all the parameters were. That led him down another path; could someone actually see what he was doing in real time? He had to consider that a very real possibility, which increased the risk of this venture significantly.

He swallowed the bile that had risen in his throat and slowly ate his protein bar while he considered his next steps. It didn't feel like a wise move to dig too much deeper until he knew exactly how secure his system was. Without even looking at the results, he minimized the search results window and started poking around in the settings to see exactly who had access. According to the settings, no one but him could access it, even remotely, but that didn't satisfy him. Sergey had to assume even Annica didn't know everything that went on down here, or he wouldn't be here. Somehow, this was hidden from everyone, but someone had to be in charge. Someone had to have configured everything. So, who?

He dashed off a quick email to Annica simply saying 'need to talk,' shut down all his windows, and logged out manually. This would have to wait until morning; he needed some down time, and to think about what to do next.

* * *

Earth, Terran Space Project Campus, Annica's Apartment

Annica opened the door to her apartment to let Konda in.

"Something to drink?" Annica asked.

"Beer?"

"Sorry, don't have any alcohol, we never… it doesn't matter. Tea? Coffee?"

Annica had finished the only wine that was in the apartment, and she hadn't bothered to buy any more. It was an old habit, but it was just automatic. She supposed it would be okay to keep some stocked now, especially since it was likely there would be more clandestine meetings like this in the future.

"Coffee's fine. Thanks," Konda said as she took a seat.

Coffee, on the other hand, Annica always had going. That was an old habit, too. Max seemed to live on the stuff. They'd even had a coffee maker installed that was fixed to the plumbing, so all she had to do was put in the grounds and hit a button. In this instance, there was already some brewed, so she poured two cups and took them over, along with sweeteners and creamers.

Konda picked up the cup and took a sip without adding anything. "Wow, good stuff."

"That's Max. I think his blood was 50 percent coffee."

Konda grinned and nodded. "Military will do that to you. Back home, I get funny looks for not drinking tea like the rest of the family, but…" She shrugged.

Annica smiled. A moment of normalcy felt good, but there was still much to do before the board meeting.

"What have you found?"

"Something interesting," Konda said as she pushed her mug aside, set up her tablet, and folded down a keyboard. "Paula Handley spent a good bit of time in Director Malmkvist's office."

"I thought there were no cameras in there?"

"There aren't, but there are plenty in the corridors. Trace the path, and there's really only a few destinations, once you get close to the director's—your—office. And if it helps, I also watched for Kellie Warren. She didn't show up on the feeds even once."

Annica nodded thoughtfully. Her suspicions about Paula were likely correct, then, which meant Sergey was in the right place, but also a possibly dangerous one. It was also slightly reassuring that Kellie didn't appear to be in on it, but that didn't make her feel better about Kellie being there with Max, and Max thinking who knew what. As she was considering how to put it all together, quickly, her phone alerted her to an incoming message from Sergey.

"Hmm," she said as she read it.

"What's up?"

"Message from Sergey, very short. 'Need to talk.'"

"Maybe he's found something interesting already?"

"Maybe, but why not just send it?" Annica asked as she tapped the screen to call Sergey, put the call on speaker-phone, and set the phone on the table.

"Director?"

"I didn't expect to hear from you so soon. You have something?"

"Not on the phone," he said. The cockiness and confidence she'd seen in him during their meeting was gone, replaced by something else.

"Come to my apartment," she said and gave him directions.

He hung up without saying anything else, and Annica looked at Konda.

"That didn't sound good," Konda said and frowned.

"No, it didn't."

Annica sipped her coffee and wondered what had happened. Sergey sounded spooked, and she hoped she wouldn't have to find another tech wizard. She realized, though, that she was definitely on the right track. If there'd been nothing odd going on in Special Projects, he wouldn't be on the way to her apartment right now.

"I just don't know how I'm going to get all the answers I need before the board meeting," Annica said with a sigh.

"We can only do what we can do. You're in charge now; things go your way. You just have to put together your own playbook, and not try to play by old rules."

"What does that mean?"

"Malmkvist was all about subterfuge. Maybe it's time to throw open the curtains and shed some daylight on the whole thing. Sometimes a frontal assault works, especially when it's unexpected."

"And ruin the TSP's reputation?"

Konda's face scrunched up. "That's already done, as far as I'm concerned."

"Sure, for us, but if what really happened here goes public…"

"We're done. I know."

"And I lose any chance of finding Max."

"Even if you figure out where he is—and that's a stretch based on what you've shared with me—"

"Which is everything," Annica assured her.

"Fine. But even if you do, what then? It's not like you can throw together another ship to go after him."

Annica sighed. "I know, but at least I'd know… and there are other agencies working on interstellar travel. If I worked with one of them—"

She was interrupted by a knock on the door and got up to answer it.

"Sergey, come in," she said after checking the door camera to make sure it was him and opening the door.

Sergey glanced over his shoulder and quickly stepped inside. "Thanks for seeing me so late."

"Of course," Annica said and closed the door.

She gestured to the table. "Have a seat. Coffee?"

"Sure, thanks," he said, but paused when he saw Konda. "Captain Sanako?" he asked and glanced between Annica and Konda.

"Just Konda, here at least," Konda said with a wave.

"She's part of the team," Annica said and walked over to fetch another cup.

"Right," he said and sat down.

Annica set a cup of coffee in front of him and resumed her seat. She noticed his leg bouncing constantly.

"What's got you off your game?" she asked.

Sergey took a sip of the coffee after adding plenty of sweetener and some creamer. He took a deep breath, seeming to try to calm himself.

"It's okay, Sergey. Whatever it is, we'll figure it out and keep you safe. You have my word," Annica assured him.

"Did you know about the third subnet?"

Annica flinched. The question sounded more like an accusation. "What? No, there are only two. The primary net and the executive net."

"Wrong, there's a third for Special Projects. Very well partitioned and encrypted. Hell, it was a puzzle just figuring out how to decrypt the files so I could read them."

Annica frowned. It was disturbing to think that there was a cache of data she didn't even know existed. Gustav must have known, but there was nothing about it anywhere in any of the director's briefings. Then again, there was nothing about Paula Handley, either.

"What's in them? The files?"

"Don't know yet. Paula was still there when I left, and I'm pretty sure she's checking to see what I'm doing."

"What makes you say that?" Konda asked.

Sergey explained the last few minutes of his time in the room. How his chair had been moved, and Paula was still there.

Konda nodded. "I'd say you're right."

"Well, that's not too surprising," Annica said, "but she can't see anything, right?"

"I don't know," he admitted. "I didn't build the security, so I don't know what is or isn't possible. For all I know, she has rights to unlock my station and retain everything that was there under my login."

"I'm afraid we're beyond my scope of knowledge on computers," Annica said. "Who would know?"

Konda shrugged.

"Whoever built the system," Sergey answered. "Who would have set up my station and given me rights?"

"That would be Shao."

"Who?"

"Shao Yating, the CIO," Annica answered.

"She'd have access to everything. You think she's in on this?" Sergey asked.

Annica considered her response. She was still waiting for the report from Yating regarding the data she'd provided on the mind control that had been used. How forthcoming she was would help Annica decide whether to trust her or not.

"I don't know yet. I don't think so."

"No offense, but you'd better hope not, or anything I find is useless."

"Explain."

"It's simple. If she's involved, any trace of what you want to find is already gone, or squirreled away on some detached storage no one else can get to. If the CIO's dirty, the technology infrastructure of the entire organization is an open book to them."

"So, she would have known what Gustav was doing?" Konda asked.

"Not necessarily," Sergey said with a shake of his head. "Only if she was looking for it. It's a big network; no one can monitor it 24/7. The way I read it, that's part of the job of Special Projects, security on a macro scale. Sure, there's an InfoSec division, but they probably just handle the surface, the nets you know about. The SP net is its own monster that needs to be controlled."

"You've put a lot of thought into this," Annica said.

"Not really, it's just stuff I... know. Not to make myself redundant, but if you want to know what's really going on in tech, she's the one who can get the answers."

"That may be," Annica said, "but even if I decide she can be trusted, she's got a full plate. We'll still need you doing the grunt work, which brings us back to why you're here. What do you need?"

"Optimally, a setup somewhere other than in that room where someone can check to see what I'm doing."

"That would raise alarms, if you were there one day, then gone," Konda pointed out. "If Handley is suspicious now, that would just confirm you were there to do something she wouldn't like."

"I know, I said optimally. Realistically, I need to know if anyone else can unlock my station and see what I was doing. It would also be good to know who's poking around my station. I assume there are no security cameras in there?"

Konda shook her head.

"Then I'd want some kind of small camera that doesn't look like a camera to put on my desk. I'd feel a bit better, and it would reveal any weaknesses in the security of SP."

Annica nodded slowly. "Makes sense. Konda?"

"I'm sure we can come up with something. It's not something we keep a stockpile of, of course, but we all have our sources from our past lives."

"Something that doesn't transmit or receive. There can't be a signal of any kind," Sergey said. "Signals can be detected and traced."

"I'll need a few days, but I can source something," Konda said.

Sergey sighed and nodded. "Let's just hope I last that long."

Annica raised an eyebrow.

"When Paula looked at me, I swear, I felt like I was being sized up by a shark. I've swum with sharks, and they didn't feel as dangerous as she did," Sergey said as his leg started to bounce again.

"I thought they were pretty much extinct," Konda said, surprised.

"There's a private aquarium in Russia. Wealthy men like to have exotic pets."

Konda nodded. "I see."

Annica's mind wandered while Sergey talked about the aquarium with Konda. Talking about anything else seemed to calm him. His leg had stopped its near-constant bouncing again. She'd have to make a decision about Yating sooner rather than later. She might be another piece of the puzzle that was necessary to put everything together, especially if she wanted to get a more developed picture before the board meeting.

"Are you going to be okay to keep going?" Annica asked Sergey, interrupting his side conversation with Konda.

He pursed his lips, then nodded. "I'm not a quitter. I'll just be extra careful."

"Good, and thank you. Keep at it. I'll see where Shao is on what I've tasked her with digging into. Konda, see if you can come up with something for Sergey, so we know who's peeking, and what they're doing."

Sergey and Konda both nodded.

"Okay, now if you'll both excuse me, I need to get some sleep. It hasn't been coming easily lately."

"I can only imagine," Konda said and got up. "Get some rest."

Sergey rose as well. "Thanks for the coffee and for listening."

"Come on," Konda said. "I'll buy you a drink, and you can tell me more about that estate. Sounds amazing."

"Well, I guess I can't say no to that." Sergey grinned, and they left Annica's apartment.

Annica quickly put the mugs in to wash and went to bed to lay down. As she nestled in, and the room quickly cooled down per her bedtime settings, she closed her eyes and thought of Max, as she did every night.

* * * * *

Chapter Ten

Landing + 39 Days

Mythos, Eos City, X-94 Over Mythos

Eva Snow and the rest of MilForce on the mission sat back in their seats and closed their eyes. She could hear someone fidgeting, thanks to the sound dampening, and knew it had to be Leopold. She and her team would rest any chance they got. They weren't in a combat zone, not really, but it was just something ingrained in the lifestyle of special operations. You rested whenever you could, because you never knew when the next chance would be.

"Relax, Mr. Fischer," she said without opening her eyes.

"Right. Relax. You might as well call me Leopold."

She could hear the nerves in his voice, so she opened her eyes and sat up. "This is the kind of thing you do, right, Leopold?"

"Well, I reckon, yeah, but this is a bit different."

"Is it? How is it different from the last first contact with one of these things?"

"They're more prone to aggression. Even the griffins we know don't like 'em; that tells me something."

"This ends one of two ways, Leopold. We part friends with them, or they die."

Leopold stopped fidgeting and looked down at his hands. "Yeah."

"*Captain Snow, you should take a look at this,*" the pilot's voice said over the intercom.

Without hesitating, Snow pulled a pair of goggles from a hook over her head and put them on. They immediately lit up, and she could see a panoramic view outside the aircraft, thanks to cameras mounted around the fuselage and wings. Arrayed in front of them were at least twelve of the white griffins in an organized formation, flapping their wings, and hovering in place.

"Shit," she said.

"*Pretty much sums it up,*" the pilot said. "*What do you want to do?*"

"What is it?" Leopold asked.

"Put on a pair and see for yourself," Snow said.

"Oh," he said after a moment.

"Exactly. I'd hoped we'd at least get to the ground before a confrontation. Looks like they're laying the terms."

"Can't we just… land?"

"Gimme a circle so I have some time to think," she said.

"*Copy that,*" the pilot said, and they felt the aircraft bank slightly.

Snow adjusted her view to keep an eye on the griffins. They maintained position, which was good.

"They didn't come after us; that seems like a good thing," Snow said.

"Well, maybe," Leopold said. He seemed calmer now that he had something to focus on.

"Explain."

"One of two things. They're waiting for a better opportunity, or it really is just about the territory. They might not attack until we're beyond some point they feel is encroaching on their habitat. Can we land somewhere close by? Maybe we can meet on territory that isn't theirs. The fact that they're showing themselves is a *good* sign. Remember, they don't have to."

Eva thought back to their first contact with a griffin, though they hadn't known what it was at the time. All they had were claw marks in the tough metal skin of an X-94 that had been down on a scouting mission before *Traveler* landed, and what had done it hadn't been caught on camera. The first glimpse they'd had was when the AI-controlled robots were retrieving containers dropped from orbit. Several of them had been destroyed, and one of the griffins had been caught on video, coming out of camouflage just in time to destroy an all-terrain robot built for the harshest conditions. They still didn't understand how they'd done it.

"True, they could probably take us down before we even knew they were there. Assuming all the different... subspecies? have the same ability."

"*We know all about assumptions, Cap,*" the pilot said. "*They're gone, so I think we can call that assumption a fact.*"

She quickly scanned around the plane, and sure enough, they'd vanished. Snow growled at herself for getting so distracted by talking to Leopold that she hadn't noticed. She heard her soldiers doing a weapon check, slides pulling back, magazines being checked for the tenth time.

"Switch to thermal vision. Weapons hot, be ready for anything. Find us a place to land, expedite."

"*Copy that.*"

"You said we were going to try to talk to them first!" Leopold said.

"Look, if I feel even a tap on this aircraft, the pilot's going to shoot the sky, and we're out of here. So tighten your straps and hold on until we're out of this. Clear?"

"Yeah, mate. Crystal."

"She automatically went through the routine of checking her own weapons by feel without taking the goggles off. The entire time, she was scanning the skies for heat signatures. Now and then, a blur would cross her field of vision, but they were moving too fast to track easily.

Suddenly she felt a thud through the fuselage, and the aircraft rolled ninety degrees.

"Going down, hold on."

She scanned the area around the plane again, and the air seemed to be full of fast-moving griffins. They moved too quickly across her field of view to track with the limited scope of the aircraft's external cameras. A new view told her the munitions that had been mounted under the right wing were gone, replaced by a row of gashes that went the length of the wing.

"They'll be going for the other—" She was interrupted by another impact, and the aircraft skewed out of control. This time, she'd seen it coming, but there was no time to do anything about it. It came in at the perfect angle and scraped the munitions off the left wing.

"Brace for impact!" the pilot yelled.

Snow took off the goggles and tightened her own straps. She had a feeling not only the munitions had been taken, but some of the control surfaces had been damaged. This was going to suck.

* * *

Mythos, Eos City, Planetary Control Center

Max rubbed his eyes as he scrolled through another page of inventory updates. Every day he reviewed the stockpile of everything, from foodstuffs to paper products. Annie's bots took care of the counting, but he was still required to sign off on it as a part of the mission parameters. Maybe it was time to change that.

"Sir, you'll want to hear this. Say again, Eagle," the comm operator said from his station.

"*Snow's bird is down. I didn't see what hit it, but something sure as hell took the wings apart,*" Eagle said over the speakers in the PCC.

All eyes turned to Max as he processed the information. They'd expected to at least be able to land. An airborne fight was possible, but they hadn't counted on the griffins coming in camouflaged. There was literally nothing they could do to stop that.

"Mark the location and return to base, Eagle," Max said.

"*Sir, there could be survivors—*"

"I'm aware of that, Eagle, but you're not going to do anything on your own. We'll put together a search and rescue party and return in force. Those damn things aren't taking my people and getting away with it. Send back whatever video you captured."

Max stared up at the speaker, and when he didn't get a response, he spoke again. "Eagle, do you copy?"

"*Copy, Captain. RTB,*" Eagle said with an audible sigh.

Max knew exactly how he was feeling. Eagle felt like he was leaving the group stranded to die, and he might very well be, but Max wasn't going to throw away another perfectly good aircraft and pilot. Snow and her team were good—the best—and if there was a way to get out of the wreck and survive, they'd find it.

He called Colonel Mikhailovna on his way out of the PCC.

"*Yes, Capitan?*"

"Snow's bird is down; we're going to need S&R teams gearing up ASAP. We're going in force, Essena. First is search and rescue, then search and destroy. This shit won't fly."

"*Understood,*" Essena said and hung up.

Losing people to accidents was one thing, but this was a straight-up attack. In the back of his mind, he knew the griffins were defending what they saw as theirs. Max also knew there'd be a significant number of the population who wouldn't like what he was about to do, but he wasn't going to let this colony fail, and they needed that ore.

"*Are you certain this is the correct course of action?*" Annie asked through his earpiece.

"You have another idea to save my people and get the ore?"

"*There are other ore deposits, Max. There must be.*"

"And my people?"

"*Mission parameters include acceptable losses.*"

Max stopped walking and turned to stare at the *Traveler*, where Annie's core was still housed.

"And what do the mission parameters say about aggressive native species?" Max asked, though he already knew the answer.

"*There is no clause for aggressive native species.*"

"Exactly," he said, and resumed walking toward the griffins who'd become a mainstay around the city.

"*I estimate 49 percent of citizens will disapprove of this action.*"

"Then they can disapprove. My mind is made up, Annie. Please just focus on decoding that flight manual."

A part of his mind realized there'd been a shift in Annie's behavior, but he brushed that aside for later as he approached the griffins. The one he'd come to think of as the leader of the local group, at least as far as liaising with humans was concerned, sat up and focused on Max.

"I should really talk to you more, and I'll remedy that if I survive this. I want you to see this," he said and indicated his tablet.

Max wasn't sure how much they understood, but at least it seemed to understand looking at the tablet. The griffin laid back down, so it was at eye level.

He first pulled up a picture of Leopold, then changed to the view from the aircraft he'd been on. Max let the griffin watch the entire attack from when the griffins had first been spotted. When the video concluded, the griffin let out an ear-piercing screech and sat up. Its feathers stood up, and Max definitely got the feeling it wasn't happy.

The screech got the attention of the other two resident griffins, who walked over to sit around Max. The lead griffin reached out with a talon and pointed at the tablet. The griffins lay down and waited.

Max got the idea and repeated the process. He showed Leopold, then the footage of the attack. Once it was done, the griffins stood and walked away a few steps. They sat head to head in a triangle, and Max waited. He'd never seen this exact behavior himself, and he was very curious.

* * *

Mythos, Eos City

"Does he live?" Ebontalon asked.

"Unknown. I recognize the area; it is in the Cloudseekers' territory," Dreamtail answered. "I knew he was going there. I did not expect them to attack so easily. They have grown too comfortable coming into the lowlands," Dreamtail said.

"That is not your decision to make," Ghostfeather warned.

"We must save him," Dreamtail demanded.

"That is not your decision, either. We would need numbers, and you will not get those without Crownfeathers."

"Then we will accompany the Terrans. They want to dig from the ground there, that is all."

"The ground is sacred to them," Ghostfeather reminded him.

"The Terrans will use many of their metal birds. Look," Dreamtail said, turning to look toward the tarmac.

"Even those will be no match for the Clouds' numbers. They will be ready," Ebontalon said.

"I do not believe we will dissuade their leader from this course of action."

"Then they will all die," Ghostfeather said and stretched his wings.

Dreamtail looked toward Max, who waited for them. His body language indicated he was impatient and angry. Dreamtail understood anger, and he had grown to like these Terrans. They were friendly, mostly, unlike those who had visited before. He wished, not for the first time, he could communicate with them more easily, but the Terrans simply weren't developed enough to understand them.

Leopold had made good progress, but even then, it was like talking to a newborn.

"We could disable their flying machines," Ebontalon suggested.

"They would kill *us*, in that case. They are soft, but their weapons have bite," Ghostfeather said.

"Then what would you do, Ghostfeather?" Ebontalon asked.

"Let them go. Let them die. What business is it of ours?"

Dreamtail knew Crownfeathers had sent Ghostfeather for just this reason, to temper his desire to care for the Terrans, but Ghostfeather's nonchalance about their deaths was almost more than he could bear.

"Ebontalon, seek guidance from Crownfeathers, quickly. I will attempt to delay them as long as I can."

Ebontalon stepped back and took flight immediately.

"He will say you should do nothing," Ghostfeather said.

"We will see," he said, and walked back over to Max.

* * *

Mythos, Eos City

Max watched the griffins and waited. The one he'd talked to seem to shift his attention between the other two as they communicated. For the first time, he paid close attention to them, and something told him they were definitely, very clearly, communicating. There were none of the exaggerated actions necessary for the humans to understand their meaning. The vocalizations ranged in pitch several octaves, accented by the occasional beak snap or shift in stance.

One of the other griffins spread his wings at one point, and Max had the odd feeling it was the equivalent of a shrug. Max crossed his arms over his chest and glanced toward the tarmac, where aircraft were being loaded with munitions.

He wondered if the griffins knew they could be spotted by the humans with thermal vision. Now that he knew the griffins around the ore site were aggressive without provocation, he'd have an edge with their technology. He was going to use four of his remaining nine X-94s for this mission. Each of them was being armed with ground-penetrating missiles, as well as two 40mm Gatling guns. Lasers still weren't used for atmospheric air combat because of thermal blooming in the atmosphere rendering the beam less effective at the ranges they needed.

Max had actually argued against bringing so much weaponry, since they weren't expecting to face anything that needed to be killed… but Malmkvist had overridden him on that one. Now, he was glad, but he also had a feeling Gustav had known they'd be needed. Old frustration boiled to the surface as he thought of Malmkvist and looked back toward the griffins impatiently.

One of the griffins took flight, and the leader walked back over to Max. The griffin moved between Max and the tarmac, sat, and spread his wings.

Max furrowed his brows. "If you think I'm not going after my people, you don't understand us at all," Max said and moved to walk around the griffin.

The griffin easily shifted his stance to stay between Max and the tarmac and snapped his beak. Not at Max, but for attention. When Max looked at him, he grounded his wings, still spread, and looked to the air in the direction the other griffin had flown off.

Max considered for a moment. "You want me to wait?" he asked, while he pointed at the ground where he was standing, then pointed up the same way the griffin had looked, and flattened his hand, and moved it back toward himself, trying to indicate the griffin would come back.

The griffin gave an unmistakable nod of his head. At least that much was crystal clear, assuming he understood what Max had said and intended with his actions.

He frowned and looked at the griffin. Max knew every minute his people were on the ground alone—assuming they were alive at all— was a minute the enemy griffins had to hunt them down. The chances of survival were actually fairly good with the X-94. The reactor would have scrammed on impact if the pilot hadn't shut it down manually, so the chance of an explosion on impact was basically nil, and it was built to survive. That model's passenger cabin was basically like a pod inside the aircraft, with its own armor casing and safety features. The pilot was, unfortunately, likely dead, but the passengers would have a better than even chance of being alive.

Max's earpiece beeped in his hear, and he tapped it to accept the call.

"*Everything okay, Captain?*" Essena asked.

"Yeah, I think so. I get the feeling the griffin wants us to wait."

"*Are you in danger?*"

"No, it doesn't mean me any harm. How long until we're loaded and ready?"

"*Twenty minutes,*" she said after a few moments of silence.

"Understood," he said, and tapped the earpiece again to end the call.

"Okay," Max said to the griffin. "You've got twenty minutes."

Max wasn't sure where to start explaining how long twenty minutes was, so he didn't even try. He still needed to get his gear, so he pointed to himself, then toward the building where his apartment was. Without waiting to see if the griffin understood, he turned and walked away.

* * * * *

Chapter Eleven

Landing + 39 Days

Earth, Terran Space Project Campus, Sergey's Apartment

Sergey woke earlier than normal, his bedsheets soaked in sweat. He sighed and got up to take a quick shower after turning on the coffee pot in his small studio apartment. His move to Special Projects had earned him a larger apartment, but he was happy here. One big room was all he needed, plus he hated moving. Packing, unpacking… it was just too much hassle.

Once he was dressed, he sat at his small café table with a cup of coffee and turned on some music. He opted for some high BPM dance music, and his leg started bouncing to the beat while he planned out his day. He felt a bit better about Annica, but he'd still run a search for her name. There was a good chance anything that targeted her would turn up, and that's one of the things he was after. He'd also check on Shao Yating. He knew Annica would be doing the same, but he needed to know if *he* could trust her. Nationality wasn't supposed to matter here, but China and Russia weren't exactly bosom buddies, and he was smart enough to know that you couldn't just throw away a lifetime of beliefs.

China had always been heavily into state-sponsored technical espionage and sabotage, and if Yating was good enough to be the CIO of the TSP, it stood to reason she'd probably been a part of it. That was probably the road Sergey would have ended up traveling if he hadn't gotten out of Russia when he had. One day, men in trench coats would have shown up at his door, told him his country needed him, and made him an offer he couldn't refuse. He shuddered, glad he'd escaped that in time.

After his third cup of coffee, he cracked his knuckles and headed out to his first full day in Special Projects. The walk across campus was brisk, and he was well and truly awake by the time he entered the welcome heat of the main building, made his way to the elevator, and down to his new work home.

He wasn't the first person there, but he was glad to see Paula wasn't in yet. No one looked up from their work as he walked to his corner, and he wondered what everyone was doing. He quickly dismissed his curiosity as he sat down, logged in, and reran his search for Annica's name in the SP subnet. While that ran, he thought about other ways to approach his task. If whoever had done this was smart, they would have sanitized everything involved in the mind control operation. Even if they hadn't, Malmkvist could have easily had a deadman switch triggered that, upon his departure as director of TSP, triggered a sweep and clear job.

Then again, techs were paranoid. They were used to being thrown under the bus, or served up as fodder when necessary to distract from the man behind the curtain. It was possible someone had an insurance policy saved somewhere, just in case all this came back to bite them in the ass. He opened more windows and started more searches, for Shao Yating, Paula Handley, and all the board members.

While he waited, he opened his messages and found an email from Konda on the primary net.

Had a great time last night; let's get together for lunch? Let me know what time, and I'll see if I can get free.

Without even thinking about it, he dashed off a quick response stating that anytime would work, his schedule was more flexible than hers. They'd stayed at the bar pretty late last night, talking. It was nice. Not even one mention of all the stuff going on, just talking about life back home. He rarely left his desk for lunch or anything, but what the heck.

The message made him think, and he took a few minutes to route all his messages to the SP queue so he wouldn't have to check three nets for messages every time he looked.

The search window for Annica slowly pulsed between colors, indicating it was done. He pulled it up and shook his head. There were fourteen hundred results. This was going to take a while.

* * *

Earth, Terran Space Project Campus

Annica rose early and decided to drive back to the house to bring more clothes. Some of her clothes had turned up when Malmkvist's penthouse suite had been cleared, but she'd had those disposed of. She didn't even want to think about it, or what people thought of her. She got the occasional sideways look in the corridors, but so far, she'd managed to avoid most people and just focus on her work. She knew that would end soon.

She drove to the gate and was stopped as was normal protocol, but that's when things got different.

"Director Reeves? Where are you headed today?" the guard asked.

"Just back home to get some things. Why?"

"Ma'am, I'm going to need you to wait for your escort. We didn't know you were planning to leave the campus today, so it'll take a few minutes."

"Escort?"

"Yes, ma'am. SOP when the director leaves the campus."

She was about to protest, but that gave her an idea.

"So anytime the director leaves, er, I leave, there'll be an escort with me at all times?"

"Yes, ma'am."

"And I assume that's something that gets logged."

The guard tilted his head, a bit confused. "Of course. I'm sorry, ma'am, I figured this would have been part of your briefing when you assumed the position."

"Not your fault. I'm afraid the transition was less than normal."

"Thank you. They should be here in a minute, if you wouldn't mind pulling over there?" he asked and pointed to a small parking area just inside the gate.

She checked her rearview; there were other cars behind her.

"Of course."

While she waited, she plotted. If there was a record of every time Malmkvist left the campus and where he went, that could be handy—unless, of course, those logs didn't exist, because the people who went with him were in his pocket. She shook her head. That would require corruption at a lot of levels. Too many to keep quiet.

Annica was so lost in thought, it took a knock on her passenger side window to get her attention. She rolled the window down.

"Director Reeves. If it's okay, I'll ride with you, and we'll have two follow vehicles," Anton Essen said.

"Sergeant Essen. Um. Sure. Two vehicles? Really?"

He opened the door and sat with his rifle pointed down at the floorboard.

"SOP, ma'am," he said as he closed the door. "You know you have a car and driver that go with the office."

"No... I didn't know that. But that's okay, I like driving."

"Mmm hmm. I think command might have something to say about it, but I convinced the guard to let us go, today at least."

"Thanks, Sergeant."

"Anton, please. I hope everything's been going... well?" he asked as they pulled through the gate.

She looked back, and the two follow vehicles were actually vans, probably holding even more MilForce. "As well as it can, I suppose."

She still wasn't sure how much to trust him, or anyone else other than the small circle she'd developed. *Well, triangle really*, she thought and grinned at her own weak humor.

"Captain Sanako hasn't said much since that day."

Annica knew the day he was referring to, and she didn't want to talk about it, but he'd helped cover for her, so she figured she owed him a little.

"That's good. She's been very helpful. We're still trying to plumb the depths of what happened."

"I figured, since she's now assigned to you. I figured she'd be with you today, leaving the campus."

"She doesn't know. Besides, she's got plenty of other things to do."

"Don't we all."

"I'm sorry if I'm interrupting your day, Sergeant, but this wasn't my idea."

"Begging your pardon, ma'am, I didn't mean it that way. Just meant things always seem to be hopping. We're getting the extra security ready for the board meeting, and if you'll pardon me saying so, it's a real pain in the ass. Rich people," he said with a grunt.

She sighed and nodded. "Sorry. I suppose I'm a bit on edge."

"Can't blame you there," he said, and paused a moment. "Listen, if there's anything I can do to help…"

"I'll keep that in mind, and I may take you up on that. Though you may regret it," she said.

The rest of the drive continued in silence, which she was grateful for. Driving helped her clear her mind, and she needed that desperately.

Finally, they arrived at the house, and she pulled into the driveway. Before she could open her door, the two vans emptied out, and there were ten men and women in body armor carrying a variety of weapons approaching the house and moving around to the back.

"What the hell?" she asked. "This isn't an assault; I'm just getting some things from my house!"

She got out of the car before Anton could answer and walked toward the front door.

"Wait!" Anton yelled as he jumped out of the car and ran in front of her.

"We need to clear the house before you go in. Key, please?"

"Not happening," she said and set her jaw.

"All set Sergeant!" one of the women yelled from her position at the front door. There was a stack of them, ready to enter like they needed to clear the building.

"Ma'am," Anton said in an almost pleading voice.

"Not. Happening," Annica said and stepped around him.

The woman in the lead at the door stepped out to block the door. "Sorry, Director, this is the procedure."

"Then I'm changing the procedure. I'm the director, right? So it's my policy. Now, it's not."

She opened her mouth, then looked past her to Anton. "Sarge?"

"Let her in," he said. "Eyes sharp."

"What's your name?" Annica asked the woman.

"Corporal Gabriela Wells, ma'am, but everyone just calls me Gabby."

"Okay, Gabby, here's how this is going to go. I'm going to go into my house, get some things, and come back out. If *one* of you wants to come in, that's fine, but you *will* respect my home. Am I clear?"

"Crystal. Ma'am, I'd feel a lot better if you let me at least go in first... that's my job."

Annica considered her for a moment, then sighed. She wanted nothing more than to tell them all to get out and go away, but with the role also came responsibility. Part of that was letting other people do their jobs. She wasn't going to let a bunch of them charge through her house, but she hoped the woman standing in front of her would understand.

"Fine," she said and held out the key.

"Thank you, ma'am," Gabby said, took the key, and slowly opened the door.

She pushed it open and swept the room with her handgun before obviously checking for tripwires or anything low, then stepped in.

"Clear!" she yelled.

"I could have told you that," Annica said before she walked in.

Annica walked back to her bedroom with Gabby close on her heels.

"I have to use the bathroom; going to follow me there, too?" Annica asked.

"No, ma'am, but I'd like to check it first."

Annica rolled her eyes and gestured toward the bathroom before she walked over to the closet to pull out some clothes. A moment later, Gabby came back out.

"All good, ma'am."

"If someone wants to make themselves useful, they can put these in my car," Annica said and pointed to the neatly stacked clothes, still on hangers.

"Can do, ma'am."

On the way to the bathroom, Annica saw a piece of paper crumpled up on the floor. She picked it up and carried it in with her. She really did have to go, so she sat down and carefully straightened out the paper to read it.

"Oh, Goddess," she muttered as she read it.

The handwriting was hers, but she certainly didn't remember writing it or putting it there. She fought back tears as she neatly folded it and tucked it into a pocket as she left the bathroom. Numbly, she grabbed her mission bag from the closet, took out a few of the things that had been packed specifically for the mission, and used the space to pack more necessary things from her dresser.

"We're done here," she said and walked out, past the waiting MilForce outside, tossed the bag in the back seat, and got into the car.

"Loading up! Let's move!" Anton barked as he walked over and got into the passenger seat.

She had to wait, because one of the vans was positioned to block the driveway, but once it was out of the way, she drove off.

"Got everything you need, ma'am?" Anton asked.

"Not even close," Annica said.

Anton must have gotten the subtext, as he remained silent for the ride back to campus.

* * *

Earth, Terran Space Project Campus,
Special Projects Office

Sergey took his time going through each file he'd found, but most of it was nothing of real interest. Everything Annica had requested for the Wormhole Traversal Project that required Special Projects was there. It was interesting to him, but it was just routine work. Not everything Special Projects did was covert, it was just work that required a very specialized, and very talented, skill set, so much of the design and execution of the core systems for *Traveler* had happened here.

He decided to filter the results and show only the files dated a week before the probe sighting, and a week after she became the director. Gratefully, that brought the file countdown to only two hundred. He copied those into a new directory to separate them and started going through them.

The first few he looked at had been more tasking for Special Projects, but they were given after the probe sighting. That meant they were things Annica had done after she'd lost control of her own mind, so he read through them carefully.

Before he knew it, an alarm on his screen popped up that it was time to head to the cafeteria to meet Konda. He hadn't come upon

126 | ALEX RATH

anything really interesting yet, and he hated to stop, since he was in the zone, but maybe it would be good to get out and clear his mind.

He minimized all the windows and locked the computer. Doubt entered his mind as he got up. There was a better than ever chance whoever had been snooping before—very likely Paula—would do it again. There was nothing he could do to stop it yet. He shrugged as he pushed his chair in and left SP to go to the cafeteria.

It wasn't a long walk, since the cafeteria was positioned near the elevators in the center of the building. He'd actually only been here a handful of times, and he looked around at the selection. Nearly every major fast-food chain was represented, as well as some local cuisine. He opted for an American-style vendor, and got himself a bacon cheeseburger, fries, and a soft drink before he turned to look for Konda in the large seating area. She'd apparently spotted him and stood to get his attention.

Sergey smiled and walked over to join her at the small two-person table. He wasn't really comfortable in large crowds, so he just focused on her and tried to tune everything else out.

"You okay?" she asked as they both sat.

"Yeah. Just don't like crowds."

"What is it about techs and crowds?" she asked as she used a pair of chopsticks to pop a sushi roll into her mouth.

He shrugged, feeling self-conscious, and took a bite of his burger.

"Oh, I got you a little something," she said and picked up a box from beside her to put on the table.

Sergey raised an eyebrow and picked it up to look at it. It was standard commercial packaging. A desk fan, a nice one. Multiple speeds, timer, air filter, even doubled as a heater.

"Um… thanks."

"I haven't seen a computer geek without one on their desk yet," she said and winked, "and this one has some special features not listed on the box."

"Oh, I see," he said, and glanced around.

She took his hand and leaned across the table after he set the box down. He was a bit taken off guard and leaned forward.

"There's a full spectrum camera in it as well. Sim card in the base behind a concealed panel. Don't take anything from this, but appearances are important," she whispered in his ear before she kissed him on the cheek and leaned back.

He felt his face flush as he leaned back and stared at her.

"Red really isn't your color," she said with a grin. "How's the project going?"

Sergey took another bite of his burger as he considered how to answer that in public.

"Boring. Nothing of real interest to do yet. Just prep work, mostly."

She nodded and turned the subject to more mundane things for the rest of their lunch.

He found that he actually enjoyed it. It was nice to have someone to talk to about something other than work, and he had to remind himself that this was all just part of the job. She'd created the public image so they'd have an excuse to be seen together without raising suspicion.

* * *

Earth, Terran Space Project Campus,
Special Projects Office

Back at his desk, and after he'd set up the new fan, Sergey went back to the files he'd been reviewing. Annica had mentioned that they were listening on a strange set of frequencies, and he found references to that effort. He opened a notepad window to take notes on things for further research, and this definitely made the list.

There were other files that referred to the 'Annica project' that had started before the probe sighting, but he hit a wall. The header of the file was readable, things like 'Annica—Initiation Phase 1,' but the rest of the text was hashed. It was just one long string of meaningless letters and numbers. That meant the file would have to be opened with either a special tool, or some sort of key would have to be applied to the file to be able to read the rest.

"Great," he muttered.

Decryption had never really been his strong suit. He was more of a creative, developing things from scratch, but he also loved a challenge. Nothing was crack-proof; he'd just have to put in the time. Sergey made a note of every file name he'd later have to work on further and kept going. Unfortunately, he didn't learn anything new from the rest of the search results, and he wouldn't until he could read what someone didn't want him to read.

He paused before going to the next list of results on Paula Handley and opened the folder that contained the encrypted files. They were all in the same place, deep in the structure, in a directory simply named 'JA.' Based on how deep they were, it definitely felt like an 'oh shit' backup directory.

Sergey licked his lips, suddenly nervous again. To him, it was concrete proof that Paula was involved. He didn't have the details yet, but the fact that those files even existed seemed to be enough to him. As he considered his next move, his screen went black. Not locked, but powered down.

"What the hell. Anyone else lose power?" another tech asked.

"Yep, okay, who tripped over the cord?" someone said, which drew a few chuckles.

The door to SP opened, and the chuckles stopped. Sergey got up to see what was going on, and he saw Shao Yating standing in the doorway. He recognized her because he'd done a brief review of her public profile the previous night before he'd fallen asleep.

"All operations are suspended until further notice. You may return to your homes, or wherever you want to go, but this room is now off limits."

"What? You can't do that," Handley protested.

"Oh, I can. As for you, Ms. Handley, don't leave campus; we have a few things to talk about. Now, everyone out."

* * * * *

Chapter Twelve

Landing + 39 Days

Earth, Terran Space Project Campus

Annica left her things in her car when she got back to campus and went straight back to her office. Once there, she unfolded the letter she'd retrieved from the house, and set it on her desk before checking her messages.

The first one she opened was a brief message from Konda. *Found something for Sergey, will deliver it to him over lunch.*

Annice nodded to herself. That was quick, and good. Hopefully it would not only set Sergey's mind at ease, but also give them a bit more insight as to who was involved in this plot.

She scrolled past a few others to a message from Yating that had arrived only fifteen minutes before Annica got back.

Came by your office, but you weren't in. I have information for you. Please contact me as soon as you are available.

Annica tapped the contact number at the bottom of the message, and Yating picked up immediately.

"*Director?*"

"Shao, you have something for me?"

"*Yes, are you in your office?*"

"Yes."

"*I'll be there in a few moments*," Yating said and hung up.

Annica thought for a moment, then sent a quick message to Konda to have her come to the office immediately. She'd either arrest Yating, or hear what she had to say.

A few moments later, there was a knock at the door, and Konda and Yating walked in together.

"I'm sorry; should I come back later?" Yating asked as Konda closed the door behind her.

"No," Annica said, and gestured to the chairs in front of her desk. "Captain Sanako works directly with me. Anything you have to tell me, you might as well tell her. It saves me a step."

Yating pursed her lips, then nodded and sat.

"So, your message indicated you had something for me?"

"Not as much as I'd like, I'm afraid, but enough. You were correct in your assessment. There were deliberate holes poked in the internal security measures that allowed Director Malmkvist to perpetrate… well, I'm honestly not sure exactly everything he did, but it certainly created your situation."

Annica leaned back in her chair and looked at Yating. She wasn't sure what to say.

"You should know," Yating continued after a moment, "that I've shut down Special Projects, for now at least. Any efforts that are necessary to the organization or mission can be picked up, but I've cut off access to the Special Projects subnet to everyone but me."

"Oh, the subnet I didn't even know existed," Annica said.

"What? That should have been part of your briefing in the standard materials," Yating said, appearing genuinely confused.

"Apparently it got left out somehow. What made you decide to make this drastic a move?"

"In investigating the materials you sent me, I did some research and found evidence that Malmkvist was working with someone in Special Projects to work, shall we say, outside the expected parameters of the organization. In order to prevent anyone from covering their tracks further than they already likely have, I shut down access."

Annica sighed. "I really wish you'd have talked to me first."

"I tried… you weren't here."

"I have a phone!" Annica exclaimed. "I put someone in Special Projects to dig for me in there, and possibly get to know those involved."

"Perhaps if I'd known," Yating said, mirroring Annica's tone. "Let me guess. Yegorovich? The new SP staffer?"

Annica nodded.

"I should have suspected when the request came through, but I was admittedly distracted," Yating said. "If I'd known, he could have assisted me in my efforts."

"I'm still not sure I can trust you," Annica said.

Konda cleared her throat.

"Go ahead, Konda," Annica said.

"We are where we are, ma'ams. All we can do is go forward, so maybe focus on how to do that? There'll be time to figure out how it could have been done better later."

Annica took a calming breath and nodded. "You're right, Konda. Thank you. I suppose it's time I brought you all the way in, Shao."

Yating raised her eyebrow. "There's more than what I already have?"

Konda looked down at her phone, then looked at Annica.

"What is it, Konda?"

"Message from Sergey. He's a bit freaked out."

"I can imagine… go see if you can calm him down while I fill Shao in on the whole picture. This will take a while. And you might as well go ahead and take Ms. Handley into custody. Have her confined to her apartment, and sweep it for any electronic devices. I don't want her talking to anyone, or wiping out anything we need. See if Sergeant Essen is available to keep an eye on her."

"Yes, ma'am," Konda said and left.

"So, what else is there?" Yating asked, intrigued.

Annica felt like she should just make a recording of this so she wouldn't have to go through it all every time, which caused her to grin for a moment. She quickly dismissed the thought and went through it all with Yating.

* * *

Earth, Terran Space Project Campus

Sergey was numb as he got off the elevator with a handful of other men and women from Special Projects. That move could either mean Yating had found something like what he'd found and decided to take decisive action, or she was in on it and wanted to stop him from getting any further than he already had.

He couldn't stop looking over his shoulder and ducked into a restroom. He looked at his phone, debated who to reach out to, and decided to send Konda a quick text. It was more likely she'd be able to respond than Annica, who was likely busy. Part of him wanted to hide in his apartment until he figured out what was going on, but something his father told him came to mind.

If you ever need to hide, hide in plain sight. If you're isolated, you're an easy target.

Sergey decided to head to one of the bars on campus. There were several, all with different themes and offerings. He opted for the one he'd been to the most often, a tech-oriented place called The Circuit Board.

When he left the restroom, he glanced around and noticed Paula leaning against a wall looking at her phone. That set him on edge again, and it took restraint not to run down the corridor. Instead, he calmly walked toward the exit. Now and then he'd pass a window or a corner with a convex mirror, and his fears were confirmed. She was following him.

Or she's just going the same way. This is the closest exit, you idiot, he thought to himself.

His father would have turned and confronted her, but his father was the type of man who could kill with his bare hands and go home for dinner without a second thought. Sergey had never had much interest in fighting. He worked out sometimes, just to keep from getting overweight, but that was about it. On the other hand, it was certainly not boring.

It was a short walk to The Circuit Board, and when he got to the door, he checked the reflection, and Paula was still behind him. He opened the door and walked in, trying not to hurry or look concerned, and went to a table in a corner where he could put his back to the wall. On the way, he noticed about half of the Special Projects team was already there. It figured this would be the SP chosen watering hole.

The floor was green, with traces and pads that made it look like an old circuit board. The traces and pads served a purpose, though. They indicated the paths and stopping points for the robot servers that brought the drinks and food from the back. There was still a bar and a bartender, but this place definitely catered to the techs who didn't want to be forced to interact with people if they didn't choose to.

Sergey noticed several of the SP team glanced up at him as he passed on the way to the table. Some of them were just seeing who else showed up, while others seemed to be suspicious or accusatory. He was the new guy, so he must have done something to piss Yating off.

He checked his phone after he sat; nothing from Konda. With a sigh, he set the phone on the table and scrolled through the tablet that was wired to the table. He usually opted for just beer on the rare occasions he went out, but today called for something stronger. Far down the list, he nodded to himself and selected his choice.

A moment later, the bartender approached and set a glass in front of him. Sergey looked a bit surprised, and the bartender smiled.

"We don't trust this to the robots. Never know when someone will bump into them. Forty-year-old Macallan is too expensive to risk," he said with a wink and walked back to the bar.

He brought the glass to his nose and inhaled deeply. It was a rare treat, but something he truly enjoyed. Another of his father's influences. Sergey had tried less expensive single-malt scotch, but just didn't enjoy it as much. *Sometimes*, he thought, *it's as much about what it is, as how it tastes.* He had an even older bottle in his apartment, a gift from his father when he'd left Russia to join the TSP, but he hadn't opened it yet. Maybe one day there'd be a reason.

Sergey watched the door as he took his first sip. He savored the flavor as it rolled around in his mouth, then enjoyed the slight burn as he swallowed. It was only slightly ruined when Paula Handley walked in the door.

Based on how far she was behind him, it had taken her longer than it should have to come in. Either she'd debated outside, or she'd talked to someone before coming in. He picked up his phone and tilted his head down as if he were looking at it, but his eyes were still on her. She stopped a few steps in and looked around the room. If she was trying to spot him, she was certainly being obvious about it.

He felt his stomach clench and tasted bile in the back of his throat, worried that she'd decide to confront him right here in public. Thankfully, she walked over to the bar and took the seat closest to the door. An interesting choice, Sergey thought. Most people, upon entering a bar—especially one like this—would walk the farthest away from the door, for several reasons. First, you avoided the chill that came every time the door opened; second, it got you farther away from anyone else who might walk in.

Sergey looked down when his phone vibrated in his hand. It was a message from Konda.

"Stay there. We know what happened; I'm on my way."

His shoulders relaxed when he read her message. He hadn't realized he'd tensed up that much, but he certainly felt much better now. He smiled as he leaned back and took another drink. The thought of seeing Konda again made him smile, then he chastised himself.

What the hell are you doing, Sergey? You're in something deep here, and you're thinking about the cute woman with the guns? Focus on the task at hand.

He couldn't help himself, though. It took some effort to maintain a neutral expression when he imagined Konda walking in, Paula making a scene, and Konda twisting Paula into a pretzel. As if summoned by his thoughts, Konda walked through the door, but she wasn't alone. There were two other MilForce with her.

Sergey couldn't hear what was said, but Konda clearly pointed directly at Paula, and the two armed men with her walked over to Paula and spoke to her. A minute later, they escorted Paula out the door, and Konda walked over to sit down with him. She took a chair so her back was to the room, and only he could see her face.

"What was that about?" Sergey asked.

"Well, we were going to be satisfied with digging deeper, but Yating acted and forced our hand. It's pretty obvious Paula's deep in this, so Director Reeves asked us to confine her to her apartment."

"You know she'll just—"

"I have a team sweeping Handley's apartment for electronics now. She won't be able to do anything."

"Oh. Right. Good thinking," Sergey said and gulped down the rest of his scotch. "You know everyone in this place is staring at us and wondering why you're sitting here, right?"

"Of course. Which is why you're going to walk out with me as if I'm escorting you out. They'll think you're in the same boat Paula is."

"And that's a good thing?" Sergey asked.

"Unless you want them to think I came in to arrest her and then have a drink with you…"

"I see your point," he said and stood up.

Konda gestured for him to go ahead of her and rested her hand on her sidearm.

He walked out, with Konda on his heels, and she followed him for a short distance until they were out of sight of the bar.

"Head to your apartment and relax. I'm sure Director Reeves will be in touch."

"Will do. Thanks," Sergey said as Konda peeled off.

* * *

Earth, Terran Space Project Campus, Director's Office

A nnica received a message from Konda just as she was wrapping up her presentation to Yating.

"Handley's in custody, and Sergey's safely on his way to his apartment," Annica said.

Yating nodded. "Good."

"So, how much of this did you already know?" Annica asked.

Annica took note of the fact that Yating had been silent through the entire thing, and hadn't asked one question, so she had a sense that not all of it was a surprise.

"I knew about the faked probe sighting. Everyone at the executive level did, including the board. A lot of money went into *Traveler*, and the decision was made that it needed to go."

Annica clenched her jaw and felt herself nearly trembling with rage. They'd decided there was too much money on the line, so they threw four hundred people into the unknown, like tossing a penny down a well to see how far down it went. She shook her head in disbelief.

"I know how callous this must sound, but there was a high level of confidence they'd arrive *somewhere*."

"How?"

Yating paused, uncharacteristically uncertain. "I don't know. I confess, I don't understand a lot of the science around space travel, but Gustav convinced everyone that it would be safe."

"Why lie to them? To Max? To all the people who volunteered for a specific mission?"

"That… wasn't my decision, and I protested it, but I was outvoted," Yating said with a sigh. "The board, they're money—they're interested in how things look to the public. I believe maybe half of them have an interest in the science; the other half are interested in capitalizing on the technology the TSP develops."

Annica nodded silently. She was torn between rage, frustration, and just wanting to curl up in a corner and cry. Everything felt hopeless. Even the board was in on lying to Max, to everyone. Now she was stuck with having to maintain the lie, at least for now. The board had the ultimate say-so in the governance of the organization, and that was where she was hamstrung. She'd have to convince them that coming clean on the deception was the best way to try to find *Traveler*. That way they weren't the only ones looking.

"Who else on staff knew?"

"A handful of personnel in Special Projects were involved in creating the probe sighting footage. That's it. They were forbidden from revealing their work to anyone else. And before you ask, yes, Paula was on that team."

"And the rest of it?" Annica asked.

"I had no idea you'd been manipulated. I didn't know about the personnel on *Traveler* who clearly shouldn't have been there. And I've never seen those... odd drawings, or whatever they are."

Annica studied Yating for a moment. It felt like Yating was telling the truth. She obviously wasn't the best at detecting deception, but something deep down told her Yating was clean, at least of some of it.

"Why are you here?" Annica asked.

Yating looked confused. "Because you asked me to come."

"No. Why did you come to the Terran Space Project? I know it wasn't for the money."

"True. I suppose it was the challenge of doing something that hadn't been done before. Leading the effort to develop a mission AI, to send humanity farther into space than it had ever been. I suppose the knowledge that the job would be all about creating new technology rather than the best budgetary application of existing technology was the big draw."

"That's how Max was, is, with flying. He always had to be the first."

"Let me help you find him, Director. Let me help you find them all."

Annica heard the change in Yating's tone, and she sounded truly sincere.

"Okay. We'll gather our little team here in my office tomorrow morning at seven to figure our next steps."

Annica sent a message to Konda and Sergey to let them know about the meeting as Yating stood and left. It looked like the covert phase of this effort was over, and it was time to go at it head-on and confront those involved. There had to be quite a few, but she'd start with Paula Handley, the only one they had any real evidence on.

* * * * *

Chapter Thirteen

Landing + 40 Days

Mythos, Eos City, Crashed X-94

Eva Snow's eyes popped open, and she did a quick assessment of herself. Fingers, toes, eyes. They all worked, so her back wasn't broken; that was something at least. Main power was offline, but the emergency red lighting had kicked on, and she quickly surveyed the rest of her team. One was obviously dead, based on the angle his head was hanging. She grimaced and said a short prayer to Odin.

"Til Valhalla," she said as she unfastened her restraints.

The aircraft had landed right-side up, which was always a plus. This wasn't the first transport she'd been in that had gone down, and she had a feeling it wouldn't be the last. She pulled off one glove and quickly checked everyone's carotid heartbeat. Only one loss; that wasn't bad, given the circumstances. She knew she'd have to answer to Colonel Mikhailovna for the loss, *if* they made it back alive.

"Rise and shine, sleepy heads!" she said in her command voice.

Almost immediately, the other members of MilForce snapped their eyes open, unfastened, and stood with weapons at low ready. Leopold groaned in response.

"Check on him," she ordered while she went to the rear to pop the door.

One of her men knelt to assess Leopold's condition while she went to the rear entry of the pod. As long as the X-94 itself was mostly intact, this door would open to the larger bay of the aircraft,

143

then they would have more room to spread out and determine a plan. She tapped a panel on the wall next to the door, and a camera, powered by the pod's backup systems, powered up. The rear of the aircraft was gone. Hell, *everything* was gone. The pod was resting upright on the ground like it had been placed there on purpose.

"Aircraft is pieces somewhere, or the pilot ejected the pod. Emergency transponder is on, so at least they'll be able to find us."

"Then what? Come down like we did? Best thing they could do would be to just forget it and let us hump back on foot," said Sergeant Casper Kracht, formerly of the German *Kommando Spezialkräfte* Marines.

"Probably, but I know Captain Reeves. He's probably in a plane himself on the way to look for us."

"He really shouldn't," Kracht said and turned his attention back to Leopold.

"What should or shouldn't be is irrelevant. We have to find a way to clear an LZ. That's our top priority. This mission is scrubbed."

"There's still a chance," Leopold said angrily and pushed Kracht away. "I'm fine."

"Mr. Fischer, I know you want to believe that," Kracht said, "but Captain Snow is right. This situation is FUBAR."

"You guys use that too, huh?" Snow asked.

"Who doesn't?" asked Sergeant Jana Nováková, one of the few women ever accepted into the Czech 601st Special Forces Group. "You Americans come up with good descriptors."

"It's what?" Leopold asked.

"Fucked up beyond all recognition," they said in unison.

"Well, I reckon it fits, but there's still a chance we can do what we came to do," Leopold insisted.

Snow licked her lips while she thought. His dedication to the mission was admirable, but right now his safety, and that the rest of her team, were priority one. The pod was intact, but for how long was a question she didn't want to think about. She knew what the griffins could do, and the pod would be just another play toy if they decided to go that route. Fortunately, they'd probably had no idea they were in here until she cracked the door. She had to assume the pilot was definitely dead.

"All right, here's what we've got," she began. "Unknown number of hostiles that, if we're lucky, don't know we're here. We can sit tight and wait for extract, which is coming, or we can evac and try to find a better position. There are trees all around us, and we know some trees don't like it when we walk around them, so it could be some of those. They all look the same to me."

"I can help with that," Leopold said and walked over to look at the small display.

"Okay, while Mr. Fischer assesses that situation, thoughts?"

"I've never been a fan of sitting in a coffin," Kracht said.

"Same. I was trapped in a bunker for two weeks once," Jana added. "That's not fun."

"We've all been through shit like this, in training, and in the world," Snow added for Jana, "but Mr. Fischer—"

"Leopold," he interrupted.

"Fine. Leopold, hasn't. He's as civvie as it gets."

"But I know more about what's around us than you do," he said and turned to face them with his arms crossed over his chest.

"I like him," Jana said. "*Velké koule.* I wonder if—"

"That's enough," Snow said.

Leopold looked confused.

"I'll explain later," Kracht said to Leopold with a grin and a wink.

"Anyway, no, the so-called killer trees ain't out there. Least not the ones we've seen."

"You fill me with such confidence, Leopold," Snow said dryly. "Our armor will keep us safe. You'll have to stay behind and follow closely in our footsteps."

"Okay, but let's assume there's some kind of communication, and they remember things. They'll know what those are," he said as he pointed at their weapons. "Keep 'em down unless you have to. If we have a chance to communicate, let me get out front."

Eve shook her head.

"Listen! Let me do what I can do!" Leopold exclaimed. "You saw what they did to our most modern aircraft. You want to fight them long term with what little firepower you have? Or do you want a chance to stop this now?"

Eva looked at Leopold, then over at Jana and Kracht, who both shrugged.

"Fine, if the opportunity presents itself, it's all yours, Mr. Fi-Leopold."

* * *

Mythos, Eos City, Max's Apartment

Max snapped the last fastener on his flight suit, grabbed his field bag, and left his apartment to go to the tarmac. He wondered about the griffins again. They were obviously intelligent. That had been proven time and again, but the fact that at least this one now showed concern for him was interesting. He really needed to dedicate more people to figuring out a good way to communicate.

"I knew you'd do this," Kellie said. She'd been waiting for him outside his building.

"Of course I am," he said without breaking stride as he turned down the sidewalk.

She hurried to get in step beside him.

"We have plenty of people who can handle this, Max."

"Yes, we do, but it's my responsibility. I can better judge the situation if I'm there and make a snap decision. You're in charge while I'm gone. Task one, pick a few people off deciphering those flight manuals to work with the griffins. I want some kind of actual communication system set up ASAP. It's obvious they know things we need to know to better our chances of survival on this planet."

"I, okay, Max, but—"

"Second, green light the crew to bring the alien craft back to the base. That's a completely different set of skills, and that needs to keep going."

"Max!" she shouted and stepped in front of him.

He could have easily stepped around her, but he stopped and fixed her with a serious gaze. "Don't do this, Kellie. Not now. We both need to focus on the mission. Nothing else. Lives depend on what we do today."

Max saw the muscles in her jaw and neck tighten. He had a feeling he knew everything she'd say to try to stop him from going, but none of it would work. It would just make it harder when he got back. If he got back.

"I have to go, Kellie," he said, and against his better judgment, wrapped his arms around her.

She returned the hug, and he could feel her sobbing against his chest.

"I'll be back, and we'll have this discussion. But not now," he whispered into her hair.

She nodded, but said nothing.

Two soldiers ran past, carrying their weapons toward the flight line, and he sighed and pushed her away.

"I really do have to go. Get on those tasks for me, okay?"

Kellie nodded and wiped tears from her eyes as she stepped out of his path.

He winked and walked on, picking up to a light jog. He'd had a moment like this with Annica when they were dating, and he was about to take off for an inter-lunar flight in an experimental spacecraft. He couldn't do it again. The last thing he needed right now was to be distracted, and now he was. The scene with Annica played out in his mind as he walked.

* * *

*M*ax zipped up his flight suit and turned to grab his flight bag, but Annica stood between him and the corner of the bed where it sat. Most astronauts didn't have their suits at home, but his position had his quarters walking distance from the flight line, so his apartment was pretty much also his own personal ready-room. Plus they were much less bulky than they had been in previous decades.

"You know I have to go," Max said and crossed his arms over his chest.

"Can't someone else do it?" she pleaded. "I'm scared I'll lose you, Max."

He sighed. "This is the job. I made that crystal clear, Annica. Look, I'll be back in a week. I fly up, do some routine ops around the Moon, and fly back. Easy."

"If the ship makes it."

"It'll make it," Max said and reached around her to get his bag.

"I love you, Max."

He and Annica had been dating for a while. Long enough that she had a few changes of clothes at his apartment, which was a first for Max. The uniform drew women, and being a test pilot just added to his mystique, but Annica was the first woman he'd been serious about. But this…

"Annica…"

"I do, Max. I know I do. Don't go. I've got a bad feeling about this. Just stay with me," she said and wrapped her arms around him tightly.

He hugged her back, and it felt good. There were parts of him that wanted to scrub the mission and stay, but the job was important, and it came first.

"I'm sorry, Annica. I really am. But the ship is loaded with supplies the people up there need."

"Then they can send something else, someone else. You can't tell me that's the only ship that can go."

"It's not, but they requested I do it in that ship. It'll cut the flight time to the Moon significantly. If this new drive holds up…"

"If."

"Yes, if," he said and gently pushed her away. "It's what I do Annica. I've told you before, I'm not changing what I do, not for anyone, because anyone who truly cares about me won't ask me to give up my dream."

She rolled her eyes and flopped down to sit on the edge of the bed. "Your dream. Why can't I be your dream, Max?"

"You make different dreams come true. But if this drive holds up, and we can get it even bigger, better, the chances of going extra-solar go up exponentially! And if I fly it…"

"Then you can leave me even further behind. Fine, Max. Go. Follow your dream," she said as the tears started to flow.

"Annica…"

"Just go," she said, and ran into the bathroom and slammed the door behind her.

He glanced down at his watch and sighed. He had plenty of time, but he'd been warned many times about distractions, and his experience had taught him those lessons were right. He picked up his bag and left without another word.

* * *

*M*ax was on autopilot as he went through preflight checks. The ship could carry a full command crew, but he'd be making this flight solo to prove it could be handled by a solo pilot. He could easily have brought the crew and just had them sit and do *nothing, but he liked being alone in a ship in space. It was his own space, where he had control of everything.*

There were thoughts of scrubbing the mission just because he was distracted, but he feared it would be the end of his career as a test pilot if he let a relationship get in his way, and it really was his first love. Flying. The scene played out over and over in his mind. She'd told him she loved him, and he'd just talked about the mission. It wouldn't surprise him if he never saw her again, and that bothered him.

"Captain Reeves? Status?" Flight Control asked in a rather annoyed voice.

Max scowled to himself. He'd been so distracted, he hadn't even heard them.

"Pre-flight checks a-okay. Reeves ready for takeoff."

"Welcome back, Captain. We're going to try something different today. Full burn to vertical to the sky. Full burn to extra-atmospheric operations. Think you can handle it?"

A switch went off in Max's mind, and the job was the only thing there. Mostly.

"Sounds like fun, Control. Let's light this candle."

"You and your old sayings. Okay, Captain. The runway is yours."

He turned to the side, where he would normally have thrown a salute to the crew detaching the fuel lines, but this time, there were no fuel lines and no crew. This ship was equipped with the first anti-matter mini-reactor to power a spaceship. So far, it had worked perfectly, and this mission would prove it could handle the load over a longer period of time.

Max took a deep breath and went through the last few steps before shoving the throttle forward as far as it would go. The jolt threw him back in his seat, and he was airborne to vertical flight in less than two seconds.

"Profile looks good, Reeves. Stay on path."

"Roger that," he said between grunts. The g-suits were good, but nothing could stop eight Gs from forcing your heart into your throat. Full acceleration ascents were rare anymore, since they could take a much lower angle approach and

exit the atmosphere more gently, but this was what the plan called for, so he did it.

The image of Annica standing in front of him appeared in his mind.

"I love you, Max."

Warning lights lit up the cabin, and emergency alarms went off. Something was wrong. Very *wrong.*

"Punch out! Punch out!" was all he could hear.

They'd at least been smart enough not to make the ejection system something he'd have to violate the rules of gravity to reach, but he couldn't remember the sequence.

"I love you, Max."

"Hold on, we're kicking you out! Now!"

The command pod ejected violently, and blackness threatened to take over his vision. He grunted repeatedly and stabbed the button that injected a large dose of epinephrine into his system to keep him awake. The clouds pushed away under the influence of the rush of adrenaline, and he fired the stabilizer jets that would stabilize the command pod, but they weren't reacting the way they should. At least not the way they would in atmosphere.

"Control, I've got a problem here," he said more normally as the g forces let off.

Nothing.

"Shit," he muttered and pulled up communications status. No signal.

He went through his routine when he punched out, which he was very familiar with as a test pilot, and frowned. He'd been too high when they'd punched him out. His command pod was now in a low orbit and without communications. Even the emergency locater was offline. That never happened. They'd never find him unless he figured something out.

He had air and power for 24 hours, so he closed his eyes, slowed his breathing, and went through a practiced meditation to clear his mind.

"I love you, Max."

He swatted thoughts of Annica out of his mind and focused on surviving. He'd never be able to tell her he loved her, too, if he didn't live through this. Ships like his were designed for every emergency, including this one, but systems that had never failed before were failing. Normally, he'd control a descent through the atmosphere, and reenter to an unguided landing, but the guidance rockets weren't behaving the way they should.

Once his mind was finally clear—or at least as clear as it was going to get— he went through his status indicators. Max stared at the power indicator, which should've been full, but it read critically low. The batteries must have been damaged along with the other systems.

"Shit."

By now, rescue ships positioned in orbit would be looking for him, but without a beacon, he was a speck in space. Then it hit him. The atmospheric entry warning system. If he could get the pod into the atmosphere, it would trigger alarms on the ground, and they'd at least have an idea of where to look by tracing back the angle of descent. In one of the more terrifying moves he'd ever made, he unbuckled and punched the hatch to the command pod. Just before he shoved himself out, he triggered the thrusters for reentry on a ten-second countdown. Based on their behavior, it would be ugly, and deadly for him if he were on board, but hopefully it would be enough. He pushed away, and the pod pushed itself toward Earth using the oxygen thrusters on his suit.

He saw the heat bloom as the pod began to burn through and activated his personal distress beacon. The range wasn't great, but it would hopefully be good enough. His suit gave him three hours of life support, and he had a feeling he'd need every minute.

* * *

With an hour to go, finally, a rescue shuttle approached with its floodlights on full bright. His plan had worked, and thirty minutes later, he was on the ground, back home at Cape Canaveral. Max knew the first order of business would be a debrief, and he was surprised to see Annica run toward him and all but jump into his arms. He was so exhausted from the ordeal, one of the rescue crew, who was luckily right behind him, had to catch him to keep him from hitting the tarmac.

"Whenever you're ready, Captain," the man said and patted his back before he walked away toward the control center.

Max was more conflicted than he'd imagined he would be. The reality was, he almost didn't come back from this one. It wasn't the first close call he'd had in his career, and he knew it likely wouldn't be the last, but now, it was different.

"I have to do this, but I can pick you up for dinner," Max said gently as he untangled himself from her arms.

The wave of emotions that passed over her face hit him hard. Pain, fear, excitement, frustration, anger, and… love. It was all there somehow in that one look. He'd always avoided getting seriously involved with anyone for this reason. He didn't want to be responsible for anyone else's happiness. His job required that he focus completely on what he was doing, and today, that focus being broken had nearly cost him his life. He really wanted to be alone for the rest of the day, but she was a part of his life now, and if that was going to continue, this was something she'd handle with him, too.

"Or you can wait in the visitor's area while I debrief, but I don't know how long it'll be."

She nodded and wiped tears from her eyes with the sleeve of her windbreaker. Well, his windbreaker. He knew she'd likely been allowed into the control center visitor's room to watch the flight, which meant she'd seen what had happened at the same time the control team had.

Max wrapped an arm around her shoulder and led her to the waiting sedan that would drive them to the building.

"Annica."

She looked up at him, still unable to speak.

"I love you, too."

* * * * *

Chapter Fourteen

Landing + 40 Days

Mythos, Eos City

Max shook his head to clear the memory just in time to avoid running into the griffin who'd positioned himself directly in his path. He looked up at the large creature and raised an eyebrow.

While he was nearly certain there was no equivalent in… griffin… it spread one wing and pointed to the sky. Max looked up, and there had to be at least thirty of the things circling over the city. What he didn't know was whether their intent was to stop him, or help him.

"So, are you going to help us, or get in my way?" Max asked, more aggressively than he'd intended.

The memory of Annica—and the near repeat of the situation with Kellie—already had him off his game, and that was dangerous. This time, there was more than just his own life on the line.

While he doubted the griffin understood what he'd asked, it must have understood at least that there was a question. The griffin pointed with the other wing toward where the X-94 had gone down and gave an unmistakable nod before he deliberately stepped out of Max's path.

"Welcome to the team," Max said and walked on with purpose.

156 | ALEX RATH

He did his best to clear his mind, but he worried. The incident at the Cape had been determined to be a malfunction with the new anti-matter core, and he'd done everything right, but nothing could convince him he couldn't have somehow saved that mission. He knew he hadn't *caused* any of the problems, but he was convinced it would've been less catastrophic if he hadn't lost focus.

He walked up to a gathering of MilForce, led by Essena, and the pilots for the mission, including Colin "Eagle" Shepard.

"Looks like we're going to have backup," Max said and pointed up.

"We were wondering what their intent was," Colin said and nodded. "Glad to hear they're on our side."

"You're not alone there," Max agreed.

"Captain Snow will keep the team alive; we must bring them back," Essena said.

"And we will, Colonel," Max said. "This is a straightforward extract at first. My plane will lead that effort. Colin, your mission is simple. Cover the extraction, then track down where those things live, and destroy it. Melt it or turn it to rubble, I don't care which. Nothing harms my people and lives to brag about it. Clear?"

"Crystal."

"Essena, you know your people and what they'll do. I'll get you in comm range—assuming they have working comms—and you'll coordinate the extract. To that end, you'll ride up front with me."

"Extraction team is ready with wingsuits, if necessary," Essena said.

"Good thinking," Max said, not even bothering to question their skill with them. Special forces troops were good at anything they decided to be good at. "I'm also considering a distance landing, and hike in to get them. We'll know more about what's possible once we're on site. I assume you reviewed the maps we had from the satellites before we lost them?"

Essena nodded. "Of course, but doubt that will be possible. Terrain is difficult."

Max nodded. His assessment had been the same, but he also knew, no matter how good the photography was, it was no replacement for personal observation.

"Okay, folks, this is going to be a very fluid situation. Be ready for anything. I'm not sure exactly what our winged friends are going to do, but let's be careful to avoid any friendly fire," Max said, looking specifically at Colin and the other pilots.

Everyone nodded.

"Okay, let's do this."

* * *

Mythos, X-94 Crash Site

It was slow going once they left the pod they'd survived the crash in. Eva moved one step at a time, probing the ground and shifting foliage with the muzzle of her rifle, wary of any plants that might take offense at their presence.

Something else I never thought I'd do, she thought. *Be on the watch for killer plants.*

The foliage was thick around them, and the colors were beautiful, if you could get past the fact that they were potentially deadly. Every shade of red, blue, and green was represented by the ground cover, and it mixed and intermingled like a modern abstract painting. Even the trunks of some saplings had a purple hue, rather than the standard brown bark they were used to on Earth. Eva made a mental promise to herself to find out more about why when they got back.

The rest of her team, and Leopold, followed carefully in her footsteps, literally. They stepped in her boot prints and nowhere else. It was tested ground they could feel confident about. To that end, with each step, she'd grind her foot to crush the foliage down further than a normal step would, and to make room for the larger boots of Sergeant Kracht.

A loud sigh from the rear suggested that Leopold wasn't quite used to such cautious advances.

"You'd prefer to just run and hope for the best, Leopold?" she asked quietly.

"Well, no. Just a little dizzy."

Eva frowned. "Are you okay to go on?" If he fell, not only could he fall on something he shouldn't, he'd make a lot of noise she didn't want. The pod was still barely in sight, and her goal was to get as far away from it as possible to avoid detection by the hostile griffins.

"Yeah. I'll be fine, mate. Let's go."

Eva nodded, though she was unconvinced. Leopold was an expert, though, so she trusted him not to put her team in danger. Step by step, she moved them deeper into the undergrowth. After another dozen or so steps, she heard the shrieking cry of what had to be one of the griffins, though she had no way of knowing whether it was friendly or hostile.

She turned to face her team and put a finger to her lips. Then she pointed ahead to where she'd spotted a large boulder. That was her first destination. Somewhere they could safely stop and assess Leopold's status.

After another half-hour of slow progress, they made it to the boulder, and she motioned for them to gather around after she'd tested the ground.

The team moved forward, and Leopold quickly took advantage of a small shelf he could use to lean back against. It wasn't quite deep enough to completely sit, but it was apparently enough.

Kracht knelt in front of him, taking his vitals, while Eva carefully climbed up the boulder to sit on the top and pull out her radio. Jana automatically took watch and scanned the environment for threats with her rifle ready to go.

Eva triggered the radio a few times, but said nothing. Just the breaks would notify anyone in range that someone was there. While she waited, she looked closer at the boulder. It looked strangely out of place, but it also appeared to have been there for quite a while. Of course, the way some things grew on this planet, that was potentially a bad guess. Still, something felt off, and then she noticed them. Claw marks, similar enough to those she'd seen in the metal of a destroyed vehicle to make her shudder. Instinct told her to look up, and she gulped when she saw two of the griffins hovering, obviously looking directly at her.

"We may have a problem here," she said without moving a muscle.

Jana looked up at her, and by chance, one of the griffins was in her line of sight. She instantly brought her rifle to bear, but Eva held up a hand.

"If they wanted us dead, I think we'd be dead already. Leopold? Now's your chance. There's only two at the moment, but the sound of a rifle will draw them all, and we didn't come in prepped for a stealth mission."

"The boulder," Leopold said.

"What?"

"I bet it's a territory marker. Are there any markings on it?"

"Yes," Snow said. "Some claw marks here on top."

Leopold nodded, but swayed a bit as he lost his equilibrium.

Casper caught him and shook his head. "I'd wager swelling on the brain; we need to get him out of here ASAP."

"I'm fine," Leopold said unconvincingly, but he stood.

He unslung his pack and pulled out a bag. As soon as he pulled it out, Eva could smell the fish, a little past its expiration date for her, but Leopold didn't even seem to notice. At least he was careful not to touch it with his hands as he undid the zip-lock seal on the bag, and flung the fish away from him. It had to be at least a ten-pound fish, and he got pretty good distance, she thought absently.

"You're feeding them?" Jana asked.

"Worked the first time. Presenting food is a well-known peace-making gesture in the wild. Or leaving food for a larger predator. It's a good way to stay alive if you're small and easily eaten."

"I can prove how hard I am to—" Jana started and raised her rifle again.

"No!" Eva said urgently, but still kept her voice down.

"We're the hunted, Sergeant. It makes the most sense for us to show we respect that," Leopold said.

"And if they don't get it?" Casper asked.

"Then you get to shoot your shiny guns," Leopold answered grimly.

One of the griffins swooped down quickly and without warning. Eva watched Jana track it with her rifle out of the corner of her eye, but she didn't fire.

The griffin sniffed at the fish, reached out its rigid tongue to taste it, then screeched loudly enough that Leopold took a few steps back.

"That didn't sound like thank you," Eva said.

The griffin lunged toward Leopold without any sort of predictable moves. Eva reached for her sidearm, but was too late. Jana already had it dead to rights and pulled the trigger. A single shot went through the griffin's head, and it fell in a heap, sliding toward Leopold on pure kinetic energy.

Leopold, who'd backpedaled as quickly as he could, hit the ground hard, and didn't move.

"Casper, get Leopold. Jana, cover me," Eva said as she unslung her rifle.

In one smooth motion, she brought the rifle into her hands, aimed at the other visible griffin, and fired a single shot. The sniper's reflexes paid off, and the griffin tumbled out of the sky, but not before it had screeched loudly enough to be heard for miles.

"We've got to move. Now," she ordered as she scrambled down off the boulder.

The environment was still a concern, but she was more concerned about the greater threat of beaks and claws that could render a human body unrecognizable.

"Jana, on point. Find us cover. I'll help with Leopold."

"No need," Kracht said, and picked Leopold up in a fireman's carry. "Just grab my rifle?" he asked, nodding to where he'd had to set it on the ground to carry Leopold. "I'd hate to lose that one."

"You'll have to tell me the story if we survive this," she said and slung the well-worn rifle over her left shoulder.

"Only if you're buying," he said and marched off after Jana, who was already at the tree line, scouting ahead.

"Deal," Eva said, which was easy to agree to, since there still wasn't an established system of barter on the planet. Everything was free.

* * *

Mythos, X-94, Flying Over Mythos

With all four X-94s airborne, Max was a bit more focused. He'd let Colin and his wingmen take the lead. They'd be the tip of the spear for this operation. A small piece of Max's mind thought *I guess you're the shaft*, and he couldn't help but chuckle at his own schoolboy humor.

"Something is funny?" Essena asked.

"No, sorry," he said with a grin—though she couldn't see it through his face shield—and shook his head.

"Pilots," she muttered.

Max looked out the windscreen and sighed as reality crept back in. The scenery he was flying over was breathtaking. Untouched wilderness of a variety of color never before seen on Earth, except maybe in one of those botanical gardens, which were manufactured to look the way they did. This was completely natural. Some of it would have to be tamed, but if they followed their mandate, which he intended to ensure they did, the majority of it would remain as wild as it was now.

His mind drifted to Kellie. He had a feeling he knew what she'd wanted to say, and he wasn't sure how he felt about it now. It was easy enough to dismiss Annica after what she'd done to him, basically abandoning him to his fate, but he couldn't just erase so many years together. The anger was still there, but time was tempering it. A small part of him wondered if she'd done what she had by choice, but he dismissed that quickly. Annica was far too strong-willed to be convinced of anything she didn't want.

"I have a signal," Essena said. "It is weak, but it has to be them."

She consulted her radio, which also included guidance information toward the signal, and pointed.

Max consulted his displays, one of which was a signal scanner, and spotted the signal. It was definitely weak, but it was there.

"Reeves to Eagle, we have a signal from the target; altering course," Max said, as he shifted course toward the signal, and transmitted the details to the rest of the flight.

"*Copy that, Captain,*" Colin responded, and the other three aircraft adjusted course as well.

Essena got up from her seat and went to the back to join the rest of the unit without a word. Max caught the look on her face, though, and he was glad she was on their side.

* * *

Mythos, X-94 Crash Site

Eva scanned the skies as she followed Casper and Jana into the cover of the trees. So far, she didn't see anything, but that didn't mean much. She remembered they had the ability to somehow camouflage themselves and made a mental note to jump on the geeks back in the city to find out how.

She got about ten meters into the cover and knelt behind a tree. She flipped down the multi-spectrum goggles mounted to her helmet and selected IR mode. Even with their camouflage, that would let her see them—and kill them. The idea of communicating with them was absolutely gone at this point. They'd threatened someone under her protection; that earned them all a death sentence.

"Much thicker deeper in," Jana said over her shoulder.

"Casper, do a quick triage on Leopold. We're not losing him. I'm going to try the radio again."

She heard him set Leopold down as gently as he could and retrieve his equipment from his backpack. Without daring to look away from the clearing, she offered up a prayer to Odin and hoped for the best. As she did, four griffins landed in the clearing. A quick peek around the edge of her goggles told her they were camouflaged. She held up her hand, showing four fingers, and pointed toward the clearing.

Eva didn't hear anything, but she saw Jana carefully kneel behind a tree near her and aim her rifle. She wouldn't fire unless Eva did, though, or she'd risk a serious dressing down when they got back. For herself, she wanted to kill every single one of them, but for now, stealth was their ally. They were most definitely outnumbered in enemy territory. All they had to do was survive until the rescue team arrived.

As if summoned by her thoughts, her radio sparked to life, and she heard static in her earpiece.

"*Captain bzzzt, bzzzzt, Mikhailovna. En route. Five bzzzzzt.*"

She waved her hand to get Jana's attention, pointed up, and then held up five fingers.

Jana nodded understanding and returned her attention down the scope of her rifle.

Her radio clicked twice, a signal from Casper that he'd seen and understood.

* * * *

Chapter Fifteen

Essena made her way to the back of the aircraft, where her team waited. They hadn't bothered with a specialized pod; they were strapped into jump seats along the exterior of the fuselage. Much more comfortable than some things they'd ridden in over the years.

"We know where they are, and have an active mic, so they are alive," she said loudly enough to be heard over the engines.

"*Holy shit. Captain, you seeing this?*" Colin's voice came over the radio. Essena was still monitoring the pilot's channel.

"*Affirm. I count at least twenty.*"

"*That signal's right under them; they're hunting, and they're camouflaged.*"

"*They think we can't see them. Good. Get bearings and go weapons hot. Clear the air, boys,*" Max ordered.

Less than a second later, they could feel the vibration of the 40mm cannons firing.

One of her men unfastened his restraints and stood up. "Hope they save some for us. How we going in, Colonel?"

Essena pulled a small tablet from a hip pouch and checked the cameras on the exterior of the aircraft. She ignored the griffins, who lost camouflage as they died and fell to the ground, and focused on the overlay showing the radio signal that had to be Captain Snow and her team.

"Is too thick for landing; we will fly in," she said, getting into her own wingsuit. "There is small clearing nearby. Will try to land there and move in to them."

She easily kept her balance as Max flew the aircraft like a fighter to bring his weapons to bear on the next target.

"Ever seen those old videos of an eagle snatching a smaller bird out of the air?" her field medic asked.

"No. Will be an aggressive descent. Eagle will clear air for us."

The medic grinned as the irony that their lead combat pilot's callsign was Eagle.

"I guess he's doing the plucking today," the medic said and put her helmet on.

Essena finished zipping up her suit and put on the rest of her equipment. She left her sniper rifle on the rack, opting instead for a submachine gun with an extended magazine, and a spare, identical weapon on her back, in addition to her normal sidearm and machete.

"*Bzzzt Snow to sky. Come in,*" Essena heard through her earpiece. "Sky" was the generic term used for any aircraft in the area capable of receiving. Eva was whispering or using her throat microphone, which meant they were likely in close contact.

"*You got that, Colonel?*" Max's voice asked.

"Yes," she said, then switched channels. It was much cleaner now. "Captain Snow, is Colonel Mikhailovna. We are one minute from drop. Team will come in with wingsuits to clearing."

"*Copy that, Colonel. Fair warning, the clearing is some sort of territorial landmark to them. We've already got two dead birds there.*"

"Good, is ours now," Essena said. "Status?"

"Secure for the moment. Leopold's injured, status unknown. Sergeant Kracht believes it may be bleeding on the brain."

Essena looked toward her medic, who gave a thumbs up, indicating she was ready for anything.

"Medic is on my team. See you in two minutes," she said and walked over to the panel to open the rear cargo door.

Unlike some aircraft, the X-94 didn't have a side hatch they could use. The only way out was to open the entire rear cargo door, which was fine. As the door slid open, her team knelt and aimed their rifles. Unlike a standard operation, where jumping was routine, their enemy could very well be right outside the door waiting for them, even in the air.

As the first crack of daylight came through, the way seemed clear, for the moment.

"IR!" Essena exclaimed over their comm channel.

Each of them reached up and toggled IR mode on the multi-spectrum goggles they'd opted to use for this mission. When Essena did, she almost gasped. The air was *thick* with targets, and they'd noticed the opening rear of the aircraft.

"We need a path, Colonel," said Captain Ivazov Kirillovick, nicknamed Krill, formerly of the Ukrainian Special Operations Forces.

She and Krill had actually been on opposite sides of the battlefield at one time, but that had just been business, nothing personal. Now, Essena trusted him with her life, which was why he was her second on this mission. He, like Captain Snow, had often been where she was too busy to be since they'd been on the planet, but he was an obvious choice to her for this mission. Krill's claim to fame was shooting Russian helicopters out of the air by sniping the pilots from over a kilometer away. Rumor was, the reality was up to three kilometers, but he'd never bragged about his work. Because it was just that. Work.

Now, he was shooting griffins out of the air one at a time. This time, he was using a standard semi-automatic rifle, but the effect was the same. One by one, red mist filled the air, and another griffin fell. The problem was, for each one he shot, another one or two would appear.

Someone had either heard them, or predicted their issue, because the air was suddenly filled with hot lead coming from their right, sweeping in close to the rear of the X-94. Seconds later, an aircraft flew past at high speed.

"*I'll do my best to give you a path, Colonel,*" Colin said.

"This is our chance; let's get down there!" Essena said and jumped.

As she exited the relative safety of the aircraft, she slung her rifle and grabbed her pistol, a Tokarev loaded with 7.62mm ammunition. It would handle the griffins just fine, assuming she got a head shot, which she usually did, even on the move.

The turbulence she encountered was expected, but hitting the cross-wave of turbulence created by Eagle's passing was new. Typically, aircraft avoided crossing each other's paths like that, but this time, it created a near cyclone in midair. She was thrown around for a moment until gravity took her past it, and it took her a few seconds longer than she would've liked to recover.

Her team faced much the same issue, but Krill recovered more quickly than she did, which was what saved her life. A griffin flew up to meet her with its beak wide open. She tried to bring her sidearm to bear, but the wingsuit kept her arm from moving where she wanted it. Just as she tilted her wrist to try to get the shot, the griffin's head exploded, followed by several body shots for good measure.

She angled herself to avoid striking the body, which could have been deadly by itself, given her speed, and even then, she felt its body graze her leg. Recovered and aiming at the clearing that was their target, she took a second to scan the environment. Any semblance of formation of the X-94s was gone. They were each turning and banking to avoid being attacked, and to kill as many of the griffins as possible.

Two more of the X94s came in and flew below them, guns firing full speed to clear a path so they could safely reach the ground. In the process, they put themselves in danger, and Essena made a mental note to gift them each a bottle of the vodka she'd stowed away in the MilForce quarters for special occasions. If they all survived.

Sixty seconds later, her team deployed mini-chutes to help them flare their descent, and they landed at a run to make their way to where Captain Snow and her team waited.

Essena hit the ground running, pulled the cord to release the mini-chute that had slowed her down just enough to land, and made her way toward where she saw Sergeant Nováková and Captain Snow kneeling behind trees, with only their rifles exposed.

They fired almost instantly, taking down griffins who'd pursued Essena and her team to the ground.

Rather than trying to slow her run, Essena went down to her knees in a controlled slide that finally killed her momentum. The rest of her team did the same, with her medic back on her feet immediately. She ran over to where Sergeant Kracht and Leopold were and got to work.

"Other injuries?" Essena asked as she knelt behind Eva.

"None, just Leopold."

"Good," she said, and selected another tree for cover as she aimed her submachine gun and took shots of opportunity at any griffin who came into range.

"How's it going up there?" Eva asked without turning away from the clearing.

"Captain Reeves will see it sorted."

"I believe he will."

* * *

Mythos, X-94, Flying Over Mythos

"Shit!" Max exclaimed as he saw Colin maneuver to cross directly behind him. "What the hell are you doing?"

"Gotta pave a road for the rescue team. You can't see it, but the damn griffins saw the hatch opening, and they thought it was feeding time. My wings will clear their descent. You find out where these bastards came from."

"Copy that; careful of that jet wash."

"Don't you worry about that. I saw Top Gun."

Max rolled his eyes, banked away from the engagement, and began his scans. He was sweeping the air for IR signals, of which there were plenty, but his goal was to track their movement and try to figure out exactly where they were coming from. Based on what Leopold had told him, he made for the nearby snow-covered mountain peaks.

He'd totally forgotten their own griffins—that's how he thought of them—were coming along. They'd wisely avoided the direct conflict, and a group of them were waiting in the distance, uncamouflaged. Had they been in the mix earlier, it would've been impossible to choose targets successfully. Friendly fire definitely would have come into play.

As he approached, they separated into two groups, forming the lines of a V-formation with an opening at the front.

"Are you kidding me?" he asked himself. The opening was just about the right size for his X-94, with some wise clearance.

"First time for everything," he said and flew toward the formation.

As he neared the group, they flew forward. There was no way they could match pace with him, even with their great speed, so they started moving well before he reached them. He realized the opening wasn't for him, it was for his guns. They must have observed the fight in the air against the other griffins, and figured out the safe zone for the spread of his 40mm guns. They *really* needed to figure out how to communicate better with these things.

The griffins engaged with Colin and his wings seemed to ignore them. Their focus was on the men and women on the ground, and the new aerial opponents. That suited Max just fine. One problem at a time.

Max lowered his speed to stay in the pocket created by the friendly griffins as much as possible. Eventually, he would overtake them, unless he converted to a vertical flight profile and moved forward more slowly, but that would make him more of a target, so he threw that idea out as quickly as it entered his mind.

They flew toward the mountains for a good fifteen minutes, and Max felt the griffins were going as fast as they could. He'd watched them fly before, and usually they'd stop flapping their massive wings and coast on the thermals, but this time, they never stopped. They were on a mission, and they weren't going to stop until it was done. That was the feeling he got.

Soon enough, they encountered the expected resistance. He saw movement ahead on one of the mountain peaks and used the magnification on his cameras to get a better look. White-feathered griffins flew out of a large cave opening like bats leaving their cave for the evening meal. The cave was up above the snow line, and to Max's mind, that explained their white plumage. Perfect natural camouflage, though they didn't actually need it.

As they kept coming, he marveled at the numbers. How many were there? And did that mean there were as many of them in the same clan as those who were leading him?

"Idiot," he said to himself, as he'd let himself get distracted.

Max toggled over to the missile racks mounted to his wings and fired off two of the four missiles he had loaded. They were specially equipped for just this type of mission, and part of his mind wondered why he had them, at the same time as he was glad of it.

The AGM-302 bunker-busting missiles were armed with a shaped charge that would blow through a meter or more of solid stone, and then the *real* explosive would detonate. It was the equivalent of a fuel-air bomb, the most powerful non-nuclear bomb on Earth, which explained the size of the missile, and why he could only carry four.

He quickly switched to his guns and mowed down any griffins who dared to enter the path of his bullets. He couldn't maneuver, or he'd risk hitting friendlies, so he took targets of opportunity—and there were plenty of them. Before he knew it, the V formation was gone, as the griffins themselves engaged in air-to-air combat. They swooped and clawed at each other, and the surrounding scene became chaos.

Max pulled back on the stick to gain altitude so he could better assess the situation, and the shockwave from the AGM-302 shook the aircraft slightly. He hoped his friends had been out of range of the concussion of the blast. With a twitch of his eye, he changed one of the views to a rear-facing camera, and he saw that the top of the mountain was gone. What was left was a crater as wide as the peak itself. The missiles had done their job, and then some. Now, the opposition knew without a doubt, he was the true threat.

The griffins who were already engaged couldn't divert their attention, or they'd be taken down by the friendly griffins, but then he saw what he'd expected, more of them coming from further away. On the IR screen, he saw a cluster coming from another mountain peak about ten kilometers away. He zoomed in again with the cameras mounted to the aircraft, and found another cave opening. He set the target and fired his last two missiles, hoping there wouldn't be another.

With the missiles expended, he switched back to his guns and opened fire. It was obvious there was some sort of ranged communication between these things. They instantly scattered, and stayed that way. At best, he could sweep across and catch one or two at a time, but there had to be at least fifty coming at him, and their rate of closure was high. Some of them dove toward the ground, and his radar detected their speeds at up to 112 kph.

"Brigid bless us," he said to himself as he banked sharply to head back toward Colin and some hope of assistance. He knew taking on this many alone was impossible.

"I may need some help, coming back your way," he said over the pilot's channel. He didn't want to worry the teams on the ground.

"*Copy that, Cap. We're almost cleaned up here. All the MilForce are deployed and doing their thing pounding the ground. Heading your way.*"

"Watch for friendlies," Max said.

"*Affirm.*"

He couldn't help the friendly griffins who were still engaged air-to-air with the white griffins. There just wasn't enough separation, and his guns weren't *that* accurate against an unpredictable moving target. They were on their own. It looked like his friends were doing pretty well for themselves, which helped assuage his guilt... somewhat.

Max pushed the throttle forward and was pushed back in his seat as the X-94 shot forward at Mach 4. His suit reacted instantly to keep all the blood in his body from pumping out of his brain, and he utilized the tried-and-true Hook Maneuver repeatedly to keep himself awake and aware. While tensing all the muscles in his torso, he repeated the word "hook" over and over in a special way. It was a centuries-old technique, but it was still taught and used by every pilot he knew. There were special suits that made it unnecessary, but he wasn't wearing one of them today.

His speed gave him easy separation from the pursuing griffins. Max hoped they'd follow him, for a little while at least. If they decided to give up and turn around, the small force the friendly griffins had sent would be severely outnumbered. With that in mind, he cut the throttle back, reduced speed to just enough to stay airborne, and lost some altitude on purpose.

"*Uhh, Cap? What are you doing?*" Colin asked.

"Playing lame. I want them to come after me."

"*Are you* nuts?"

"If they turn back, our friends are outnumbered at least five to one."

"*Copy that. We're clean over here; on our way.*"

* * *

Mythos, Flying Over Mythos

"Their machines are impressive," Ebontalon observed, as they flew at top speed, but still couldn't even come close to keeping up with the humans' metal wings.

"They call them planes, and yes, they are. Let us hope they will be enough. Our numbers are not enough to tilt the balance," Dreamtail observed with a bit of bite in his beak.

"You are fortunate Crownfeathers sent any of us at all," Ghostfeather snapped.

"Yes. He is forward-thinking, unlike some others I could name."

Ebontalon gave a small screech of amusement at the stab.

"Let us focus on our task. What shall we do? Look." He gestured with a talon as the Cloudseekers turned their attention from the ground to the humans' planes.

Dreamtail was immediately concerned. He had determined that the humans meant to leave their planes and help Leopold and the others. He had seen them descend on lines at the Deathbringer's ship, so he knew how it worked. The Cloudseekers were using their transparency to avoid detection.

"The humans will not see them! We must warn them!" Dreamtail screeched a warning.

"They will not hear you through that metal skin," Ghostfeather said nonchalantly.

"I think the humans see them. Look," Ebontalon said.

Surprised, Dreamtail watched as the rear of one of the planes opened like a gaping maw, and the humans with the fire sticks—*guns*, he reminded himself—shot them, even though they were camouflaged.

"I suppose they're more ready than we thought. Can we go now?" Ghostfeather asked.

"Leave if you wish; we will stay," Dreamtail said.

"My orders are to remain with you," Ghostfeather said with a bit of a sigh.

"Then we will take their leader, Max, to the Cloudseekers' home. Their time in this territory is over. The humans will have it," Dreamtail said confidently.

"That is not what Crownfeathers said! We are to support them to keep them *safe!*"

"How better to keep them safe than to eliminate the threat? Their leader is breaking off. He knows we wait for him. Look," Dreamtail said, and flew toward where they knew the Cloudseekers nested.

He screeched a series of orders, and the flight of griffins took up a standard travel formation. They positioned themselves just outside and behind the wingspan of the griffin ahead of them.

"We must make room for the large guns. I believe they are indiscriminate in what they kill."

"Barbaric," Ghostfeather snapped, but maneuvered to join the tail end of the right wing of the formation.

"Lead the right, Ebontalon. I will lead the left. We will take him to their home and end them."

"I cannot say I will be sorry to see them gone."

Ghostfeather nodded his head in the human way without thinking about it, then chortled.

"Be careful, Ghostfeather," Ebontalon warned. "You take up too much of their ways."

"We must learn from each other, must we not?" he asked.

The rest of the griffins followed without question. Most of them were nameless. Not all griffins were as self-aware and as intelligent as Dreamtail and his fellows. The majority were referred to as drones. They could follow basic orders and survive, but their communication was stilted and childlike. That was not their fault, and Dreamtail refused to look down on them. Unfortunately, in this case, they would be spent against the Cloudseekers' talons to keep the humans alive.

It wouldn't be the first time the drones had been used in battle. That was, after all, one of the things they truly enjoyed. Fighting. That was also why they were usually kept far away from the humans. They had not had to deal with the Cloudseekers for some cycles, but they were aggressive in their attempts at territorial expansion, and Dreamtail thought this conflict was inevitable. This time, the humans would actually help them without even knowing it.

Max positioned his plane perfectly between the wings of the flight, and Dreamtail was again impressed at how intuitive the humans were. Perhaps there was hope for them on their homeworld after all. Dreamtail almost missed a flap of his wings when the large metal tubes launched themselves from the wings of the plane. Well, more accurately, they dropped off and then flew forward.

The Cloudseekers had seen their approach and were coming out to meet them. Good. Dreamtail had not seen battle in some time. It would not be an easy one, but his confidence was high.

Based on what he had learned of the humans' weapons, he expected an explosion when the metal tubes struck the mountain, but the reality was something he had never dreamed of. They somehow managed to get inside the mountain itself and utterly *destroy* it. For the first time, Dreamtail was afraid of the humans. They were far more dangerous than he had given them credit for. If they could do that to solid stone...

His thoughts were interrupted by the buzzing sound of the smaller guns from the plane. Small they were, but deadly. Cloudseekers dropped from the sky in numbers too high to count, but there was still plenty to do. Max was smart enough to know when to stop and seemed to veer off. Good, he had seen their other nest opening. Now was their time to fight.

"Death to the Cloudseekers!" he screeched, folded his wings back, and dove to attack.

* * * * *

Chapter Sixteen

Landing + 40 Days

Mythos, Eos City

K ellie watched Max walk away and fought back tears. She'd known him what seemed like forever, and she'd always cared about him. Now that Annica was out of the picture, they were getting closer, finally, but Annica wasn't totally out of the picture. What had just happened proved that. *You have to be ready to be okay with that*, she told herself.

For now, she had a job to do. With another wipe of her face, she set off toward the PCC with purpose.

"Annie?"

"*Yes, Kellie?*" the AI answered through her earpiece. Annie was always listening.

"Go through the files and select the best personnel to work with developing some sort of formal communication with the griffins. Xenolinguists, vets, whatever."

"*Of course, Kellie,*" Annie said. "*Are you okay?*"

"I'll be fine. Thank you."

"*You know I am always here, Kellie. You can talk to me if you need a friend.*"

Kellie glanced sideways toward her ear. "I thought you didn't like me."

"I do not like or dislike anyone, Kellie. I am here to further the mission, and you are key to its survival. If there is anything I can do to help with that, it is my job."

"I see… well, thanks, but I'll be okay."

"Of course."

Kellie couldn't help but roll her eyes at the idea of the AI wanting to be her therapist as she walked into the Planetary Control Center.

"Status?" she asked as she sat in Max's chair on the raised platform in the center of the room.

"Rescue team is spinning up. Departure in two minutes."

"Good. Once they're off, green-light the alien craft recovery team. Max wants that done now."

"While we're busy with this?" someone asked, surprised.

"What else are we going to do?" she snapped. "Without satellites, we can't monitor the situation, and we can't be sure they'll have the altitude for line-of-sight communications. We might as well get something done, and Captain Reeves wants this done. Any questions?"

"No, ma'am. I'll get them started."

Kellie nodded, satisfied. She was glad to have something to focus on other than worrying about whether Max would return from his mission.

The operation to retrieve the alien craft had been planned down to the last detail, so she hoped it would be a straightforward operation. On the other hand, she'd learned this planet had a way of messing up even the simplest of tasks, and this wasn't simple.

She watched on the surveillance cameras as the BN-12s prepped and lifted off. For this operation, another X-94 would be up on overwatch to provide radio contact with the PCC for the duration. In this instance, if something went wrong, they should be able to respond and assist.

Annie would also be assisting with the effort, which was another reason for the X-94 to be in position. It had been determined that the placement of the hoist straps would be absolutely vital to ensure a balanced load for the BN-12s, and Annie's measurements down to the micrometer would assist with that. The load teams were good—the best—but there were just some things computers were better at, and this was one of them.

* * *

Mythos, Alien Crash Site

Sadie grumbled to herself as she left the BN-12 that had landed to disgorge the load team. As the chief engineer, she'd been tasked with overseeing the groundwork to make sure the load was properly distributed. It made sense, sort of, since she'd been at the head of the team that had come up with the plan, but she felt redundant, since it was Annie who'd be the final word on readiness. As an engineer, she understood redundancy, but this time it seemed like she wasn't even necessary.

"*Is everything okay, Ms. March?*" Annie asked, as if she could sense her mood. "*Your vitals seem oddly elevated for what is a routine task for someone of your capabilities.*"

"It's important that we get this right the first time; there are no second chances," Sadie said, lying about the reason her vitals were off.

"*That is why I am here to assist, Ms. March. It is good to have something of consequence to do. Don't you think?*"

182 | ALEX RATH

Sadie raised an eyebrow. Was the AI actually trying to relate to her?

"Everything on this planet is of consequence, Annie. It's all about survival."

"Oh, of course it is. I just mean, based on the information I have, it seems like the engineers are always in the background making things happen, but it is the project leaders who get all the credit."

Sadie stood beside the alien craft and gestured for the straps to be lowered as the strap teams got into their positions. Everything was planned down to where each person would stand, and where the straps should land so they could be placed around the ship.

"Well, that's not how things work here. Now if you don't mind, I need to focus."

"Of course. Please let me know when you are satisfied, and I can verify every-thing is where it should be, based on your calculations. I am only here to help."

Sadie took a deep breath to calm herself, then set to work, guid-ing the straps into place. There had been some digging around and under the ship to make room for the straps, and it looked like every-thing was done to her specifications. She'd expected to have to fix something—thus the hand trowel on her belt—but it turned out to be unnecessary. With the straps in their starting location, the work of getting them just right began.

She couldn't shake the feeling she was being watched by some-one other than those she expected, and looked up. Sure enough, there were a handful of griffins hovering nearby, overseeing the op-eration. She wondered what they hoped for. Did they hope the ship would wipe out some of the invading humans? Or did they just want this foreign thing out of their forest?

"They watch everything we do," Annie said unprompted.

"I suppose I would, too, if a bunch of things showed up near my home and started tearing shit up," Sadie said and walked around to check the strap positions for the third time.

Strapping up the ship had taken an hour of painstaking adjustments, sometimes moving them just a centimeter until she was happy. Finally, she gestured for the BN-12s to take up the last bit of slack, and there was an audible *twang* as the cables were pulled tight.

"Ready for final verification, Annie."

"*If you could do a walk around with the scanner, please?*" Annie asked.

Sadie nodded and walked slowly around the alien craft, at this point nothing more than a glorified mobile platform for the scanner she held.

"*Perfect. No adjustments necessary, Sadie. It seems I was redundant today. Please green-light the lift team. I will notify the PCC.*"

Sadie's eyebrows shot up as Annie used the same language that was in her head. "Right. Thanks."

"Take it up. Fly safe," she said into her radio and watched.

Centimeter by centimeter, the alien craft lifted away from the ground. Just before liftoff, the team had gone around and made sure no new vines had decided to attach to the ship and throw the balance off, so she expected it to be smooth, and it was.

The return trip would take over an hour because of the low speed and coordination necessary for the effort, but she hadn't wanted to risk going any faster. All it would take was one unexpected gust of a crosswind to throw off the balance. She trusted the pilots—the best lift pilots on the planet—but sometimes things just went out of control.

* * *

Mythos, Eos City, Planetary Control Center

"*Lift team is away, Kellie. ETA to landing is an hour and twenty-five minutes, based on flight plan,*" Annie said over the speakers on Max's desk.

"Thanks, Annie. Do we have a team selected to work with the griffins?"

"*Yes, Kellie. They are already reviewing all the existing footage of their communications with Leopold and Max. Of course, they want to work with them directly.*"

"Of course. We'll get that set up as soon as we can. Please monitor the lift flight carefully for anything that could endanger the mission."

"*I am always watching for anything that will endanger the mission, Kellie.*"

Kellie felt a shiver run down her spine. Something didn't feel right about what Annie had said. It seemed a bit all encompassing, but she shrugged it off as being oversensitive after the encounter with Max.

"*Looking good from here, PCC,*" Sadie said over the radio link.

"Excellent job, Sadie, congrats. Now get yourself back here," Kellie said.

"*Roger that. I'm being picked up now. I'll be back in a few minutes.*"

Kellie nodded, though Sadie couldn't see her. One of the X-94s had landed and would shuttle Sadie back, while another flew high over the BN-12s to watch the return flight and measure everything for unexpected deviations. Even the flight plan had been devised specifically based on known wind patterns to take the path that offered the least possibility of unexpected wind gusts that could cause the alien craft to sway or shift. A direct flight would've cut at least thirty minutes off the flight, but the experts had said this was the way, so this was the way.

Sadie's return flight, however, would be fast. The X-94 would get her back as quickly as possible so she could oversee everything from the PCC, where they already had all the information she'd requested up on the multiple monitors at the front of the room. Wind directions and speeds measured from the BN-12s themselves, flight position based on the X-94 overwatch observation, weight distribution from sensors on the strap anchors, and on and on.

The alien ship was heavy, but lighter—she'd been told—than an equivalent ship from Earth. Everyone assumed that was because of the material it was made of, which they'd been unable to even scratch the surface of. Back here in Eos, there were more tools and more capabilities, so Kellie had no doubt they'd be able to take the thing apart and find out how it worked.

Azeema el-Mir and a small team were standing by near where the ship would be placed. As soon as the ship was set down and unstrapped, she'd 3D print a building around it, rather than having to move it into an existing structure. It would take several days to print, since Sadie and the engineering team had given Azeema the specifications that would be necessary to withstand a substantial explosion. It would be no less than a huge, thick-walled hangar.

Originally, it was simply going to be put to the side on the tarmac, but they'd decided to pour a new base structure, separate from everything else. The craft would be placed on that, and then a hangar built around it to contain it. Once it was up, it would be secured and guarded around the clock by MilForce, not to keep anything secret, but to keep anyone from getting hurt by unknown technology. So far, nothing on the ship had proved dangerous, but that wasn't guaranteed to hold once they attempted to disassemble it.

* * *

Mythos, Eos City

Kellie stood on the tarmac and watched as the two BN-12s with the alien craft hanging under them came into sight. She could have watched and seen more detail from the PCC, but this was something she wanted to see in person with her own eyes. The flight had been thankfully uneventful. The way their luck had been going with the griffin assault on the mining team, she'd half expected some freak thunderstorm to spring up and ruin the transit.

Careful, Kellie, it's not on the ground yet, she thought to herself and looked around at the sky for threatening clouds.

With nothing dangerous in sight, she watched as Sadie stood in front of the poured base where the craft would be set down. Lines had been painted on the surface, indicating exactly where it should rest. Sadie would guide it down herself, with the assistance of loading experts who understood how to communicate with the pilots.

Slowly, the aircraft descended, and the alien craft came closer and closer to touching down. As if the planet were refusing to give anything up without a fight, a light breeze kicked up, which caused Kellie to frown. Fortunately, it wasn't enough to make any difference to the large craft, and it was set down without incident. As soon as it was on the ground, a team ran in to unfasten the harnesses, and the BN-12s lifted away to go to their own landing spots.

It was all Kellie could do not to run over to it. Maintaining the appearance of calm, she walked what she hoped looked casually over toward the alien craft. She'd seen the video of it, but she'd never actually made it out to the site, and she wanted to see it up close and personal. Even though it had been checked multiple times, no one was allowed inside the craft without protective gear, just in case. She remained outside the still-open hatch.

The observations she'd heard were right. It looked so much like an old space shuttle from Earth that the resemblance felt like it couldn't be a coincidence. Then again, aircraft were aircraft. There were some things that were just universal. Wings, control surfaces, and so on. Still, she had the feeling there was much more than met the eye with this thing. It had been sitting out in the forest for some time, but it still looked like it had just come off a factory line, as if it were simply impervious to grime or weather.

She walked around back to get a look at the propulsion system, something she personally had knowledge of. On a space shuttle from Earth, there were three gimbaled jets. This craft seemed to have more than twenty small openings that were positioned such that they could act as one large thruster. Without seeing it lit up, it was impossible to know exactly how it worked. Yet. That was part of the team's mandate—to figure out how it flew.

As much as she wanted to suit up and go inside, she could hear the equipment that would print the hangar moving into place, and she cleared out of the area so they could get started. The sooner that was done, the sooner the teams could get to work figuring out how this machine worked.

MilForce was already on station, and she was surprised to see Sergeant Villegas.

"Can't take a few days off, eh?" she asked as she walked up to stand beside him.

188 | ALEX RATH

"Me? Time off? Nah, I'd rather be doing something. I'm not here to be a tourist."

"Do I sense some judgment there, Sergeant?" she asked, only somewhat jokingly.

"Not at all, Ms. Warren. Don't get me wrong, I'll take my time off and relax once things are more... settled. There's just too much to do right now. Since the colonel wouldn't let me go out and un-screw what was screwed up, I figure this is the next best thing I can do."

"You know that attack wasn't your fault, right? Your team did great, getting everyone out alive."

"Yes, ma'am. Just wish I was there to get some back."

"I have a feeling you'll have plenty of chances for that as time goes on, Pedro," she said and patted his shoulder.

She and Pedro had worked together to capture Ragnarsson's mole, who'd kept them from regaining control of the core computer system after the attempted coup. It had also been what was keeping them from saving Max's life, so she'd taken some small joy in knock-ing Ragnarsson out. They'd formed a bit of a bond.

"It's hard to explain."

"Look, I get it. Why do you think I took such joy in kicking that bastard in the face?" she asked.

"Was a good kick. You should train with us sometime. Never hurts to stay in practice."

"I think I will. Thanks. I could use a distraction."

"Trouble in paradise?" he asked jokingly.

"I'll see you around, Pedro," she said and walked off. The in-tended joke had hit a little too close to home.

* * * * *

Chapter Seventeen

Landing + 40 Days

Mythos, Flying Over X-94 Crash Site

Max was glad the griffins actually followed him. He had no doubt some of their friendly griffins would be lost—that was inevitable in a battle of this scale—but he wanted those numbers to be as low as possible. Colin and his wings flew over him and engaged the griffins who'd followed, and it was a massacre. The X-94s had range and power, and the griffins couldn't even get close. It was over in a matter of minutes.

Just as he was about to fly back toward those he'd left behind, seven griffins came into sight, flying toward them. Two appeared injured, as they were flapping their wings a bit awkwardly. Max wanted nothing more than to help them, but he wouldn't even know where to tell them to land so their medic could take a look.

Max decided to gain some altitude so he could contact Eos.

"Captain Reeves to PCC," he said as he keyed the radio.

"*Max!*" Kellie all but yelled into her microphone. "*Are you okay?*"

"Other than a potentially burst eardrum, I'm fine. So is everyone else. Well, we are anyway. Looks like our friends took some pretty serious losses."

"*I'm sure you did your best. What about Captain Snow and her team?*"

"Sounds like Leopold's injured. They're getting him ready for evac now. Make sure Doctor Chadda has a team on the tarmac ready to take over."

"*Will do,*" she said. "*Are you heading back?*" she asked hopefully.

"I'll stay here until we're all on the way. Probably another half hour at most."

"*Copy that. Stay safe.*"

Max sighed as he watched two of the X-94s switch to vertical flight mode so they could drop lines. The troops on the ground would anchor them, and a system would be set up to bring everyone up, one by one. The most difficult would be Leopold, who would likely be moved on a stretcher, but he wasn't concerned. This was what MilForce trained for before breakfast.

He knew what was waiting for him back in Eos. All he'd want when he got back would be a shower and a bed. To sleep. But he knew that wouldn't happen. Kellie wouldn't wait, and now she'd felt what it was like to have him fly off into combat.

Max wasn't sure what he was ready for, but he knew making any kind of decision right now was a horrible idea. He was on a high from their victory, but he was also exhausted. Add to that concern for Leopold as well as the injured griffins, and his plate was full.

His attention was drawn to the griffins, as they moved to depart. He swore the lead griffin, the one he recognized as having stopped him earlier, gave him a nod before they flew off, but that must have been his imagination.

"Griffins are departing. Looks like it must really be over, or I don't think they'd leave," he said over the open channel.

"*That's good to hear. How did they do? I've been a bit busy coordinating a retrieval here,*" Colin said.

"Down to seven," Max said.

"*Damn…*"

"Yeah. We'll see how this plays out."

"*They knew what they were getting into. Let's hope we can still be friends.*"

"No kidding. I'd prefer not to have them as enemies."

Max spent the next half hour while the recovery took place contemplating the future of Eos. With this handled, they'd be able to bring out the mining equipment and really get to work. It looked like survival was handled, and now it was going to be about what was next. But what *was* next?

* * *

Mythos, Eos City, Planetary Control Center

The cheer that went up from everyone in the room when Kellie announced that the assault on the mountain griffins was over nearly brought her to tears. She'd been a part of teams in the past, but never one like this, because everything they did could mean the difference between surviving and not.

She sent a quick message to the load team and mining crew to load up the BN-12s with the full mining rig and equipment as soon as they were turned around from the lift mission. The sooner they got those materials in, the sooner they could get their satellite coverage back. She wanted that for many reasons, not the least of which was being able to keep an eye on Adel Ragnarsson's movements. Something told her his part in things on this planet was far from over, though he was literally halfway around the world.

With the major events under control, Kellie decided to treat herself, and headed out of the PCC to grab some food. It was sometime between lunch and dinner, but mealtimes on the Mythos tended to be flexible. The few restaurants that had opened up pretty much served food all day and all night, since there was a lot of shift work among the colonists. The nice thing was, everyone pretty much got to pick their own schedule—except PCC staff and MilForce, of course.

She walked into Bernadette Trintignant's restaurant, which had quickly become a favorite, and found a seat easily in the almost empty establishment.

"Kellie! You're back again! Ready for something new?"

Kellie put on a smile, though she wasn't sure she truly felt it. "Of course, Bernadette. What do you have today?"

"Ahh, something new, as always. I have what's possibly the ugliest fish I've ever seen, but it is tasty!"

"Bring it on. Thanks."

One of the servers put a bottle of water and some silverware down for her. While she waited, she thought about Max. He'd be back soon, and then what? The way they'd left things, she wondered if they were going too fast. But what was too fast? They were stranded on a planet with no hope of even *hearing* from Earth ever again. She loved Max. She was sure of it. In fact, she'd always loved him, she reflected, but now it was different. Before, it had been a love of friendship because it had to be. Now…

"Here you are!" Bernadette exclaimed proudly and set a grilled fillet of fish in front of her with a side of fresh vegetables.

"Smells delicious, Bernadette, thanks. Don't suppose you have any wine held back? We have a bit of a cause for celebration."

"Oh, I suppose we might have something," she said and gestured to one of the servers as she sat down across from Kellie.

"You're my first vict—I mean customer for this fish," she said with a wink and a grin. "Tell me what you think."

"No pressure," Kellie said with a smile, forgetting her worries for a moment as she took a forkful of the fish.

It nearly fell apart on the fork, it was so tender, and it all but melted in her mouth. She groaned and nodded. "Oh my goddess, Bernadette. You can keep this all for me if you want."

"Oh, no, Kellie. I'm afraid I have to share with everyone, but the fish is huge, so there'll always be plenty. Besides, I wouldn't want people to get bored!"

"I don't think I could *ever* get bored of this," she said and quickly took a larger bite.

"Slow down, or you'll choke. Here, this should pair nicely," she said and poured from a carafe of wine the server brought over. "So, what are we celebrating?"

"Oh. Well, we have the alien craft safely back, and Max has cleaned out the griffins who were stopping us from mining, so we should have our satellites back soon."

"That is excellent news! Well, I won't disturb your meal further. Please, enjoy," Bernadette said and went back to the kitchen.

Kellie forced herself to slow down and enjoy the meal as she reflected. There really was a lot to celebrate. Her personal conflict aside, things were going very well for the city.

* * *

Mythos, X-94, Flying Over Mythos

Finally, everyone was loaded up, and they were headed home. *Home*, Max thought, *yeah, home. And Kellie.* He sighed as he brought himself back to that subject. It was something he knew he'd have to face as soon as he landed, and he wasn't sure what to do about it. It was obvious to him that he still cared about Annica, but he'd never see her again, so why keep his life on hold? Kellie was great, she'd always been a good friend, and now she was more.

But is it love? he thought.

Annica's betrayal had destroyed him—was still destroying him in some ways—but he couldn't let that rule the rest of his life. He also didn't want to get hurt again, though he doubted Kellie would suddenly turn on him and abandon him to an unknown fate like Annica had.

"Why can't anything be simple?" he asked himself.

"*Nothing worth doing ever is, Max,*" Annie responded. They must be back in range of *Traveler* already.

"Sorry, just talking to myself."

"*I know. It is healthy, you know. Sometimes. You know Kellie really cares about you. She was very concerned during your mission.*"

"I didn't ask you to spy for me, Annie. Kellie and I are off limits. Clear?"

"*Understood, Max. Would you like a status update on ongoing projects?*"

"Might as well," he said and refocused. There'd be time to think about his personal life later.

"*The mining equipment is being moved to the tarmac to be loaded once the BN-12s are turned around. The lift of the alien craft was successful, and Azeema is printing the hangar now. At Kellie's request, a team has been designated to work on communication with the griffins. They are anxious to work with them in person. Also, I finished my review of the flight manual, and I believe that is what it is. Well, emergency procedures, as you speculated. We will know more as we are able to work with the alien craft more closely. I have already identified what I believe are the numeric symbols, from comparison with the displays that had hard printed characters. Exactly which numbers they are, and the unit of measurement, remains unknown."*

Max nodded as Annie went through each item.

"Sounds good. We'll work on figuring that out."

"Is there anything else?" Annie asked, her tone a bit short.

"Are you offended, Annie?"

"I cannot be offended, Max."

"Are you sure?"

There was a longer pause than he expected from the AI.

"Is there anything else, Max?"

"No, thanks, Annie."

Max frowned. The longer the AI was online, the more it seemed to exhibit human-like characteristics. That was always a risk with AI, and that was why they were generally used for short-term missions only. Annie was the first of her kind, so there were a lot of unknowns, including how she'd react over time to being just a computer.

Finally, they were back home. Max landed and taxied his aircraft to turn it over to the ground crew.

He exited to a round of applause from the ground crews, as did the others when they landed. Doctor Chadda and her team took control of Leopold quickly, and they headed toward the hospital.

"Take good care of him, Doctor!" he shouted.

She waved without shifting her attention from her patient. No less than he expected. She'd been a miracle worker through the entire mission; from the moment they'd gone through the wormhole, she'd been there to handle whatever came up. She'd also saved his life when he'd been injured in the coup attempt.

"Seen Kellie?" he asked one of the ground crew.

"Last I saw, she was headed toward Main Street. Probably to grab some food. She's been busy all day."

Max nodded his thanks and went toward Main Street. Food sounded like a good idea.

* * *

Mythos, Eos City

On a hunch, Max headed toward Bernadette's place, and found Kellie sitting back in her chair with an empty plate in front of her.

"Mind if I sit?" he asked.

Kellie jumped slightly in surprise, then stood. She only hesitated for a moment before she wrapped her arms around him, and he returned the hug.

"I'm sorry about before—" he began.

"No, no, you were right. It wasn't the time. Come on, sit down. Bernadette has a new fish you *have* to try. Then we can talk whenever you're ready."

As if on cue, Bernadette walked out with a plate and set it in front of Max, along with a bottle of water.

"One of the flight crew guys called and told me you might be on the way," she said with a wink.

"Thanks, Bernadette," he said and smiled.

"Quite welcome. If I'm not mistaken, we're about to have a lot of company... just so you know."

"Ah, right," he said and looked at Kellie. "Later, okay?"

She nodded and smiled. "Whenever you want."

"Thought you'd celebrate without us, huh?" Colin said loudly as he walked in, followed by the other pilots, and about half of the Mil-Force members from the mission.

Max chuckled, and Kellie got up to give Colin a hug as well.

"Oh, hey, careful. Your boyfriend's pretty good at hand-to-hand. I don't want to get in trouble," Colin said with a laugh.

"Don't worry, I can take him," Kellie said and winked. "Welcome back, everyone. Well done!"

Suddenly the restaurant was mostly full, and the servers were busy filling glasses and serving food. The atmosphere was jovial, as there were many good things to reflect on that day. Part of the way through, Max got a call and stood up to get everyone's attention.

"Just got a call from Captain Nováková. Leopold's doing well and will make a full recovery. Slight concussion, but nothing else."

As he sat down, Essena walked in, carrying bottles that looked suspiciously like contraband.

"As much as I am hesitant to do this in front of the captain, you earned it," she said, and set a bottle of vodka down in front of each of the pilots, excluding Max.

"Hey, what, nothing for the man of the day?" one of the pilots who didn't know Max as well asked.

"Captain Reeves does not partake, you dolt," Essena said and slapped the back of his head good-naturedly. "He keeps mind clean of pollutants, unlike the rest of us."

"Shit, I didn't even think," Kellie said and pushed her wine glass away as she looked at Max.

"It's okay," he said with a smile. "Just because I don't doesn't mean you can't."

"I know, but…" She sighed, and a pained look crossed her face.

He shook his head and pushed the glass back in front of her. "It's okay."

"No," she said and pushed it away. "I think I want my head clear today," she said.

"I think I don't!" Colin said. "Unless you have another mission in mind," he said and looked at Max.

"Drink up boys; you earned it. I think I'm going to excuse myself, though. I prefer to maintain the illusion of you all as consummate professionals," Max said as he stood. "Care to take a walk?" he asked Kellie and offered a hand.

"I think I would," she said as she took his hand and stood.

"Hey, you two don't do anything I wouldn't do," Colin said and grinned.

"That doesn't leave much off the table, Colin," Max shot back as they walked out.

"True…"

* * *

Mythos, Eos City

They walked a short distance in silence, neither of them sure where to start the conversation. Max finally spoke. "About before…"

"No, I'm sorry. You were right," Kellie said.

"There was a mission back on Earth when Annica and I were still just dating. She tried to stop me from going, and… it all went to hell. Closest I ever came to dying on a mission that wasn't combat."

"I remember that one, I think. You shoved the capsule back into orbit as a beacon. You two were inseparable after that," she said, a bit of disappointment coming through in her voice.

"That's the one. I was distracted during the mission. The investigation said it was all mechanical errors, but…"

"But it could have been a lot worse. Deadly worse."

"Right."

"I told her then, that's my life. That's what I do, and no one is going to stop it. You need to understand that, too, if this is going anywhere, Kellie. I do the things other people can't, won't, or don't."

"You're a stubborn jackass, is what you are. Other people *could* do those things."

"Can't argue the first part. The second part, I can. I've done things no one else on the planet has done, Kellie, with the sometimes exception of Colin. There are times I simply can't ask other people to do what I can do. It's not ego. It's that if I can do it, I feel like I should."

"But these people need you *here*, Max. You're also in a position you've never been in. You have all these people who look up to you, who count on you to be there when they have a problem that needs to be solved. I do my best, but I'm not you. I'm not the commander of this mission. You are."

Max considered her words as they walked and nodded thoughtfully. She was right, he supposed. He was used to leading on a squadron level, but never this many people. On the ship, it had been easier. Here on the planet, there was so much that needed to be done, he felt like he should be doing his fair share rather than sitting on his ass, telling people what to do.

"I do my best, but honestly, I think they still just see me as Annica's replacement," Kellie said after he was silent for a few minutes.

"Stop right there," he said and stopped walking. He kept hold of her hand and turned her to face him. "You're more than qualified for the post you hold, or you wouldn't be in it. If anyone has a problem with that, they can talk to me about it, and I'll set them straight."

"You think anyone will actually say anything? Especially now?" she asked, nodding to their held hands. "No one wants to piss you off, Max, especially after Adel."

"Smart move," he said and continued walking.

"Where are we going, anyway?" she asked.

"Driving range. You're going to learn to play golf."

She laughed and shook her head. "Oh, no. I tried once, and I swear, I nearly knocked myself out with the club."

"Then you had a shit teacher."

* * * * *

Chapter Eighteen

Landing + 40 days

Terran Space Project Campus, Annica's Office

Annica leaned back in the chair in her office and sipped her fourth cup of coffee. It was going to be a long day, and that meant coffee, and plenty of it. She'd been up far too late the night before, formulating plans and trying to figure out what her goal was. Obviously, she wanted to find Max and join him, soon, but that didn't seem realistic. The follower ship, TSP *Replenisher*, wouldn't be ready for another three years. The build plan on it would have it ready a year before it was supposed to leave to join *Traveler* in Alpha Centauri. She wondered what Gustav had planned to do with it, since *Traveler* was obviously not in Alpha Centauri.

Then she realized there must be *some* way of getting it wherever *Traveler* had ended up. Which meant somewhere, there was some sort of navigation chart or instructions on how to get there. Unless he'd simply planned to let *Replenisher* disappear into the wormhole and strand them the way he'd done Max. She sighed as it hit her that he'd probably planned to do just that. Gustav had shown he wasn't concerned about the people he was responsible for, and *Replenisher* would only have a complement of two hundred, half the population of *Traveler*. In the span of a moment, hope had quickly turned to disgust. Still, it was a lead to follow. She added that to the list of things to investigate on the notepad opened on her computer display.

Just as she finished, there was a knock on the door, and it opened just enough for Konda to stick her head in.

"Ready for us?" she asked.

"Come on in, Konda."

Konda entered, followed immediately by Sergey and Shao. It seemed they were all punctual, at least. She checked her clock, and noted that it was five minutes before seven. A small smile crossed her features as she remembered what Max had said about timing. If you're early, you're on time; if you're on time, you're late.

"Good to see you smiling this morning," Konda said as she sat at the small conference table so she'd have a place to rest her tablet.

Sergey and Shao joined her at the conference table, and Annica rose to join them as well. She stopped on the way to top off her coffee.

"Coffee, anyone?"

"I have my tea," Yating said and raised a travel mug.

"I'm set," Konda said, indicating her own travel mug.

"Apparently, I'm the only one who didn't come prepared. Sure, thank you," Sergey said and walked over to help himself.

Once Sergey was set with his dose of caffeine—with, she noticed, a lot of sweeteners—Annica logged in to the terminal at the table and brought her list up on a display on the wall where they could all see. It contained all the things she'd thought of to investigate, and she was sure the list would grow, now that the team was assembled.

"Here's what I have so far. Let's build out the list, then figure out how to tackle it," she said and gave them all time to absorb what she'd put together.

1. Where is Traveler?

2. Who knew the probe sighting was faked? Who knew why?

3. What does Paula Handley know?

4. Who else in SP was involved?

5. Was anyone else on the ship involved? (known, Ragnarsson, Empyre, Courtni)

6. Who are the 'friends from out of town' Gustav referred to?

7. What's the plan for Replenisher?

"There's... nah, it's nothing. Forget it," Sergey said and took a drink of his coffee. "Damn, this is good. You get the good stuff."

Annica grinned. "Thank Max, if we ever see him again. Anyway, what were you going to say?"

"Nothing, it's stupid."

"At this point, anything could be relevant, or maybe trigger an idea from someone else, Mr. Yegorovich," Shao said.

"Shao's right. What is it?" Annica asked.

Sergey shrugged. "There's an old movie I watched a few times, can't remember the name of it, but it—well, it referred to aliens as 'friends from out of town.'" The latter he said with air quotes.

"Aliens," Konda said flatly.

"Hey, I said it was nothing."

"It might not be," Annica said thoughtfully.

"You're not seriously considering that," Shao said.

"Why not? Hell, I'll consider *anything* if it'll help me find Max. What's the harm in putting it in as a possibility, if only to rule it out?"

"Time wasted," Shao said.

"Maybe," Konda said. "I don't know about China, but in Japan, we have a First Contact plan in place. The details are obviously confidential, and I didn't have access to them, but I know it exists."

204 | ALEX RATH

"If there's no other life out there…" Sergey said.

"It's an awful waste of space," Annica finished. "Okay, it's on the board as a possibility, but let's not dive down a rabbit hole on this. There's plenty to tackle. So, who wants to pursue what?"

"I'll question Paula," Konda immediately offered. "I might bring Anton in, if that's okay? The Germans have a pretty good reputation when it comes to interrogation."

Annica considered. She'd already thought of bringing him in after the ride to her house. "Okay, he's in. Brief him on as much as he needs to know for now. I swear, I'm going to record this all, so I can just play the recording for anyone else who comes in."

"That's actually not a bad idea," Shao said, though Annica had been joking.

"I'm sorry?"

"This is going to go public eventually. You should have something prepared. Something that could be… leaked at the right moment."

Sergey raised an eyebrow, then nodded. "She's right. That's good tradecraft. Release what you want known in the right way, and people will think that's all there is."

"Okay, Sergey, you're volunteered to assist me with that."

He pinched his lips together and sighed. "One day, Sergey, you'll learn to keep your damn mouth shut."

That was just what everyone needed to break the seriousness of the moment and have a little chuckle.

"Okay, so Konda will handle Paula, and Sergey will help me craft something releasable that we can also use to induct new members of the team. Shao, you'll dig into Special Projects?"

Shao nodded. "That is what I am best suited for, certainly. Obviously, Sergey would likely be of assistance there. In technology, throwing more people at something is rarely the solution, but given the volume of data we have to tackle, I think at least one more person would be welcome."

"What about the rest of Special Projects?" Sergey asked. "They just cool their heels? Bored techs aren't a good thing. They often find less than productive ways to fill their time."

"Most of them are playing video games," Shao said. When Sergey looked at her, questioning, she explained, "We monitor the computer activity of everyone on the team, no matter where they are on campus. Well, we monitor everyone, but I get a report on members of Special Projects."

"Oh."

"Anyway, that sounds like a good start. I'm usually one to look forward, but in this case, we need to look back a little bit to figure out how to move forward," Annica said.

Everyone nodded their agreement.

"Last item… this damn board meeting."

Konda wrinkled up her face. "Those people are a pain in the ass. We have teams all over campus breaking their backs to set everything up just right. Why MilForce has to do this, I understand from a security point of view, but damn. Making sure the water in a certain shower gets to a certain temperature? Assholes."

"Then this might make you feel better," Annica said. "I want them all under 24/7 surveillance. Everywhere. Everything they do or say, I want it captured."

"That's… going to be difficult. They each bring their own security teams, and they sweep for bugs."

"Then you'll need to be better than they are."

"I can help with that," Shao said.

Konda turned to Shao and raised an eyebrow. "Really?"

"Everything but Hum-Int is based on technology. It's within our scope."

Annica nodded. Hum-Int—human intelligence—was things like social engineering, but technology was at the heart of pretty much every surveillance operation. That made sense, though why TSP would need that kind of expertise was... well, it would have been surprising a few weeks ago. Now, not so much.

"Okay, pull out all the stops. I want to know what they know, and when they knew it. We already know they green-lit the faking of the probe sighting. I want to know why."

"Other than money?" Konda asked.

"There has to be something else going on there. Maybe not all of them, but *someone* knows more. Also, let's keep this in mind. If they don't like what they hear, they *can* replace me."

"Let them try," Konda said with a near growl.

"Konda..."

"I'm just saying. I feel like we finally have a leader worth following. I'm not giving that up. If they replace you, I'm out of here. Screw them."

Sergey nodded. "Same."

"No. I want you to promise you'll stay. All of you. If they replace me, chances are I'll be all the way out. They'd want me completely out of the way. But I need you all here, working on finding Max, no matter what."

Konda and Sergey looked at each other and nodded, then turned to nod to Annica.

"Okay, you got it," Konda appeared to answer for both of them.

"The board members will start arriving this evening, I believe, and the rest will arrive tomorrow. Is that enough time?"

Shao pursed her lips. "It should be. We can do much of the surveillance with what is already in place, with a little creative programming."

Annica opened her mouth to ask what that meant, then decided she didn't want to know. "Okay. On that, the less I know, the better, I think. I don't plan to outright lie to the board if I can help it."

"Plausible deniability. It's a thing," Konda agreed.

"I can help with that," Sergey said with a nod to Shao.

"I had a feeling you could. Thank you, Mr. Yegorovich," Shao said with a nod that seemed to have more behind it than agreement.

"Okay, in any case, I think we all have plenty to do. I'll be spending most of the day prepping for the board and figuring out what I'm going to say."

"Good luck with that," Sergey said as he stood.

"Yeah, let us know if you need anything," Konda said as she stood as well.

"Have a good day," Shao said, rising to join the rest. "Sergey, I'll be in touch soon; we don't have much time."

"Oh, uh, where am I working?" Sergey asked. "SP is still shut down, I assume?"

"It is, and will remain that way," Shao said. She pulled a thumb drive from the jacket pocket of her tailored pants suit. "Slot this into any machine, and it'll be like you're in the SP. Just... be careful where you use it. It'll completely wipe any computer it's used on when you remove it."

"So don't use it on my own rig, got it," he said as he accepted the drive. "Got a laptop I can borrow?"

"Sure, we'll issue you one for this purpose."

"Okay, sounds like we're all set. Good luck everyone," Annica said as they left. Konda, the last one out, closed the door behind her and left Annica alone to get on with the work of preparing for the board meeting.

* * *

Once they were all outside Annica's office, Sergey turned to Shao.

"Shall we get that laptop so I can get to work? I'll do some digging while I think about what to put together for some kind of accidental release."

"Sure, follow me," Shao said and walked off.

"See you later?" he asked Konda.

"Sure thing," Konda said with a smile before she headed toward MilForce country.

Something stirred in Sergey as he followed Shao. There was a time when he would've admired Shao's figure as he followed her, even though she was Chinese, but all he could see in his mind's eye was Konda's smile.

By the gods, Sergey. Get a grip, he thought as Shao badged her way into an equipment room.

When he followed her in, he found himself in techie heaven.

"This is the main equipment storage—well, one of them," she explained. "Everything is RFID tagged, so just grab what you need. The system will check it out for you."

She walked over to a terminal and typed rapidly for a moment.

"I've given you full access. Anything in here you need is yours. Just guard it carefully; you're now one of about five people who have access. The rest are on my staff to do setups on campus as needed. Any questions?"

"No... I'm good, thanks," he said as he eyed a latest generation laptop he'd only heard rumors about. It wasn't even supposed to be released yet.

"Oh, one of my cousins owns the company, so I get early access," she said.

"Nice to know people."

"Indeed. Well, I'm going to get to work. I queried what you'd been looking at, and I think you were on the right track. I'll leave you to continue your work and take other avenues while I assist Captain Sanako with intel."

"Sounds good, thank you."

She nodded curtly and left him alone, and he took a few moments just to look around. He was used to equipment storage rooms, and most of them were less than spectacular. Here, pretty much everything was brand new, still in its box. He helped himself to one of the new laptops, an OS boot thumb drive, since the laptop would wipe itself between work sessions, and lastly, a faux-leather laptop case. He went ahead and unpacked the laptop from its shipping box and packed everything into the case. There wasn't even a power cable, since it ran on what was supposedly a lifetime, self-contained power supply. That was yet another major leap in recent technology.

He looked around as he tried to think of anything else he'd need, then shrugged. He had everything else in his apartment and preferred to use his own gear whenever possible.

Sergey thought about the power supply as he walked to his apartment. The only other power supply he knew of that was truly 'lifetime' was the reactor on *Traveler*, and he assumed on *Replenisher*. Rumor had it there was a similar supply deep underground on campus that had served as the model for the *Traveler's* supply, but it was just rumor, to him anyway.

Back in his apartment, he set up the laptop and wirelessly connected his keyboard, mouse, and triple-monitor setup. As it booted up, his jaw dropped on the boot screen. In the lower left corner was the Terran Space Project logo, beside the words "Power supply patented by."

He knew the TSP had invented some of what it had needed for *Traveler*, patented it, and sold licenses for more funding, but he'd had no idea they'd actually done that with the power supply. Did that mean this was some kind of micro-anti-matter power supply?

"Time for that later, Sergey," he said to himself. "You've got real work to do."

He took a moment to grab a soda from the mini-fridge he kept under his desk for extended gaming sessions, then plugged in the thumb drive he'd gotten from Shao. The screens went black for a moment, then up came the same login process he'd used at his desk in Special Projects. After authentication, his windows popped up just as they'd been when the power went out in SP.

Sergey cracked his knuckles and resumed digging into the members of the board of directors. He wanted to arm Annica with as much information as he could. Meanwhile, a part of his mind considered how to put together something to 'accidentally' leak information.

* * *

Konda called Anton on the way to the interrogation unit and met him outside the room where she'd had Paula Handley brought in. She stood, watching her on surveillance monitors, when Anton walked up.

"What's up, Captain?"

"You're being retasked, Sergeant. You work with me, and thus with Director Reeves now."

"Okay," he said and shrugged. "What do you need?"

"Information," she said as she looked up from the monitors. "There's a lot going on, Anton, and I can't go into everything now. We just don't have time. Suffice to say, Ms. Handley there has information we need."

"I'm going to need a little more than that," he said.

"She knew the probe sighting was faked. She knew Annica had been mind-controlled. Hell, she might have been in on it. We need to know what she knows about why. She also may know something about where *Traveler* actually ended up, and Annica is understandably curious about that."

"Parameters?"

"She doesn't want any enhanced techniques used."

"Hmm. That limits things a bit, but I think we can get somewhere. What do you have on her background? Family?"

"Let's see," Konda said, and pulled up her personnel records which, as with every TSP employee, were incredibly extensive.

"We have to take anything we see here with a grain of salt. Special Projects was involved in the background checks, so…"

"She could have edited hers. Got it."

"I'm going to go ahead and see what she'll say to start with. Observe and pop in when you think the moment is right."

"Will do."

* * * * *

Chapter Nineteen

Konda put her sidearm and knife in a lockbox just outside the interrogation room. She didn't think Paula could overpower her and take her weapons, but it was standard procedure. A part of her hoped Paula tried something so she could get a few licks in for free. She'd made Sergey uncomfortable, and for some reason, she wanted to make her pay for that.

"Good morning, Ms. Handley," she said as she closed the door to the interrogation room behind her. "I'm Captain Konda Sanako. You may call me Captain, or Captain Sanako. I trust you've been treated well while in our custody?"

"What the hell am I doing here?"

"Well, you can talk, so I'll take that as a 'Yes, everything has been fine, Captain Sanako,'" she said in a mocking voice as she sat across the table from Paula.

"You're here for a variety of reasons, but we're going to focus first on what you know about why Gustav Malmkvist brainwashed Director Reeves and put her under a mind-control program."

"I don't know what you're talking about," she answered a bit too casually. "We done?"

Someone truly innocent would have expressed outrage at being accused of something like that, or at the very least, been confused

213

about the whole idea of it. The denial was purely routine for Paula Handley.

"We know you spent a good bit of time in Director Malmkvist's office. What we don't know is why, and you're going to tell us."

"Why don't you ask him… oh wait, you can't. That bitch shot him."

"So you were lovers?"

Paula wrinkled up her face, disgusted at that idea. "Ew! Wow, you really don't know anything, do you?"

"We know a few things about a few things. We're just trying to fill in some blanks before the board decides to shut down the TSP altogether."

"I followed orders," she said with a shrug. "I design software; that's what I do. What's done with it, I really don't care. And if you think I'm scared about TSP shutting down, you're wasting your time. Trust me, I can make money anywhere there's a computer."

"Oh, I'm sure you can, Ms. Handley. But if we shut down, I might accidentally forget about someone locked up in secure facilities."

"Yeah, nice try. Got anything else?"

Konda was getting nowhere, and she knew it. Paula was simply not fazed by the whole experience. She felt she had nothing to fear and had done nothing wrong. The problem was, Konda had no concrete evidence that she'd done anything actually illegal unless she knew what Gustav had planned to do.

"Let's go to something simple. Why fake the probe sighting?"

Paula shrugged. "I wasn't in on that project, but I knew about it. Video isn't really my thing, you see. Anyway, I honestly don't know.

He was never much for explaining why he wanted something, he just asked for it, and we provided it."

"So what did you work on specifically?"

"Oh, lots of stuff that's probably above your pay grade, *Captain*," she said with a sickly sweet smile.

"I'm afraid that isn't going to fly. I'm cleared for anything, Ms. Handley," Konda said, and pulled a folded piece of paper from her uniform jacket.

She unfolded it and slid it across the table to Paula. Konda had had a feeling this might come up, so she'd had Annica provide a document giving her full clearance to any security level.

"Well, that's nice. Could be faked, though," Paula said and slid it back across the table with barely a glance. "You know, there are some amazing things people can do with computers these days. Sorry, not convinced."

"Let me make this perfectly clear," Konda said as she carefully folded the paper and slid it back into her jacket. "You're not getting out of here until I'm convinced you haven't violated any laws or TSP policies. So you can talk, or sit and rot. Annica's prepared to move forward without whatever you might or might not know."

Anton walked in without knocking and motioned to Konda. "She's just pretending to know something. She's probably one of the plebs of Special Projects. The little girl's there so Shao can show she's got females in there as well. Might as well just toss her back in a cell. She's got nothing we want. I think the only reason she was in Gustav's office so much was for… personal reasons," he said with a sly wink.

"Oh, I see. Well, whatever you have to do to keep your job, I guess."

"Oh, please, Gustav never had that particular pleasure," Paula said, disgusted.

"Oh, really? Then explain this," Anton said, and used a tablet mounted to the wall to pull up some of the surveillance video from near Gustav's office.

"You recognize that corridor?" he asked.

"Of course," she said and rolled her eyes.

"That's you, isn't it? Going toward his office?"

The video quality was excellent, and there was no mistaking Paula walking in the direction of Gustav Malmkvist's office.

"Sure."

"Now, this is about thirty minutes later. You're wearing a different outfit," he said as he fast-forwarded the video. The timestamp showed thirty-two and a half minutes had elapsed, and Paula walked by the other way, wearing something completely different.

"That never happened!"

"Our video doesn't lie, Ms. Handley. We don't manipulate it to fool people into throwing their lives away."

"That can't be right," she said, and finally a crack in the arrogant exterior began to show.

"Want to see it again? Tell you what, let's go to a different day," he said, and the screen went blank for a moment before another recording appeared on the screen. Again, it showed Paula walking in the direction of Malmkvist's office.

"There you are again, just two days later. Couldn't get enough of the old man, I guess. Maybe you were *his* Special Project," he said with a lewd grin.

Konda leaned back in her chair and stretched. Anton was good, and she let him play this out. She didn't show the fact that she hadn't noticed the differences herself. She'd been more concerned with the fact that Paula was there at all, though she was surprised she hadn't noticed.

Without a word, he fast-forwarded the video. This time, over an hour had elapsed before Paula showed back up on camera. She was wearing the same thing, but her hair, usually up in a ponytail or a bun, was down.

"Guess he liked to play with your hair while he—"

"Enough! This is fake!"

"You wish it was. How do you know he didn't use the mind control program you created on *you*? Maybe you didn't want to, but he always got what he wanted. Just ask Director Reeves. She's intimately familiar with the advantages that worm took."

"He… what?"

"Oh, yes. When we cleaned out his penthouse to make room for the new director, we found her clothes there. It was obvious she'd been staying there."

"Oh. That wasn't—that was never part of the plan."

"What plan?" Konda asked, seeing her opening.

"That," she said pointing at the monitor, "has to be fake."

"You'd know something about fake video, wouldn't you?"

"I already told you, I knew about it, but it isn't my expertise. And Gustav would have never used it on me."

"How sure are you? Have you had an STD check lately? Pregnancy test?"

"Wait, what?"

"Well, he was old, but with the medications he took, anything's possible," Anton said with a shrug. "Come on, Captain, let's let her brew on this and decide if she'd like to cooperate. I'm sure we could

218 | ALEX RATH

find a doctor to pay her a visit, if she should decide to be cooperative."

Without giving Paula a chance to say anything, Konda rose, Anton opened the door for her, and they both left. Anton closed the door softly behind him.

"I can't believe I didn't notice that," Konda said after the door was closed.

"Because it wasn't there," Anton said with a grin.

"You... how?"

"Oh, my skillset is wide and varied, Captain Sanako."

"I suppose this might be the time to mention we have another request from the director."

"Oh?"

"We get to put surveillance on the board. All of them. Everywhere they go, everything they do, everything they say."

"That'll be—"

"Tough, I know. We'll have Shao's help with the tech."

"That'll help. Who else is in on this?"

"You, me, Shao, and Sergey."

"Sergey. That's the kid I've seen you around with?"

"He's no kid, and yes."

Anton raised an eyebrow, and she realized she might have sounded a little defensive over Sergey.

"He's cute and smart, leave me alone," Konda said.

He grinned, then chuckled. "By Odin, you've got a *crush* on the geek."

"Shut up, or I'll twist you into a pretzel just for practice and pretend you're Gustav."

Anton shifted his chuckle into a cough, then cleared his throat. "Look. I think she might be ready to talk."

She looked at the monitor mounted outside the room and saw Paula sobbing with her head down on her arms on the table.

"I guess she's not as streetwise as she wants to think she is. I'd never fall for that."

"You fell for the probe just like everyone else, Captain. Never underestimate the mind's ability to believe what we want or what we fear the most. Even after all these years, females still struggle for recognition in high-profile tech roles. It's male dominated. The idea that she was being used for sex will have gotten deep into her subconscious fears."

"You're just full of surprises."

"I assume you didn't bring me into this for my charming wit."

"Let's go," she said and opened the door.

They walked in, and Konda resumed her seat, while Anton stood and leaned back against the door once he closed it.

Paula looked up, a bored look on her face. The tears had obviously been fake.

"Ready to talk?" Konda asked.

She sighed. "You must be desperate to fake video like that. Not a bad job, either. You know what, I'll tell you what you want to know. I have nothing to hide. What is it you want to know exactly?"

"Everything."

* * *

Earth, Terran Space Project Campus

S hao left Sergey to browse the offerings of the TSPs best technology—well, second best—and went to another storage room just outside her own office. This room's access was even more limited, which was to say, only she had access. The equipment in this room was there for a rainy day, and it was currently pouring. So far, she'd never had cause to use any of it, but now was the time.

As soon as the door closed behind her, the lights came on, and she was in the designed man-trap, and a second layer of security, which included a finger-prick for blood DNA, presented itself. She put her finger on the small platform, felt the needle, and then sucked on her finger while it processed. After a few seconds, the door unlocked and popped open. Not only was the room secure, it was pressurized. Only properly releasing the security would remove the positive pressure that literally held the door closed.

"Welcome back, Shao," a male voice said in Chinese.

It was a simple program, but she liked it. It triggered each time she entered the room.

"Just a little shopping," she said to herself as she looked around at the shelves of latest generation surveillance and spy equipment, all produced by and acquired from the Chinese government.

From cameras no larger than a human hair, to signal interception equipment the size of a grain of salt, this room contained the absolute latest in nano-technical surveillance gear. She selected a few containers, tucked them into a small bag, and secured the room before she went to her office.

With the bag resting on the corner of her desk, she sat down and started going through the files and activities of everyone in Special

Projects, starting a few weeks prior to Annica not being herself anymore.

Shao had never really known Annica personally prior to this, but she'd known who she was, and she'd respected her. Annica wasn't there just because she was Max Reeves' wife. She was there because she was a well-known and respected engineer. She'd been an integral part of the design of *Traveler*, among many other things. She'd also unknowingly designed the security that surrounded Shao's personal collection of toys.

She knew Annica had dabbled in many things early in life, but once she and Max had become an item, she'd really dug into engineering, specifically space flight and everything surrounding it. Shao figured it had to do with something Max had said or done, but the reason didn't matter. Annica would have been a part of the Terran Space Project with or without Max, and her skills on the mission would have been invaluable.

Kellie Warren, who'd taken Annica's place as Max's executive officer for the trip, was barely adequate in Shao's eyes, but she'd positioned herself well, and was on the roster as Annica's alternate. She was more of a Jill-of-all-trades, so she supposed that would be useful, especially given that *Traveler* hadn't ended up where it was supposed to be, so they were having to make it up as they went.

She looked first at activity patterns. Who worked when? She immediately found some commonalities that were too frequent to be coincidence. Paula Handley and two other members of the team would leave around the normal time, but be back in SP at almost exactly 2 am. That was too odd a time for it not to have been coordinated.

The next thing to do was figure out what they'd worked on during those late night sessions, so she began the laborious task of going over the keystroke recordings that existed for every station in Special Projects. It was a well-kept secret not even the director knew about, but Shao had brought her suspicion that everyone was out to get her when she'd come from China. It was nothing more than an insurance policy and not something she'd ever looked at previously. The keylogger had never been meant for her benefit, but for the benefit of the organization. Even with her background, she truly believed in the TSP's mission.

She sent a quick note to Konda and Sergey with instructions to drop by her office for a care package. She also opened up a personal directory to Sergey, which included the keylogger master software, though not access to what it had already captured, as well as the passwords for every network and firewall on campus. That should give Sergey what he needed to assist Konda with setting up the surveillance operation for the board members.

With that done, she began the task of assembling the keylogger logs into some semblance of readable text for review. Eventually, she'd have to bring Sergey in on this as well, but she wanted to get a head start.

* * *

Earth, Terran Space Project Campus, Director's Office

Annica sat back down behind her desk once the team had left, and decided to first tackle the list of what she should record to be released. How to record it would come later. She hoped Sergey would be able to come up with something for that. She opened a notepad app on her computer and started typing.

I was mind controlled and forced to let my husband go to unknown space alone

The probe sighting was fake; we don't know where Traveler *and its four hundred people are*

Known antagonists were placed on Traveler *through deception*

She leaned back and looked at the short list she'd quickly typed. It was short, but it was massive in scope, and it was enough to get started. She knew part of this would be recounting what she'd found out after she'd killed Malmkvist, and she didn't relish some of that going public, but appearances didn't matter. As she looked through the list, the thought rose to the surface. *Why me?*

Why, of all the crew of *Traveler*, was she kept behind? Granted, her role was secondary, and she was never meant to be the head of any department, but Max had to have been off his game after reading the letter she'd been forced to write. She wasn't arrogant enough to think that her absence alone had put the mission in major jeopardy, but add to it the uncertain destination, and what it may have done to its commander, and the risk parameters went up.

Maybe that was it—to put Max off his game enough to let Ragnarsson take over? But if that was the case, why not replace Max before the mission departed? Malmkvist was a jackass, but he was the director of the TSP; he could have made that decision, though it would have been nearly impossible to explain to the public. Max was the face of the mission—hell, he was the face of the TSP. While the Terran Space Project had done a lot for Earth in helping more people get to the Moon or Mars, this mission was the big one. It was what drew the funding. Maybe that's why Max had still been in charge when it left. A lot of the funding was probably because people trusted Max to handle the mission, while they wouldn't trust some unknown character.

Besides, she thought, *if Ragnarsson's face hit the press, he would've been recognized and reported as who he really was.*

A grin crossed her face. That was it. Whatever she released would include the faces of the criminals Malmkvist had sent along on the mission. That would not only add credibility to what she said, it would bolster any desired efforts to find *Traveler* out of a simple desire to bring fugitives to justice, even from wherever they were. Precedent on that had been set when fugitives who'd tried to make a new life on Mars were tracked down and returned to Earth. This new destination was certainly much further away, but it was still something some people would want done.

She dashed off an email to Sergey to drop by her office sometime within the next 24 hours, at his convenience, to go over the details and figure out how to get this done.

* * * * *

Chapter Twenty

Landing + 40 Days

Earth, Terran Space Project Campus, MilForce Section

Konda leaned back in her chair and waited.

"Where do I start?" Paula asked.

"At the beginning," Konda said. "When did you first feel like something was going off the rails from the publicly-stated mission of finding a new home for humanity?"

"About two months before the mission left. We were tasked with wiping out the real backgrounds of a few people. I honestly can't remember their names. Anyway, they were shady as hell, but we were told they were critical to the mission, so we had to clean them up."

"Adel Ragnarsson?" Konda asked.

"Yeah, that was one of them, I think. The other two were weird, had one name, like Prince, you know?"

"Empyre and Courtni," Konda supplied.

"Yeah, that sounds right. Anyway, we did what we were told. Cleaned them up so they'd appear to be perfect upstanding citizens to the folks who did the surface checks. One person got a little wise, but... oh, goddess. He killed her, didn't he?"

"Probably," Konda said; though she wasn't privy to what Paula was talking about, she made a mental note to check on it.

"Anyway, that's when it started. And some of the guys were tasked with listening on some really odd frequencies. Something so

225

high, it just didn't make sense for communication. You'll want to check into that. I honestly don't know anything about it. That was siloed."

"Go on," Anton prompted.

"That's also when the order came in to fake the probe sighting. I didn't work on that, either, but I knew it was happening because I saw the work in progress before it was done. You have to understand, we just follow instructions down there. We don't get to ask why. Asking questions is a good way to lose a job. Or apparently a life," she finished in a small voice.

"You've talked a lot about what you didn't work on," Konda said. "What *did* you do?"

Paula sighed and looked down at the table. "The mind control program; it was mine. Well, I took something that existed and made it better."

"What possible use could that have that wasn't bad?"

"It was supposed to go with *Traveler*, in case someone lost their mind in space or something, to help them."

"You bought that?" Anton asked incredulously.

"When you're a tech and you get to work on cutting-edge stuff, you tend to just do what you're told. You don't get it."

"Oh, I think you'd be surprised," Konda said, thinking of missions she'd been on that had been dubious, but had she'd carried out because of the challenge. "Who else was it used on?"

"I don't know. I wrote it and turned it over to Director Malmkvist. After that…" she said with a shrug.

"And Director Reeves?"

"No, that wasn't supposed to happen. Honestly, we don't pay much attention to what happens up here on the surface. We work, we eat, we sleep, we work. We're about the tech."

Konda studied Paula for a moment. She found it hard to believe, but then again, it could have been much like her own job before she'd joined the TSP. She'd done her missions, hadn't asked why, and hadn't cared what the result was as long as her mission goal had been met, so maybe it wasn't so hard to believe after all.

"Okay, what else did you work on?"

"I helped with the background cleanup, and…"

"And?" Anton asked.

"Annie. Oh, goddess."

"Annie?"

"The AI. It's not well known, but there's an AI on the ship."

"What? A real AI? I thought that was impossible."

"Well, it is… and it isn't. Machine learning has been a thing for a while, but Annie's a true AI. She has all the knowledge we have and is there to help Captain Reeves and the crew with anything. There's no problem she can't solve."

"You seem to think that's a bad thing," Konda said.

"The whole team worked on her, but she was my focus. It was without a doubt the most complicated piece of programming I've ever done, but… the final layers were added by Director Malmkvist. He finished the personality imprints."

"So he could have 'taught' her anything he wanted."

"Yeah. Imprinted his ideas of right and wrong. See, that's the hard part about an AI. The fear all the way back to the origin of the idea was that the AI would realize it was smarter than humans and decide humanity should serve it, rather than the other way around. I built in what are considered the three base rules of AI, but…"

"But they could be overridden by some asshat who thinks he knows better?"

"Yeah."

"Can we find out what he did?" Anton asked.

Paula shook her head. "The only copy of Annie is on *Traveler.* I was prohibited from retaining any of her code. All the work was done on a single drive, which was then installed in *Traveler.*"

"Does Director Reeves know about Annie?" Konda asked.

"I don't know whether she does now or not. No one knew. Even the techs who installed her just thought it was a database drive. We did use Director Reeves' voice print, though. It was supposed to be a nice surprise," Paula said.

"Instead, it'll just remind Max of the wife he thinks left him. Nice," Anton said.

"There are other prints available. There's a machine default I programmed in. It's a modulated version of an average voice print, so it doesn't sound like anyone specific."

"Still, I'm sure that was a rather rude hello. Who on the ship knew about it?" Konda asked.

"Just Captain Reeves, and there was a note about it to his second, in case something happened to him in transit. That would travel down the chain of command to whoever was in charge at a given time. It couldn't be activated until they were through the wormhole."

"So for all we know, this damn AI took over?"

"I mean, it shouldn't be possible. The core programming prevents it!"

"But Malmkvist could have undone that."

"I don't think…" Paula sighed. "I don't know."

"I think that's enough for now. I have some other things to take care of," Konda said. "Anton, would you escort her back to her cell?"

"Sure thing, Captain."

Once they left the room, Konda walked over to her tablet and sent the recording of the interrogation over to Annica in raw form.

* * *

Earth, Terran Space Project Campus, Sergey's Apartment

After several hours of digging, Sergey shook his head, got up to stretch, and walked a few laps around his studio apartment. So far, he couldn't find anything that wasn't on the public record about the board members. That was the thing about rich people; there were always people digging into their personal lives, so there wasn't much more for him to dig up.

His phone *pinged*, and he walked over to check it. It was a message from Shao. He now had some new toys to play with to help Konda set up the surveillance. Maybe that would net something, and it had to be more interesting than reading articles from gossip rags or digging into what Wikileaks had found. He sat down to look through what he'd been provided, and his eyebrows went up.

"Son of a bitch," he muttered as he saw the keylogger.

The mere fact that she had one sitting around, and he assumed she hadn't just procured it, meant she probably had it in use now. So that's what she'd meant when she said she monitored all activity. She'd meant it quite literally. He grinned when he saw the master password and IP lists—that would be a huge help, and it meant that Shao truly trusted him. With that, he could get into any computer on the network from the backend, with a little creative programming of his own.

He sent a note to Konda to let him know when she was ready to visit Shao. After he sent it, he added another line. *Lunch, maybe?*

While he waited for a response, he set up his own little spy net. He used the IP list and firewall access to put sniffers on every device in the rooms that would be used by the board members. He also installed the keyloggers on the computers in those rooms. Once it was installed, he checked behind it for any kind of fingerprint that would show a user it was there, no matter their level of technical knowledge. It took about ten minutes for him to find one random-looking registry entry that masqueraded as a part of the kernel, the central and most necessary part of the operating system of any device. The only reason he knew it was the keylogger was the installation time stamp, which took another ten minutes to find.

He considered searching his own computer for such an entry, but decided it didn't matter. It was probably there, and if he removed it, it would appear as if he had something to hide. Besides, if she was smart—and she was—it would automatically reinstall itself. With that in mind, he set up a new routine in the firewall. Any new devices that connected to the campus Wi-Fi would automatically have the keylogger installed in the background. It would appear to the user as if they were accepting a user agreement with a boilerplate template he downloaded and quickly customized, which they had to accept in order to access the network, then it would quietly seat itself deep in the device.

Just as he finished setting that up, his phone *pinged* with a different tone. It was the one he'd set up for when a message came in from Konda.

Come to the MilForce zone in thirty minutes. Anton will be joining us, so we can bring him fully up to speed.

Sergey frowned slightly. He'd hoped for some time alone with Konda, but he understood the need to bring Anton up to speed before they bugged the rooms of the board members. With thirty minutes to use up, he decided to do a quick dig on Anton to see who he really was.

With his new Special Projects access, he had access Anton's full personnel file, and he read through it quickly. He was impressive, to say the least. Some of the operations he'd taken part in were heavily redacted, but that wasn't a surprise. The TSP wasn't a government that had access to everything, just everything done on campus. He checked Anton's movements and didn't see anything suspicious, like frequent visits to see Director Malmkvist when he'd been in office, so he was satisfied.

Satisfied that Anton wasn't some sort of spy—not that he'd expected him to be—he set off for an area of the campus he'd never even considered visiting, an area of the building referred to as the MilForce zone. It wasn't technically off limits, but everyone pretty much treated it that way. So many guns made some people nervous. Sergey wasn't one of them.

* * *

Earth, Terran Space Project Campus, MilForce Section

Sergey cross the unmarked border into what was considered th MilForce zone and smiled involuntarily when he saw Konda waiting for him. The presence of the person who must be Anton was only a mild distraction.

Konda smiled back, which made him feel all warm inside. There was definitely something there.

What is it about life-threatening situations that seem to do things like this, he thought. He remembered his mother and father telling him about how they'd met. It had been during one of his father's ops, and she'd been one of the protected detail. They'd fallen for each other quickly during the op, and it had been history from there. As far as he knew, they were still together.

"Sergey Yegorovich, meet Sergeant Anton Essen. He's assigned to our team now, so you'll probably be seeing more of each other."

Sergey and Anton shook hands. "Nice to meet you, Sergey. I've heard good things," Anton said.

"Oh, really?" Sergey said.

When neither of them expanded on that, Sergey nodded and ended the handshake.

"I hope your morning has been as productive as mine," Sergey said.

"Oh, we definitely got some intel. Come on, let's eat and compare notes," Konda said and gestured for him to follow.

Sergey wasn't sure what he'd expected, but it wasn't what he saw. The cafeteria was a miniature version of the main cafeteria, with many of the same offerings, and was immaculately clean. He'd imagined something... else. There was one large difference, in that around the walls of the room hung the flags and banners of special forces units from around the world. It was impressive, and at the same time, a little intimidating to think how much skill in killing there was in this one small section of the campus.

"Careful, you'll catch flies," Konda said.

Sergey snapped his mouth shut with a grin.

"Sorry, just never seen so many of these in one place."

"That's not even all of them," she said. "There wasn't enough room."

They were early for lunch, so the cafeteria was mostly empty. They made their food selections, then they chose a table in a corner for privacy and sat. Sergey made a mental note that Konda had chosen to sit beside him rather than Anton. *That was a good sign, right?*

"So, you first. What have you dug up?" Konda asked Sergey.

"A lot of nothing. The thing about rich people is they're already under a publicity microscope, and there's nothing in the TSP records about them anywhere that isn't what you'd expect to see about someone who pumps money into the organization. I do have the list of who's invested what, so we know who the really big players are, but that's about it."

"Fortunately, we did a little better. Granted, we had a better source," Konda said and explained everything that had happened with Paula, and everything she'd told them. By the time she finished, they were done eating.

"Wow, that was… She thinks she was raped?" Sergey asked.

"Well. Yes. It was necessary to get the intel we wanted," Anton said unapologetically.

"Yeah, but she knows it wasn't real now, right?"

"No. I believe she has more to tell," Anton said.

Sergey shook his head and sighed.

"You disagree with my tactics to get potential life-saving information?" Anton asked with a bit of an edge in his voice.

"Have you ever talked—really talked—to a rape victim? I have. It's not something to screw with. That can do some serious damage to someone. It happened to a friend of mine back home. She was never able to leave her house alone again."

"We'll fix this as soon as we feel like we have everything we need," Konda said. "I know it sucks. Honestly, I don't feel too good about it, either. I feel like I need a shower. But remember, Director Reeves was taken advantage of, *raped,* using the software Paula put together. She's as responsible as Malmkvist, as far as I'm concerned."

Sergey considered that. It went back to an age old argument. Can someone who produces something be held responsible for what the tool is used for? The answer was still ambiguous and differed depending on who you asked and what the tool was.

"Well, we can't wind the clock back, so what's done is done, but please... get that off her shoulders as soon as you can? I'm not a fan of hers, but that's just... please?"

Konda nodded. "I promise. As soon as I feel like she's come completely clean, I'll tell her the truth."

Anton nodded agreement, but didn't seem to have any emotional investment in the situation.

"Moving on," Konda said, "we need to bring Anton the rest of the way in. All he really knows is what turned up while we questioned Paula."

Sergey nodded. "Well, you've been in this for the long haul, so go for it."

Konda nodded and expanded on what Anton had already gleaned during the interrogation. Sergey watched his reactions, and he could tell Anton was quickly realizing just how screwed up things were.

When they were done, Anton just shook his head.

"Unbelievable," he said.

"Believe it," Sergey said. "And now we get to do something about it. Ready to go visit Shao, Captain?"

"You can still call me Konda. Only Anton has to call me Captain," she said with a wink.

That caused both Sergey and Anton to grin, and it brought a bit of levity to a serious situation.

"And yes, let's do that. The first board members will be arriving tonight, so we need to move."

In agreement, they stood, policed up their trash, and headed out toward Shao's office.

* * *

Earth, Terran Space Project Campus

Konda and Sergey walked side-by-side on the way to Shao's office, while Anton followed closely behind. To an outsider, it must have looked somewhat like they were escorting Sergey, but Konda felt almost like it was the other way around. While Konda and Anton had both done surveillance, of a sort, the technology would be the big arrow in their quiver this time, and that was Sergey and Shao.

The pneumatic pocket door slid open on its own as they approached, and Shao stood up behind her desk.

"Mr. Yegorovich, Captain Sanako, and... Sergeant Essen, I believe?

"Yes, ma'am," Anton confirmed.

"Pleasure to meet you. I'm afraid we're short on time as I've just received word that the first board member's security team will be arriving within the next two hours, so we'll dispense with the pleasantries. I have a few things that may be of assistance," she said as she walked around her desk and extended a bag toward Konda.

Konda took the bag and shouldered it with a nod.

"Inside you will find a variety of equipment, all of it state-of-the-art. Most of it you'll never have seen before."

Anton grunted, and Konda glanced over her shoulder and saw the doubt on his face.

"Sergeant Essen, Germany's impressive, but China's the master of spies. Trust me. But if you think you have better…"

"No, thank you, Shao," Konda said before Anton could speak. "Our inventory of surveillance gear here on campus is—well, there wasn't much anticipated need for it, so it's mostly for maintaining security on the perimeter and so forth."

"Makes sense. I always like to be prepared for anything and… let's just say, my position allowed me certain allowances in storage space, and privacy, that you likely aren't the benefactor of."

Konda nodded, and Anton remained thankfully silent.

"Mister Yegorovich, everything in there can be handled by the software you now have access to. If you have any questions, which I doubt you will, just call me directly."

"Will do," Sergey said with a nod.

"Did you make any progress this morning?" she asked them.

"Paula talked after a bit of persuasion. Nothing physical, as Director Reeves ordered, but it worked. I'll be preparing a full report for Director Reeves, unless you want a briefing now."

"I would indeed like that, but I'm afraid you don't have time. I'll just wait for the report and see how it jives with the material I'm reviewing. Mister Yegorovich?"

"The press pretty much does our job for us on the board members. They're all wealthy, so they're the targets of hackers and press hounds day and night. Nothing we can use."

Shao nodded thoughtfully. "I thought as much. Have you come up with an idea for Director Reeves' 'leaked' video?"

"The board meeting, actually. We'll set up a camera, so it'll look like someone recorded it secretly."

"Perfect," Shao said with a dangerous grin. "That'll lend credibility that it's completely unfiltered."

"And the board members will be the first to come out and say it wasn't them, because if I understand correctly, no media devices are allowed in the boardroom."

"You're correct. It's also contained in a Faraday cage, so signals in or out are impossible."

Konda nodded. Technology wasn't her forte, but even she knew a Faraday cage was a network of electronics that blocked any and all signals from penetrating its confines. It made for the ultimate technological clean room.

"She must have some ideas, too. I have a message to drop by her office. I guess I'll do that once we're done?" he asked Konda.

"Sure. Let's get this done now. The sooner we're set up, the happier I'll be."

"Thank you all for your efforts. Sergey, I'll be in touch. I may need some assistance with a few things. The volume of data I have to peruse is a bit much for just me," Shao said.

"Anything I can do to help," Sergey responded.

"Okay, let's get a move on," Konda said, nodded to Shao, and turned to leave.

* * * * *

Chapter Twenty-One

Landing + 40 Days

Earth, Terran Space Project Campus,

Residential Apartments

Sergey walked into the apartment the first board member—the one arriving that day—would use, and stopped just inside the door.

"Is this an apartment or a house?"

"A hundred and seventy-five square meters is the average for the apartments kept for them, so a small house," Konda said.

"Such a waste. They sit empty most of the year," Anton said with a grumble.

"I guess the reasoning is, we wouldn't be here without their money," Konda said as she set the bag on the dining room table and opened it. "Well, she's right. I'm impressed."

Konda pulled out the variety of containers and shook her head. "I've never seen stuff so small. What the hell is this?" she asked and picked up a container of what looked like salt.

Sergey pulled out his tablet and scanned the network. The transmissions made it very clear what was what after he entered the password to a new firewall.

"They're signal interceptors, routed through a secure firewall in our system. We'll be able to intercept any data they send or receive on their personal devices. Damn, this stuff is scary."

Konda looked slightly confused. "Won't we get that when they hook into our Wi-Fi, anyway?"

"They might not all use it. Some might have satellite phones or something. These will even pick up those signals. Let me check the range," he said. "Go over to the far end of the kitchen."

Konda took the container to the far corner, which would let him get as far away from it as possible on the other side of the apartment. Given the size, he'd expected a limited range, but he'd been wrong. There wasn't a spot in the apartment he could find where it didn't pick up.

"You can put it anywhere, we'll still get the data," he said as he returned to the dining room.

"These must be the cameras," she said and examined a container of what looked like 2cm-long hair clippings.

Sergey consulted his tablet again, found the signals, and brought them up.

"Damn, that's impressive. Yep, cameras, apparently with audio pickup as well."

"These could be... dangerous, in the wrong hands," Anton said.

"So can guns," Sergey said.

"Valid point," Konda said. "Okay, let's get to work. Sergey, I think Anton and I can handle the placements, if you want to get to Director Reeves' office. We're running out of time, and we'll probably want to avoid dealing directly with her once the board members are on campus."

"Well, I will. You're her personal security, which is good. You can keep her safe and keep an ear on what's going on. Rich people treat security like they don't exist."

"Hadn't thought of that," she said.

Sergey considered for a moment. It would be easier if he cataloged which equipment was in which room as it was placed, but she was right, he needed to discuss his plan for recording the presentation with Director Reeves.

"Okay, here, give me your phone. I'll install a signal scanner, and you can record the ID codes for the devices as you go. That'll make it easier for me later."

Konda handed him her phone, unlocked, and he quickly installed the scanner from local storage and opened it.

"Here. Let me show you," he said and turned so he was standing beside her.

She shifted in closer, so she was almost leaning on him, and it took him a moment to refocus on what he was doing.

"Just move it close to the device, type in a note, like which room it's in and where it is, and save. I'll be able to retrieve that and create a log of which device records what. Easy," he said with a smile and handed her phone back.

"Wait, won't the bug sweep teams find it if it's that easy?" Anton asked.

"I assume Shao thought of that. For me, I'd say yes, probably so," Sergey said with a shrug. Then he thought for a moment. "Unless… we can shut them down, and then remote start them once we're sure the sweeps are done. Anyway, I'm sure Shao thought about that. Just let her know when you're done. I'm off. I know you'll be watching her back, Konda. Just… keep yourself safe too, huh?"

Konda smiled. "You're cute when you think I'm the one you have to worry about."

"I'm cute all the time," Sergey said. "You two have fun. I'll see you later?"

"Count on it."

Sergey left the apartment and banged his head lightly on the wall of the elevator as he rode down.

"I'm cute all the time? Really, Sergey? Could you *be* more of an idiot?"

* * *

Earth, Terran Space Project Campus,
Residential Apartments

Konda opened the containers and used the provided tweezers, equipped with tiny, rubber-coated tips, to carefully remove some of each of the devices.

"You take the kitchen and living area; I'll get the bedroom and bathrooms," she said.

"Will do, Captain. I suppose he is cute, in a puppy dog following you home kind of way."

"Oh, stop it," Konda said and blushed.

"Hey, if you like the spaghetti-arm type, that's all you."

"He may not be a super soldier," she said loudly as they both went to their respective rooms so she could be heard, "but he could tear your life apart with a computer to the point that even you would question who you were."

"Is that so?"

"I checked on him. His father is SVR."

"No shit?"

"No shit. So be nice, or his dad could disappear you."

"I went up against some of them once. They're sneaky bastards. Tough, too," Anton said as he moved to another room.

"Don't write Sergey off. He may not lift weights, but I get the feeling he can handle his fair share."

"You're really into him, huh?"

"Yeah, I guess I am. Who'da thunk it?"

* * *

Earth, Terran Space Project Campus, Director's Office

Annica looked up from her presentation preparations at a knock on the door.

"Come in," she said loudly.

Sergey poked his head in. "Ready for me?"

"Oh, good, come on in Sergey; we're out of time."

"I heard. The first one is arriving tonight."

Annica was confused and tilted her head.

"Shao told us," he explained.

"Ah, right. So, I had a few ideas. Have a seat."

She explained how she planned to include photographs of the known plants in her presentation, along with a general outline of what she planned to present for the video.

"Well, I had an idea about that," Sergey said. "What if we just record your presentation for the board? We make it look like someone snuck a camera in, then published it later. It'll serve several functions."

Annica shook her head. "Won't work. Every member has their own team sweep the room before every session, and the room is a Faraday cage."

244 | ALEX RATH

"Sure, but what if you run into technical issues and have to call in a tech to assist? I'll have to talk to Shao about how to do it, but I think the devices we're using can be turned off and on remotely. All I'd need to do is to be in the room to activate it. We can place it dormant so it would pass the scans."

"Aren't you a sneaky bugger?"

"My dad would be proud to hear you say that."

"I'm sure he would, and will, be proud of the work you're doing, Sergey."

Sergey shrugged, slightly uncomfortable with the praise.

"Not the type who'd ever say so, huh?"

"Not exactly."

"I get that. But trust me, he is, and he will be," she said with a smile.

"I hope so."

"Okay, I like your idea. Will the recording be decent quality?"

"As if it were shot by a professional, and we can place it any-where."

Annica nodded. "Okay, do it. Thanks, Sergey. I'll let the guards know you're coming in to do a tech check on the equipment in the room."

* * *

Earth, Terran Space Project Campus, Board Room

Sergey went directly to the boardroom, which was on the top floor of the TSP Headquarters building. It *was* the top floor, for the most part. There was a small gathering area, complete with leather couches and chairs, and a bar. At the other end of the room was a large pair of solid wood double doors, guarded by two well-armed members of MilForce.

He walked up and presented his ID.

"I'm Sergey Yegorovich with Special Projects. Director Reeves asked me to run one last tech check on the system in the room."

One of the guards, a large man with no neck, snatched the ID from his hand and scanned it.

"Go ahead, you're cleared," he said and handed the ID back while the other guard unlocked the manual lock with an actual key and opened the door.

"Wow, old school," Sergey said.

"Can't be hacked," No Neck said. "Hurry up."

"Right, thanks," he said and walked in.

The door closed behind him, and he took a moment to take the room in. It was multi-tiered and reminded him of something like a government setup. There was the dais, where Annica would be for her presentation, and three tiers of desks. Each desk had a computer workstation, which wasn't connected to the outside network, if what he'd been told was correct.

He decided, just in case someone walked in, he should at least do a cursory check, so he sat down at each terminal, one by one, to make sure it worked. There wasn't much there. Notepad, a folder where Annica could place documents or anything else she wanted them to be able to review on their own labeled "Director's Notes," and the day's preloaded weather report.

Sergey noticed how comfortable the chairs were and made a mental note to see if he could get something similar in his apartment, since he hadn't upgraded to the larger suite he was entitled to in Special Projects. Then again, the damn things probably cost as much as a month's rent would off campus.

With all the terminals checked, he walked up to the dais to check the terminal there. He went through the routine of checking the large display behind him to make sure it mirrored properly, and everything checked out. While he as there, he looked out to spot a good place to put the small, hair-sized camera.

The desks were out. They'd be checked carefully by the security details for anything out of the ordinary, and might actually be cleaned, which would wipe the device off onto the floor. That went for any flat surface, now that he thought about it, which ruled out most of the room. Then it hit him. The lights.

The dais was lit from every angle by lights along the walls and in the ceiling. The result was there was no shadow cast by the person standing at the front of the room, which was more visually pleasing. It also meant there were a lot of surfaces that normally wouldn't be touched.

He walked to the back of the room, grabbed one of the chairs, stood on it, and placed the small camera on top of one of the lights. A tiny drop of a light adhesive he'd brought for just that purpose held it in place.

That done, he got down and brushed the chair off so there was no evidence of a footprint. There was a light impression, so he decided to sit down in it again to give the leather something else to conform to.

Suddenly, the door opened, and a man in a uniform walked in. The lights pointed at the dais made it difficult to see any details, so mostly what he saw was an outline.

"What the hell do you think you're doing?" the man asked

"What I was told to do by Director Reeves. Who are you?"

"Colonel Shawn Carey, leader of the MilForce contingent here at headquarters. And you are?"

"As if your guards didn't tell you, I'm Sergey Yegorovich. Nice to meet you, Colonel Carey," Sergey said as he stood.

"And why did this equipment need *another* check?"

Sergey shrugged. "It's all fine. I guess Director Reeves just wanted to be 100 percent."

"Any why would she direct you to do this, and not Ms. Yating?"

"Again, I don't know. Director Reeves got me the post in Special Projects, so I guess she's taken an interest in my career," Sergey said, thinking fast.

He figured the colonel had probably already looked him up and knew that Annica had gotten him the job in SP, which would be seen as unusual.

"Are you done in here?"

"Yeah. Like I said, everything checks out."

"Good, get out. I'll take this up with Director Reeves myself."

"You do that. Have a nice day, now," Sergey said as he left the room.

* * *

Earth, Terran Space Project Campus, Director's Office

Annica startled at a harsh knock on her door. She frowned slightly as she wasn't expecting anyone, and none of the people she was working with would be so forceful.

"Come in," she said and disengaged the lock on the door. Her voice would come out of a speaker mounted outside the door.

The door swung open rapidly, and Annica stood.

"Colonel Carey, did we have an appointment?"

"We did not. What the hell are you up to, *Director* Reeves?"

"The business of the Terran Space Project. And you?" she asked as she resumed her seat.

"You know full well that MilForce reviewed the equipment in the boardroom. Why send that snot-nosed kid to check behind our work?"

Annica studied Colonel Carey for a moment. He'd always been one of the rougher tools in the TSP toolbox, but he was certainly riled up today, for some reason. She did consider it odd that this was the first time he'd come to see her since she'd assumed the role of director. Of course, she could have invited him, too.

"Mister Yegorovich is an incredibly experienced and qualified member of Special Projects. No offense, but MilForce isn't known for its technical acumen. As this is my first time presenting to the board, I wanted to make sure everything was ready to my own satisfaction. I believe that's within my rights as director."

"A member of Special Projects you personally appointed. Odd."

"Is MilForce in the habit of questioning the hiring decisions for Special Projects, Colonel Carey?"

"I question things that seem out of the ordinary for the safety of everyone on this campus."

"Then where were you when I was brainwashed by Gustav Malmkvist?" Annica asked harshly.

She hadn't meant to say it; it just came out. Ever since she'd come out of her induced state, she'd partially blamed MilForce for not investigating such an odd occurrence as her deciding not to go on the mission. It hadn't been easy to take Konda into her confidence, but she'd known her long enough to trust her, and now Anton by association. Colonel Carey was an unknown quantity.

They'd had dinner together a few times with the rest of the people directly involved in the *Traveler's* mission, but she'd never really gotten to know him. He did remind her a lot of Colonel Ascher, the MilForce commander for the mission. Rough around the edges.

"A full investigation was done, and you answered our questions to our satisfaction," he said, flinching back as if he'd been struck.

"Really…"

"Yes. I had no idea. No one had any idea, not until you killed Director Malmkvist. I watched that investigation carefully, obviously. I was satisfied with the job Captain Sanako and Sergeant Essen did, and there was enough evidence to back everything up."

"Did you know the software existed?"

Carey shook his head.

"None of this explains why you're conscripting my people without an explanation," Carey said. "You should have come to me with all this."

"Quite honestly, Colonel Carey, I don't know who to trust. You always seemed pretty chummy with Gustav, the times I saw you together."

"He was a friend," Carey said with a frown. "Though I guess I didn't know him nearly as well as I thought I did."

Annica studied Carey for a moment. She wanted to trust him, but something nagged at her. He knew what had happened to her, but hadn't come to see her once, until now. Then again, she hadn't asked him to visit, either, which, in retrospect, she probably should have, if only to gauge his standing in all this. She'd been so focused on tracking down *Traveler*, the rest of the running of the TSP had been shoved to the side. She should have called a meeting with all depart-ment heads, but she hadn't. She'd let her own motivations take over. Much, she reflected, as Malmkvist obviously had.

"Let me help you, Director Reeves. What do you have so far?"

It seemed an innocent enough question, given the circumstances, but Annica couldn't shake the feeling he was just trying to find out what she already knew.

"I'd love to sit and chat, Colonel, but I really have to get ready for this presentation to the board. I promise, we'll talk after the board meetings are done, and they've left. For now, I need you to let me do what I'm doing without interference."

"I'll do what I can, but I can't ignore it when things seem to be drifting away from the core mission we've established."

"Neither can I, Colonel. Now, if you'll excuse me? I really do need to get back to work."

"Please, let me know if there's anything I can do to assist," Carey said before he turned and walked briskly out of the office.

Something wasn't right about Carey, but she couldn't put her fin-ger on it. She quickly sent out invitations to Sergey, Konda, Anton, and Shao to join her in her office for a working dinner. After that, she checked each of their receipts, tracked by the ID they used to 'pay' for everything, and ordered everyone whatever they'd ordered most frequently to be delivered.

* * *

As Annica had expected, everyone arrived slightly early to her meeting summons. About the time everyone sat around the small conference table, the food was deliv-ered. Annica offered up sodas, tea, or stronger choices to everyone, and they ate mostly in silence. She had a feeling she wasn't the only one who'd had a full day.

"How did you know what to order?" Konda asked.

"Everything's tracked. When you register your ID for your food, it goes into a database," Shao said. "I know this is what I most frequently order, so that must have been the criteria?"

"Right you are," Annica confirmed.

"Damn. Can't even eat without being spied on," Anton said.

"A consequence of the digital age, Sergeant," Sergey said. "You'd be surprised by the things that get tracked."

"Probably not. Intel is key in our game," Anton responded with a grin.

"I suppose so," Sergey said with a nod.

"Anyway, if we're all done, let's get down to business. I need to get to bed early tonight. I have a feeling the next few days will be a marathon," Annica said.

"They will," Shao confirmed. "I dread visits from the board. They're always poking into things that don't really matter. Sometimes, I think they do it just to throw their weight around."

"We could always throw them around for you," Konda said.

"Let's hope it doesn't come to that," Annica said. "Now, how about a quick five minute brief from everyone? Let's see where we all are."

One by one, Sergey, Konda, Anton, and Shao provided updates. Everything so far was preparation. The bugs had been planted, and Sergey confirmed they all worked before putting them in a dormant state until they could be sure the bug sweeps were done. Konda and Anton gave a quick briefing on what they'd found out from Paula. Shao was the only one with something of a surprise.

252 | ALEX RATH

"I've been reviewing keylogged data," she said.

"Damn. You have keyloggers everywhere?" Sergey asked.

"Just on the Special Projects systems, unfortunately. I *wish* I'd had them everywhere. Though that's something I intend to rectify as a matter of digital security."

"Keyloggers?" Annica asked.

"They literally record every keystroke made on a computer," Sergey answered for Shao.

"Wow."

"We used to have to install them on intel ops," Konda said. "Well, we guarded the people who did."

"Why? We have all the correspondence and all the work product, don't we?" Annica asked.

"Maybe. The keylogger also records what someone wrote, then decided not to send for whatever reason. You'd be surprised how many messages get typed up, then trashed. There's also the possibility that some things have been permanently deleted."

"I thought everything was backed up immediately?" Annica asked.

"It is, but Special Projects has access to the backups. They're pretty much the only ones in the organization, other than me, who could completely eradicate data."

"Anything of use yet?"

"Nothing yet."

"So what about this AI Paula talked about?" Konda asked.

"Yes. Annie. I wasn't aware that Director Malmkvist had touched it at all," she said with a tiny frown.

"What could he have done?" Annica asked.

Shao shrugged. "If it was still being imprinted—which, based on what you've told me, it was—nearly anything. He could even have changed her mission parameters. What she considered right and wrong. Anything."

Annica sighed. "Great. Not only does Max have to worry about the people that shithead sent along, he could have a psychopathic AI to worry about. What can the AI do?"

"Anything," Shao answered. "It's hardwired into the ship itself. If needed, the AI can take control of any ship system, though it's programmed not to do anything that could bring harm to humans."

"Unless Gustav changed that," Annica said.

"That was Paula's fear as well, once she thought about it," Konda said.

"What's your take on her? Does she actually care? Or is she just out to destroy the memory of someone she thinks took advantage of her?" Annica asked.

"I think Paula cares about Paula. That's as far as it goes," Anton answered.

Konda nodded. "She didn't care when she'd heard you'd been impacted by the software she worked on. She was more upset that you'd killed her buddy Gustav. When we led her to believe he wasn't as friendly, or too friendly, she turned on a dime and started talking. Speaking of, we're going to want to get the other techs in a room."

"I'm working on identifying which of the SP team had a part in any of this, though I suspect it was most of them, in some fashion or another. It could easily have been so compartmented that they worked on pieces, with only one knowing what the whole project was," Shao said with a shrug.

"Sounds like we have a plan. As for me, I'm almost done with my presentation for the board. Also, I got a visit from Colonel Carey today."

"Oh, shit," Konda muttered.

"He was none too happy that I'd conscripted a few of his people without consulting him, but frankly, I couldn't care less about his sensibilities. He stood by while all this happened, so as far as I'm concerned, he was involved, if only by being an idiot and not spotting anything odd."

"I didn't mention it, but we did conduct an investigation when you didn't go on the mission," Konda said.

"I know. He told me. Still, something about him doesn't *feel* right. Why didn't you think to mention that to me, Konda?"

Konda looked down at her empty plate. "I was embarrassed, because the investigation cleared you."

"Were you involved in it?"

"No, neither of us were. I was too close to you, or at least that was the reason given to me," Konda answered.

"Seems like someone close to me would have been the perfect person to evaluate my state of mind, don't you think?"

"That's what I said! But Colonel Carey disagreed. You should also know, he knew about me bringing in my friend after you shot Gustav and allowed it."

"Well. We'll get to him soon enough. I'll want to check on every head of department, which I should have been doing all this time. Shao, I'm afraid that's going to fall on you. I want you to dig into what the CFO and Colonel Carey might have known."

Shao nodded.

"Okay, it's getting late, and tomorrow's going to be a long day. I suggest you all get some rest," Annica said and stood, signaling an end to the gathering.

* * * * *

Chapter Twenty-Two

Max woke with one of the suns penetrating his eyelids and grumbled that he'd forgotten to close the blinds the night before. The reason was half draped over him. He smiled and wrapped his arms around Kellie.

"Wake up, sleeping beauty. Another day has begun."

She groaned. "Five more minutes."

"Nope, time to get up," he said.

He tried to throw the covers off, which were in a significant state of disarray. It took several attempts to get them untangled from them both.

"Fine," she said and sat up. "I'm awake, but do we *have* to get out of bed?"

He admired her body and sighed. The team would be waiting for him before getting started on the alien craft, as the hangar should be done.

"I'm afraid so. I need a quick shower, then I have to get to the new hangar," he said as he got up and walked to the bathroom.

"Max?"

"Yeah," he called as he turned the water on.

"I love you, you know?"

Max sighed and leaned on the counter. He'd known it was coming, but he still wasn't sure how to respond. He cared about her, but he wasn't sure he was ready for that yet. Then again, what was holding him back? His feelings, or his fear of being hurt again?

She walked into the bathroom. "You don't have to say it, Max. It's okay. I can't understand what you might be feeling, but it's important to me that you know how I feel. Okay?"

He turned back to the shower to check the temperature, unable to meet her eyes.

"I care about you, Kellie. I just…"

"It's okay," she said and put a hand on his shoulder. "Take your time. You must have a lot to sort through still, now that things are getting calm enough to really think about it."

He smiled and turned to face her. "What did I do to deserve you?"

"You're you," she said, and slipped past him into the shower.

"Hey!" he protested.

"You're welcome to join me."

"I suppose they can wait on the alien craft a *little* longer," he said and got into the shower with her.

* * *

Mythos, Eos City

As Max and Kellie walked up the sidewalk, hand-in-hand, a pair of X-94s and both BN-12s lifted off.

"Must be heading to the mining site," Kellie said.

Max nodded. "I green-lit the transport while you were getting dressed. The sooner we get that ore, the better."

Kellie nodded. "Should have the first satellite ready in a few days."

"Good. More to follow, once regular loads start coming back. I'd better get to the hangar. The team is waiting."

"I'll ask again, why do you have to be there for that?"

"Because I still haven't decided whether to tear it apart or try to get it working as it sits. Now that it's here, I can have more experts actually looking at it, including Annie, without the delay of being relayed."

Kellie sighed. "Be careful, okay?"

"I will," he said and gave her a quick kiss before they parted ways. He continued to the hangar, and she walked off toward the PCC.

Max walked into the suit room of the hangar and put on his environment suit. Then he continued through a decontamination chamber into the hangar itself, where a five-person team waited, all suited up and waiting for him.

"Sorry for the delay. Had a few things to take care of."

"No problem, Captain," Colin said.

"Colin? What the hell are you doing here?"

"It flies," he answered simply.

"Fine, but no more surprise additions. Essena, we all clear?"

"Nothing appears to have changed, Captain."

"Very good. The first thing we have to decide is what to do with it. I know the original plan was to take it apart to see how it works. Now, I'm not so sure. I'm wondering if we should try to get it powered up."

"Yes!" Colin said. "I want to fly it first."

"Not to fly it, Colin. To see if we can figure out their language. Find out their power source and more about the materials."

"Damn," Colin muttered.

"Annie, have you and the linguists made any progress on their language?"

"*I'm afraid not, Max,*" Annie said. "*There is not enough to go on. We do not know whether the characters are letters or syllables. There are some diagrams, but none of them have led to any breakthroughs. Cryptography has also gotten involved.*"

"Good call. Okay. Given that, we're going to try to power this thing up."

"Are we sure that's a good idea, Captain? For all we know, it's got some kind of recall routine, and could try to fly off by itself as soon as it has power."

"Let's hope not," Sadie March said.

"That's why you're here, Sadie. If anyone can figure this out, it's you. Let's get started."

"*The entire craft has been sanitized and cleaned, but I recommend you keep your suits sealed,*" Annie said.

"Thanks, Annie. Yes, everyone keep your suits sealed. No unnecessary risks."

"Only the necessary risks, got it," Colin said.

"I'm going to take a look at the propulsion system in the back," Rhonda Matthews said.

Rhonda had been their chief astronaut in space, but she was also one hell of a mechanic.

"Sounds good, Rhonda, thanks," Max said. "Come on, Colin, let's check out the cockpit. Maybe something will stand out to us."

Everyone went into or around the ship, as their jobs demanded, and got to work. The radio was constantly active, with people reporting their activities and any findings that might be relevant. Finally, it all got to Max.

"Okay, folks, I know we want to record everything, but don't transmit unless you come up with something everyone else needs to know. Clear?"

There was no answer, but the radio went quiet, which was good enough.

"Now I can think," Max muttered to himself as he and Colin got to the cockpit.

"Damn, these seats are narrow. Even *my* skinny ass can't sit in them," Colin said.

"Yeah, they were definitely thin and tall, but very human-like."

"I have an idea; be right back," Colin said and left.

While he was gone, Max looked over the switches, buttons, and panels around the cockpit. It was familiar, but foreign at the same time.

After a few minutes, Colin came back in with an armload of blankets. He put enough of them in the left seat so they filled the void, and Max could sit on top of them.

"Good thinking, Captain."

"Thank you, Captain."

Max sat, and while he was afraid his head would be too high, he realized it had put his head about where the aliens' would be.

"What do you think?" Max asked.

"Looks about right to me. So, try to start it up."

Max considered the thought. That was what he wanted to do, certainly, but it was risky.

262 | ALEX RATH

"Clear the hangar," he said over the radio. "I'm going to try to start it up, and I don't know what's going to happen."

"You know I'm not going anywhere, right?" Colin asked.

"Nor I," Essena said from the opening to the cockpit.

"You have to stop doing that, Essena," Max said after his heart moved back to where it was supposed to be.

"Not my fault you are not aware of surroundings."

Max knew better than to argue with either of them. Neither Colin nor Essena were going to leave him alone to try this.

"Hangar clear, Max," Annie said. *"Good luck. If you must do this, follow your instincts. Do not try to read the text, just go by feel."*

Max nodded and took a deep breath. He let it out slowly, then looked around him. Everything was slightly out of reach due to the aliens having longer arms, longer legs, and everything else. He tried to envision the alien hands reaching out, and his hands followed his vision. He flipped one switch, tapped a button, then reached up and flipped several more toggles.

When nothing happened, he considered resetting everything, since they had imagery of where everything had been before he'd started, but Colin reached past him.

"You forgot initial system boot," he said and pushed a button that was slightly larger than the rest.

As soon as he did, the cockpit came to life. Displays lit up, and the interior lights came on, but they were very dim.

"Suit lights off," Max said and turned his off.

Essena and Colin followed suit, and Max saw what the aliens would see—a dimly lit cockpit, with all the displays lit up and ready. Ready for what was the big question.

"Okay, no one touch anything else," he said.

"Don't worry. Who knows what the hell this thing can do?"

Suddenly, some kind of buzzer went off repeatedly.

"Everyone out!" Max yelled and got out of the seat.

"Wait," Colin said and stopped him. "Could be an altitude warning. The craft is grounded, but has no landing gear."

"And even if we knew where they were, I wouldn't trigger them when we're flat on the ground," Max said.

"I do not like this," Essena said.

"Yeah, I'm not a fan of warning buzzers, either," Max said, "but Colin's probably right."

"So stop it."

"I don't want to hit the wrong thing at this point," he said. "Okay, let's shut it down. We were planning to put in a hoist, anyway, so we'll do that next, so we can lift it off the ground. Maybe they'll auto-deploy."

Max went in reverse order of the switches he'd toggled, and after he was done, hit the larger button again. The system shut down, and the buzzer ceased its noise.

"Okay, we're done here until we can get this thing lifted. Essena, I assume you have a recording of what I did?"

"Of course."

"Good, let's get that edited out and instructions drawn up so anyone on the team can repeat it."

"*I'll take care of it, Max,*" Annie said.

"Thanks, Annie. Short day, everyone. Engineers, feel free to look around, but the main work needs to be installing a hoist strong enough to lift this thing. Sadie and Rhonda, that's you."

"*We're on it,*" Sadie answered instantly.

Max led the way out of the craft and stood back to look at it with his arms crossed over his chest.

"Something bugging you, Cap?" Colin asked.

"Yeah. Why did that work?"

"Maybe it was just the button?"

"Maybe, but let's say it wasn't. That means they went through a shutdown sequence before they gathered in that little room to die."

"I hadn't considered that... what does it mean if that's true?" Colin asked.

"It was a suicide mission? Why the hell were they still in the ship? None of this adds up."

"*Max, I am picking up a transmission from the alien ship,*" Annie said.

"What?" Max and Colin both exclaimed at the same time.

"*It started as soon as you turned the ship on, and has not stopped.*"

"What is it?"

"A single tone, C, two octaves above middle C, to be precise. It is broadcasting on a broad spectrum of frequencies."

"Why aren't our radios picking it up?"

"I filtered it out as soon as I detected it, which was before you would have heard it."

"Distress signal?" Colin asked.

"Okay, I'll buy that, but why did it just start now?" Max asked.

"I'm more worried about who, or what, is going to respond to it."

"Change of plans. Rhonda, work on the lifting mechanism. Sadie, I need you on the manufactory making satellites as soon as materials get back. Skip whatever steps you can. We need to know if something or someone else is out there."

"I'm on it," Sadie said and rushed out of the hangar.

"Colin, fly out to the mining site and tell them to hurry the hell up."

"You got it," he said and also ran out of the hangar.

"Rhonda, can you handle this?"

"Sure, I'll bring in some of the other engineers. Can we cannibalize from the hangar on *Traveler*? That'll make it faster."

"Do it. Essena, with me," Max said and went to get out of his environment suit to head to the PCC.

* * *

Mythos, Flying over Mythos

"What is that noise?" Ghostfeather asked as they flew back toward Eos after tending to their wounded.

"I do not know, but it appears to be coming from the humans," Dreamtail said. "We will investigate."

Dreamtail picked up speed, and Ebontalon and Ghostfeather matched pace. They had spent a day at home with their wounded, to make sure none would have long-lasting injuries. They had lost several in the fight with the Cloudseekers, but without the humans, it would have been a fruitless attack. Now, it seemed, the few remaining Cloudseekers had fled to other territory. They would go in shame and become servants to another clan. It suited them, Dreamtail thought.

The Cloudseekers had always been too arrogant for their own good, always seeking to expand their territory beyond what they could control or maintain. It was part of the job of the griffin to take care of the land that was their domain. Rotted trees were pruned, stale water was drained, or a channel raked out to join it to flowing water. Everything in the Treewatchers' territory was well tended. That was why they had fought back when their pristine forests had been attacked by the humans' machines. They would still do their best to restrict the humans' expansion, but it had been agreed that they would have some small part of the Treewatchers' territory as their own.

The fact that the humans had ventured into the Cloudseekers territory was, in Dreamtail's mind, a happy coincidence. Granted, they had lost twelve of their own in the attack, but countless Cloudseekers had died in exchange, thanks to the humans.

This battle had taught Dreamtail something important. If the humans truly wanted something, they had the ability to take it—even from the Treewatchers, if it came to that. Their metal birds were more powerful than he had imagined. That was impressive and frightening at the same time. A surprising consequence of the victory, though some hesitated to call it that due to their losses, was that more of their clan wanted to meet and interact with the humans. Dreamtail thought that was a good thing. It would help his clan understand them, and help the humans see them as friends. He certainly did not want to be their enemy.

There were those, of course, who saw the humans as an imminent threat and thought they should be hunted. Some suggested Dreamtail could easily remove their leader—and he could, but he knew it would be the last thing he ever did. The humans protected their leader and each other.

As they neared Eos, he pinpointed the noise to a new building near where they kept the metal birds, *planes*, he reminded himself.

"We will investigate," he said and changed course toward the new structure.

"Good, I am getting a headache," Ghostfeather grumbled.

As he was about to land, Dreamtail saw their leader, Max, come out of the structure, and swooped in to land near him, followed closely by Ebontalon and Ghostfeather. That put them on the hard surface, which he hated the feel of under his talons and paws, but it was necessary to get the humans' attention.

* * *

Mythos, Eos City

Max pulled up short when the trio of griffins landed basically right in front of him.

"What the…"

The lead griffin pointed at the hangar with an extended wing and screeched loudly.

Max winced; the screech was louder than any he'd heard from them. He figured maybe they wanted to know what was inside it, so he pulled his tablet from his hip pouch and pulled up the feed from one of the cameras in the hangar.

He showed it to the griffin, but it didn't get the response he expected. The griffin's talons dug into the ground, leaving grooves in the hardened surface.

"I think he's unhappy," Essena observed.

"Ya think? I figured they'd be happy we had the thing out of where it was."

The griffins were chittering and screeching amongst each other. It was overwhelming to see. It reminded Max of when they'd gone off alone before the mission.

"The sound. I bet they can hear it. Annie, would that pitch be within hearing range for an eagle? Let's assume the anatomy is similar."

"It would, and it would likely be piercing, much as if it were coming over your radio. The broadcast frequency is above the range of human hearing, but it may be within theirs."

"Play it over my tablet. Now."

The sound came from the tablet, and Max immediately wanted to drop it and plug his ears. The griffin had a similar response, but it was more violent. One of the griffins stepped forward and slapped the tablet out of his hand with a clawed talon. Max screamed as the talon tore through his hand and hit the ground.

Essena raised her rifle and pointed it directly at the griffin's head. Before she could fire, it backed up, and the lead griffin stepped in the way.

"Go! Now!" Essena demanded.

The lead griffin spread his wings as if to protect his comrades.

"Don't shoot!" Max said, and gasped. "Get me transport to the hospital. Now!"

Max looked down at what was left of his hand as he screamed out in pain. He could see bone, and that was never a good thing.

As Essena got on the radio to call for a medic, the griffins flew up and off into the distance.

* * * * *

Chapter Twenty-Three

Kellie walked into the hospital and saw Essena standing outside one of the triage bays. She walked up to her and put her hands on her hips.

"What happened?"

Essena briefly explained the exchange, and Kellie sighed.

"So it was probably going for the tablet. Max's hand was an accident?" she asked.

"Could be. Captain Reeves stopped me from shooting it."

"Probably a good thing. You're good, Essena, but three on one, I think you'd lose. How is he?"

"Doctor Chadda is trying to save hand."

"Oh, goddess. Okay, I won't disturb her, but stay on station," she said needlessly. She knew that Essena wouldn't leave his side. This was twice on her watch he'd been injured. Neither had been her fault, but Essena seemed to take things personally.

She needed to understand the attack. Everyone would be looking to her for answers, and there'd be no shortage of people who wanted revenge for an attack on Max.

"Where's Leopold?"

"Not sure."

Kellie nodded and went to the main reception desk to find out. Once she had a room number, 104, she went there directly.

She knocked once and walked in, tablet in hand, to find Sergeant Jana Nováková sitting by his bed holding his hand. They were both laughing at something.

"So you haven't heard?" Kellie asked.

"Heard what? Hey there, Ms. Warren," Leopold said.

"Max was attacked by one of the griffins."

"What?" Leopold exclaimed and bolted upright in bed, which seemed to make him a bit dizzy, as he immediately leaned back with Jana's help.

"Leopold is still recovering," Jana said with a frown.

"Well, I need his help to understand what happened, and to decide whether to hunt these things down or not. Clear?"

"Show me," he said. "Help me sit up," he said to Jana.

Jana used the bed controls to sit Leopold more upright while Kellie walked to the other side of the bed.

She pulled up the surveillance footage and let him watch it on loop as she explained.

"Max managed to start the alien ship, but it began emitting some high-pitched signal. If their auditory system is similar to an eagle's, it'll be a high-pitched tone that's constant. They seemed pretty agitated about the hangar, so Max showed them the craft, and then played the sound. That's when one of them lashed out. I think it was probably at the tablet making the noise, but I need to be sure."

Leopold watched the footage and listened to her explanation, then nodded, instantly regretting it.

"Ugh. Remind me not to do that. Yeah, I reckon it was the sound. That one's always been the grumpiest of the three. I think sometimes he resents the leader for keeping them around."

"What makes you think that?"

"Just the way he acts. He's always just a bit further away than the other two when I'm talkin' to 'em."

"So you don't think it intended to hurt Max? This is important, Leopold."

"Nah, I reckon not. He's grumpy, not stupid. I reckon the leader's giving him an earful. They're smart, Kellie. They'll have figured we're not people they want to piss off after seeing the planes in action."

"Or they figure we're too large of a threat, and they tried to take out our leader."

"If he'd wanted to take Max out, he could have. Make no mistake on that."

Kellie nodded. She believed Leopold and wanted to give the griffins the benefit of the doubt, but word was spreading fast, and calls for blood were on top of her message queue.

"This won't be an easy one to diffuse. How are you doing?"

"Still a bit rough, I'm afraid. Doc said my brain bounced around in my skull like a ball when we crashed. And here I thought my brain was pretty big."

Jana giggled, which sounded odd, coming from someone who looked every inch the soldier.

"Well, you may have to talk to everyone from here, then. I'll do my best, but they trust you when it comes to the griffins. Think you'd be up for that?"

"If the alternative is people hunting 'em down, yeah, I'll make it happen."

"Don't push yourself too much, Leo," Jana said seriously.

"I'll be fine, mate," he said and patted her hand.

"Okay, I'll let you know. In the meantime, think about what you'll tell them. This is one hell of a powder keg I'm going to try to diffuse."

"They're animals at the core, and it lashed out at something that caused it pain. Simple as that."

"Thanks, Leopold. I'll be in touch," she said. "And get well soon; we miss you out there."

"I'll do my best."

Kellie left and walked outside the hospital. There was already a gathering of people being kept out of the hospital by a handful of MilForce.

She held up her hands for attention. "Everyone, calm down!" she shouted.

That had some effect, but not enough. Sergeant Villegas happened to be one of the MilForce members stationed outside and turned to face her.

"How's he doing?"

"He'll survive. Doctor Chadda is trying to save his hand, but it's touch and go."

"Touch and go... that's bad, Kellie."

Kellie grimaced.

He grinned. "Sorry, battlefield humor. Hold on."

Sergeant Villegas turned to the assembling crowd and raised his voice. "Everyone, be quiet, and Ms. Warren will tell you what's going on."

A few more were quiet, but the demands for answers continued.

"Shut up!" he shouted at the top of his lungs.

It seemed even the nearby wildlife obeyed, and there was complete silence.

"The floor is yours, Kellie."

"Thank you, Sergeant," she said, then turned toward the crowd. "Max is in the care of Doctor Chadda. He will be fine; it was only his hand that was injured. She's trying to save it, but even if she can't, she's a miracle worker when it comes to prosthetics, and we have the most advanced printers in the world."

"Let's get that griffin!"

"Make it pay!"

"Stop!" she shouted. She explained about the alien craft and the sound coming from it. Then she went through what had happened when Max had played the sound directly through the tablet. She went on to explain that Leopold agreed, which seemed to have some effect.

"So, what, it gets away with maiming Captain Reeves?" someone asked.

"Those griffins just lost over a *dozen* of their own to help us get land for mining! Yes, if that's how you want to put it, they get away with taking a swipe at a tablet Captain Reeves happened to be holding. It could have been any of us. Now, go back to whatever you were doing. Doctor Chadda will release an update when there is one."

There was grumbling in the crowd, and they seemed reluctant to leave, though a few walked away.

"You heard Ms. Warren, disperse!" Pedro shouted.

They seemed to take him more seriously, and everyone wandered away from the hospital.

"Thank you, Sergeant," Kellie said.

"Don't mention it. I don't get to yell too often. Feels good to clear out the lungs, ya know?"

Kellie couldn't help but grin and shake her head.

"There ya go. Don't worry, I'm sure he'll be fine. Doc's the best. She took good care of me."

"I know she is. Thanks."

"Now, you should probably let everyone else know what's going on. There's a lot of grumbling, and now that people have weapons…"

"Shit. You're right. Thanks again," she said and rushed off to the PCC to draw up an official statement to read to everyone. She knew she needed a script for something like this.

Inside, she was battling her own desire for revenge. She loved Max, and flying was his passion. Would the injury put a stop to that? If so, she'd seen pilots who'd been grounded, and they were rarely the same afterward.

* * *

Mythos, Eos City, Hospital

Max slowly opened his eyes, and the first person he saw was Doctor Chadda.

"We have to stop meeting like this," he said with a groan.

"That would be good, Captain Reeves. I've put in a nerve block, so you won't be able to move or feel your right arm."

"So what's the verdict?"

"You have options. Sort of."

"Okay…"

"I can save the hand, but you'll never fly again."

"Not an option," he said.

"Or we can print a prosthetic," she continued. "It'll be completely functional, but it'll take a while for your body to adjust."

"I fly by feel, Doc."

"The prosthetic would, if all goes well, attach to your nerves. You'd be able to feel as good, if not better, than a natural hand. I've worked on pilots before, and with the prosthetic, more than 90% returned to active duty. The alternative is a 0 percent chance."

"I guess 90 percent is better than 0. Do it."

"I thought you'd say that. I just have to go start the printer. Is there anything you need?"

"Where's Kellie?"

"Sleeping, most likely; it's the middle of the night. It has been an eventful day."

Max groaned, imagining the reaction of the rest of the population to the attack.

"Ms. Warren managed to diffuse the worst of the calls for revenge, but MilForce is keeping a close eye on things. There are some who want to hunt the one who hurt you down and return the favor."

"Well, I suppose it's good to be liked."

"This is serious, Max."

"I know, I'm sorry," he said with a sigh. "I assume Colonel Mikhailovna is outside. Send her in, please?"

"You assume correctly. Please tell her she needs to get some rest?"

"Will do. Thanks again, Doc."

"Thank me when you fly again," she said and laid a hand on his shoulder briefly before she left.

He looked down at his heavily bandaged hand and shook his head while he waited for Essena. "Dumb move, Max. Dumb move."

Essena walked in, trying to appear not to rush.

"Captain Reeves."

"Essena. I'm fine. Thanks for not causing a major incident."

"Should have killed it," she said simply.

"No you shouldn't have. It was my fault. I should have known the sound would provoke a reaction."

"Stupid thing should have known better. I was too slow."

"Essena, I'm alive. That's what matters, okay? Now, go get some rest."

"I stay until you are better. It is my responsibility."

"Do you honestly think I'm in any danger here, Colonel?" he said, intentionally using her rank to bring her mind to business.

"I have guards outside."

"Of course you do," he said and rolled his eyes.

"People were very unhappy, Captain."

"I understand that, but I doubt they wanted to hurt *me*, and I seriously doubt the griffins are going to come back anytime soon. Now please, go get some rest. I need you well rested and alert, not asleep on your feet."

She drew up, seeming to take some offense to the suggestion that she was too tired to do her job.

He raised his left hand after trying and failing to raise his right.

"You know what I mean, Colonel. Do I need to make it an order?"

"No, Captain. I will have guard posted outside."

"Thank you, Essena. For everything."

She nodded, turned smartly enough for a parade ground, and marched out of the room.

Max laid his head back and sighed. He *had* to stop finding his way into medical bays.

* * *

Mythos, Eos City, Hospital

Max looked up and smiled as Kellie walked into his room the next morning. She leaned down to hug him, and he returned the hug with his left arm.

"So, what's the verdict?" she asked.

"I'll be getting a new hand," he said with a sour look on his face.

"I suppose the alternative was never flying again?"

"Bingo."

"It'll be fine, Max. You're a fighter. You've proven that already on this planet."

"I know, it's just..." He stopped and sighed.

"What?"

"Nothing."

There was plenty, but none of it he wanted to voice. He'd known pilots who'd been injured and had prosthetics. They usually worked great, and some even claimed they might lose the other hand just to get another one. But he'd seen the impact it had had on some of their relationships. Some of their spouses couldn't stand the touch of the prosthetic, no matter how much it looked or felt like a real hand. He was afraid the same thing would happen here with Kellie.

"What's our status?"

"Well," she said, consulting her tablet, "mining operations are going full bore. Get it," she said and glanced at him. "Full bore?"

He chuckled and shook his head. "What else?"

"MilForce, as well as Hugh as his people, are watching the populace carefully. There are some just sitting around with rifles pointed at the sky, waiting. They want blood, Max."

"Think it would help if I spoke about it?"

"Maybe. I think some of them just want an excuse to get something back. Control maybe?"

"Okay, I'll draw up some notes, and we'll plan something this afternoon. What's Leopold's take on it?"

"It was the sound; he's sure of it. He's just a few rooms down the hallway."

"Sounds right. I was an idiot. I just wanted to make sure I knew what had them all riled up."

"Well, you found out. Try not to do that again, okay? I've got Annie working on some way to block the signal and the sound, but that would require a lot of metal we don't have."

"How's the hoist coming along?"

"Rhonda's working on it, and Sadie's helping when she's not checking on the manufactory. They hope to finish it by the end of the day. We're rushing the first comm satellite through testing, and Colin should be taking it up this afternoon. We'll put that one in a geostationary orbit so we have coverage all the time."

"Sounds good."

"First load of ore should be coming back today sometime, too. I've put a BN-12 on permanent detail. It's sitting at the site, waiting to load, and will bring it back as soon as it hits the weight limit."

Max nodded, trying to think of anything else he needed to track.

"Beyond that, everything's as normal as it can be, while the city's leader is laid up in the hospital. The griffins haven't been seen since they flew off."

"Probably wise. We'll figure something out about that later. I have no intention of abandoning a relationship with the locals."

"I knew you wouldn't, but we really need to figure out communication. The team is working on it, and they're working a bit harder now, I think, but it's going to take interaction to really make any progress."

"Yeah, I know that'll be a bit trickier now, but we'll get there."

"It's taking Doctor Chadda and Sergeant Nováková both to keep Leopold from going out there right now."

"I bet. How's he doing?"

"Pretty serious concussion; he'll need a few weeks before he's back to full capacity."

Max nodded and looked down at his right arm again.

"Hurting?" she asked.

"No, can't feel a thing."

"I don't care, Max."

He looked up at her with a raised eyebrow.

"You're you. I don't care if your hand is a prosthetic. I love who you are. It's your heart and your mind, not your hand. Though I don't mind that either," she said with a sly grin.

Max cleared his throat as Doctor Chadda walked in unannounced.

"Am I interrupting something?" she asked.

"Not at all. How's the progress?" Max asked.

"We're ready if you are. The operation will take several hours, so if there's anything that needs your attention, now's the time."

"I think we're good. Kellie?"

"Yep, all set. Thanks."

* * * * *

Chapter Twenty-Four

Landing + 41 Days

Mythos, Eos City

"*K*ellie, *I have an idea,*" Annie said as Kellie watched Colin take off with the first communication satellite.

"Kind of busy right now."

"*Watching a plane take off? Kellie, there are much better uses for your time, like stopping the noise that caused the griffin to attack Max.*"

"You said it would take more metals than we have material for."

"*I did not take all the variables into account. We can cancel the noise. Since it is contained in the hangar, we can simply rig the hangar walls with a noise canceling system to absorb it before it leaves the hangar.*"

Kellie frowned. The reason for the AI was not to miss small things, and now she'd missed something fairly significant.

"*I have the plans for the system drawn up, and it can be done with the parts we have available, if we are willing to cannibalize part of my ship.*"

"Your ship?" Kellie muttered, then said out loud, "Are you okay, Annie?"

"*I can run a full system diagnostic if you wish, but I am fine, Kellie.*"

"Please run that diagnostic. Let's just be sure, okay?"

"*Of course, Kellie.*"

"And send those plans to Sadie. What would have to be removed from *Traveler*?"

"Speakers. They can come from the cabins where the colonists have already moved out."

"That's fine. Send them along, please."

Kellie watched Colin's X-94 disappear into the air, becoming a tiny dot, then nothing, as he flew up to place the satellite. It would be good to have communications again without a plane to relay the signal. The one satellite would be enough to cover both the alien crash site and the mining operation, which was as far afield as they'd gone up to this point.

"Kellie. Sadie here."

"Go, Sadie."

"Got the plans from Annie. I'm a little annoyed I didn't think of it, to be honest. I've already got some techs getting what we need. I figure we can have it done within the hour. The hoist is almost done."

"Excellent news on both fronts. Thanks, Sadie."

Kellie checked her watch, which had been reprogrammed for the new 20-hour day. It was noon. To combat the constant light, every apartment was outfitted with room darkening curtains. Easily made since the foliage around the area could be converted to fabric by the manufactory, and they had literally tons of that lying around.

She decided to walk around and get a feel for the attitude of everyone since the attack on Max, and she saw the results. In several places around the dedicated part area, people sat back on benches. Not unusual around noon, but what was unusual was that most of them were holding rifles, or in fewer cases, handguns. Not just holding them, they had them ready to aim and shoot.

She walked up to one of them she recognized.

"Scott, what exactly are you doing?"

"Waiting," he responded.

"For?"

"For one of them damn things to show itself so I can wing it. Seems only fair."

"Scott, I explained this. It was an accident."

"Really? An accident? Trust me, on Earth, that would be assault."

"Actually, it wouldn't," Hugh said as he walked up to join them. "Sorry, Kellie. I was just making my rounds and saw you. Figured I'd come check on Max personally."

"What do you mean it wouldn't? That's bull!" Scott exclaimed as he rose to his feet, keeping the rifle carefully pointed at the ground.

At least he has good gun discipline, Kellie thought.

"If you were holding something I determined to be a threat to my person, and I struck your hand to get it out of your hand and injured you, it would be self-defense."

"But… that's wrong! That was Captain Reeves! Damn bird should have known better!"

"Trust me, Scott. If Kellie here can accept it, so can you and everyone else," Hugh said.

"I don't buy it, Hugh. Just don't buy it. Those things are dangerous."

"Scott, if it had wanted to kill Max, it would have. The griffins went to fight with us; they helped us get access to where we can mine the ore we need. Why would they want to hurt us after that?" Kellie asked.

"They did, huh?"

"They did," Hugh confirmed.

"And they lost about a dozen of their own. We lost no one, just Leopold with a concussion, but he'll be fine, and that was because the white griffins attacked their plane," Kelly added.

"Oh."

"So maybe go put that away," Hugh suggested.

"Maybe I'll go on a little hunt. Bernadette's always looking for something new. I could use some more leather, anyway," Scott said.

"You be careful out there, Scott," Hugh said.

Scott waved, wandered out of the park, and walked out toward the edge of the city.

"Well, that's one," Kellie said and sighed.

"It'll be okay, lass. Time will calm them down. They just want to protect their leader."

"I get it, I do, but calmer heads must prevail. We really don't want an all-out conflict with these things."

"No, we don't. We'd win, but it would be bloody for sure, on both sides."

Kellie nodded.

"I'd better get back to work. Thanks for the assist, Hugh."

"Any time."

* * *

Mythos, Orbit Over Mythos

Colin hummed to himself as he flew up through the atmosphere of Mythos to establish a geostationary orbit from which he could launch the satellite. It wasn't fun, but it was one of the roles he and his aircraft were perfectly suited for.

"Eagle to PCC, verify position."

He waited while the radar on the *Traveler* found him and tracked his position for a few minutes.

"Spot on, Eagle. Clear to deploy," a professional voice came back over the radio.

"There's someone who's lived in a control room," Colin said to himself as he unbuckled and moved to the back of the X-94.

He triple checked the seals on his suit and depressurized the cargo bay in the rear of the aircraft. Once the light went green to indicate his pressure matched the outside, he opened the hatch. Another minute of waiting, and then he looked out into the black. The X-94 lacked a robotic arm of any kind, so the deployment would happen by hand.

He used a strap from the bulkhead to the satellite to pull himself along and activated the computer package on the satellite.

"Deploying now," he said as he unfastened the restraints.

A small push, and the satellite floated out the back of the aircraft. It was the first of many he'd likely deploy, but this one was key to operations on the planet.

"Clear of the aircraft."

"Copy, clear of the aircraft. Establishing contact."

Colin watched as the satellite unfolded after a command from the ground made the connection. First, the solar array unfolded. He would have to remain there until all the checks were done, so he hooked himself to one of the straps and floated there, enjoying the zero-g.

The motor on the solar array paused for a moment, and he cursed under his breath. Then it started again, and he breathed a sigh of relief that he wouldn't have to go out into the black to repair anything yet.

"Solar array is up. Testing nozzles."

286 | ALEX RATH

Colin saw several small jets fire off, and the satellite changed position slightly to maximize its reception of solar rays from the system's three suns.

"*Contact looks good. Position is fixed. Power is online. Mission accomplished. Good job, Eagle. Come on home.*"

"Copy that, PCC. Thanks."

* * *

Kellie couldn't help but smile as everyone in the Planetary Control Center cheered when the communications satellite came online. She imagined it had been much the same when Earth had launched their first satellite, except that on Mythos, they'd known what they were missing when they hadn't had it.

"PCC to mining site. Comm check," she said as she keyed the radio on Max's desk.

"*We're receiving, Kellie. Great news. Good job,*" Azeema responded. "*How's Max?*"

"He's doing okay. Doctor Chadda is giving him a new hand as we speak."

"*He's alive; that's what's important.*"

"Agreed. Thanks, Azeema. How are things looking out there?"

"*Extraction is going well. There are rich veins near the surface, which works out well for us. I expect we'll be sending back the first load in a few hours. Not surprising, since no one has ever mined the planet.*"

"Sounds good. Minimal environmental impact," Kellie reminded her.

"*Always. These tools were designed for that purpose.*"

"Good. Talk to you soon," Kellie said and leaned back in her chair, satisfied.

The first load coming back would be a huge boon for the city, and none of it would be wasted. Usually in a mining operation, anything that wasn't ore—tailings—was junk to discard and leave in heaps. Here, they'd be used by the massive 3D printers for buildings or anything else they needed. Nothing would be left behind as waste.

Even if the printer had materials remaining after whatever building it was working on, it would be laid out, and artists would use it to create some form of sculpture wherever it was placed. Other times it would print a part of a wall that would eventually enclose the main part of the city. It wasn't considered an urgent need, so it wasn't being printed as a whole, but doing it piece by piece as there were spare materials was another of Azeema's ideas.

Kellie decided to check on the progress of the noise canceling in the hangar and left the PCC. As she approached the hangar, Sadie and Rhonda were both outside, rubbing their temples.

"You two okay?"

"We may not be able to hear the tone, but damned if it doesn't hurt after a while," Rhonda said.

"Earplugs don't help. Just drills into your brain. Even the noise canceling in the helmet doesn't help," Sadie added.

"Sorry. How's it coming?" Kellie asked.

"Almost done. Two more to attach, then wire it up, and we can turn it on and see if it works."

"*It will work*," Annie said over Kellie's radio. "*Diagnostic is completed, Kellie. All systems normal.*"

"Okay, Annie. Thanks. Why doesn't the noise canceling in their helmets work? And why will this work if that doesn't?"

"Diagnostic?" Sadie asked.

"The fact that Annie didn't think of this solution sooner bothered me," Kellie explained.

"Proximity overrides the helmet's capabilities. It is the same as if you stood next to the manufactory. No noise canceling can defeat that level of noise so close to the machinery, but we are able to keep the sound in that contained space. Otherwise, it would be heard from where you are now."

"She's got a point there. Oh, well, hopefully it works. At least the hoist is done. Maybe they can get the damn thing to stop doing it on its own," Sadie said.

"Maybe, but let's not count on it. Take whatever break you need, but we need that system in place as soon as we can get it."

"I need a few more minutes at least," Rhonda said.

"I'm with you there," Sadie agreed. "We'll get it done as soon as we can without going nuts," she said with a grin.

"Thanks. I'll leave you to some peace and quiet," Kellie said with a wave and walked toward the hospital.

* * *

Max's eyes popped open, and he was instantly awake. The light didn't hurt his eyes this time.

Doctor Chadda smiled at him as he looked around. He was in a normal room instead of an ER triage room now.

"You did very well, Captain. Your body seems to be very receptive to the new material."

"So it likes my fake hand?" he asked with a grin.

"Something like that. It's going to take some practice, so don't get frustrated. If I did my job, with Annie's assistance, I must say, you should have some basic function right off the bat. Though I will warn you that I've activated a limiter for now. The strength the prosthetic will have could literally tear it off the bone if you try to use it before you're used to it. While it has more strength than a normal hand, it can still only handle what your flesh and bone can handle."

Max looked down at the prosthetic hand, which he couldn't tell by appearance was a prosthetic at all, except for all the bandages at the attachment site just above his wrist.

"Go ahead, take it for a test spin. We'll be doing some specific physical therapy, but you should be able to move it around. Since it wasn't a violent amputation we had to work against, we were able to carefully... well, the details aren't important. Let's just say, this provides the best possibility for optimal results."

"So you got to pick where to cut everything?"

"Basically."

Kellie walked in through the open door just as he lifted his arm to bring his hand in front of his eyes and experimentally flexed his fingers. She stood in the doorway and smiled, and if he wasn't imagining it, wiped a tear from her eye.

"Doesn't even feel... heavier, but it definitely feels weird."

"That'll come with time," Doctor Chadda explained. "Eventually, your nerves will get used to it, and it'll feel normal again."

He turned his hand over, as if examining an antique to see if it was all in one piece. He brought up his left hand and compared them side by side. Even the fine hairs on the back of his knuckles looked completely normal.

"Amazing work."

"Thank Annie for that. She was able to take footage we had of you and zoom in on your hand. She guided the printer to make it look exactly like your old hand, including the small scar in the crook of your thumb and first finger."

"Annie was involved in doing this?" Kellie asked.

"Of course. I'm good, Ms. Warren, but having an AI to assist with the construction of a prosthetic is priceless. She's able to get into details I couldn't possibly do in such a short period of time. It would take me a week to program what she did in an hour, and that's if I helped no one else."

"*I was glad to be able to be of assistance, Doctor,*" Annie's voice said from the speakers in the ceiling of the room.

"Thank you for your help, Annie. I can't tell you how much I appreciate you both," Max said.

"Yeah. Thanks Annie," Kellie said, though Max thought she didn't truly mean it as much as she tried to sound like.

"Well, my work here is done, and I do have other patients. A therapist will be in shortly to give you some exercises and work with you," Doctor Chadda said.

"Thanks again, Doc. Hopefully this'll be the last time you have to save my life."

"Let's hope so, Captain. Take good care of him, Kellie."

"Oh, I will," Kellie said with a smile.

Kellie walked to the right side of Max's bed and looked at his hand, then into his eyes.

"It looks… normal."

"I know, right? Amazing."

"Whoever selected Doctor Chadda, we owe them a huge thanks."

"I'm afraid that'll be impossible," Max said sourly. "She was Annica's pick."

"Oh. Well, at least she did *something* positive for the mission."

"She did a lot. But she's not here, and you are. How's everything going?"

"Pretty well. Annie came up with a noise canceling approach that'll hopefully keep that tone confined to the hangar. Also, Colin put the comm satellite up, and we have comms again."

"Well, you've been busy. Maybe it's time for me to retire."

"Oh, hell no you don't. I'm handling things while you recover. You're welcome to it once you're out of here."

Max chuckled.

Kellie reached out hesitantly. "Does it hurt?"

"Not at all," he said and took her hand in his new right hand, being careful to control his grip.

"Afraid you'll break me?" she asked jokingly.

"Actually, yes. Apparently, this thing has super strength or something. But there's a limiter on it right now, so it should be safe."

"It is, for now," a man in scrubs said when he walked in, having overheard his last comment. "I'm Doctor Viebey, but you can call me Pat. I'll be working with you on your therapy, and I assisted Doctor Chadda with the operation."

"A doctor for therapy?" Kellie asked.

"Well, Captain Reeves here gets the best, and I'm it," he said with a grin. "I was a combat medic, so I worked with a lot of soldiers and pilots post prosthetic. I probably have more experience with them than anyone on the planet," he said and held up his hands. "Both prosthetics."

"And they're good enough to perform surgery?" Max asked, impressed.

"And more. Trust me, Captain, you'll fly again in no time, and probably have a better feel for the stick than you did before."

"Oh, goddess, don't tell the other pilots that," Kellie said.

"We don't have the materials to do voluntary replacements… yet, but I'm sure that could happen in time. On Earth, it was basically illegal, though there was a black market in cybernetics."

"Which I stayed completely away from," he added when both Max and Kellie gave him a *look*.

"Right," Kellie said.

"In any case, are you ready to get started?"

"Sure. The sooner we get this started, the sooner I can get back to work," Max said.

"Yes, please," Kellie added with a grin. "I'll let you two work," she said and leaned over to kiss Max on the cheek before she left.

"That's all I get after this?" Max asked.

"Later, flyboy," she said and laughed as she walked out of the room.

"Well, looks like I'd better get you cleared to be checked out," Pat said and walked to his right side.

He put a case down on the bedside table and opened it. Max looked over and saw that it contained a variety of grip and manipulation tools and toys, from the looks of it.

"Let's get started," Pat said with a smile and pulled out the first item.

* * * * *

Chapter Twenty-Five

Landing + 41 Days

Earth, Terran Space Project Campus,

Special Projects Office

The next morning, Sergey walked back into the Special Projects room, and even though he'd only been there a few times, it felt like coming back home. Shao had opened it back up, but only for him and the rest of Annica's hand-picked team. It was the best place in the building for them to gather, out of sight of prying eyes, when they needed to be in the same room. For Sergey, it was where he'd work on the intercepts and continue his research.

He grabbed a soda from the fridge and sat down at his desk. After getting through the login process, he decided to activate the first set of surveillance equipment for the two board members who'd arrived the night before. It was only supposed to be one, but another had decided to come in early. The rest would be arriving throughout the day, and the first meeting would be that evening. Well, he considered it a meeting, but officially it was an informal reception for the board. That would be held in the antechamber outside the boardroom, which was already covered by TSPs normal surveillance, so there was no need for anything special to be done there.

He held his breath as he sent the signal for the cameras and signal interceptors to go live. The worst-case scenario was that guards would be doing a sweep at the moment he turned everything on. Thankfully, that didn't happen, and all his monitors lit up with the views from the cameras that had been placed. Thankfully, they were all empty. No one was wandering around with equipment that would pick up the transmissions. Waveforms also came up, showing the signal interceptors in each room. Those he checked carefully to make sure there was nothing in the rooms to interfere with his signals or anything that would detect them. That, too, was clean.

Most of his monitor space was now dedicated to surveillance, which left him only one quadrant of one monitor open for his other work. Eventually, Anton would show up and help him with the surveillance, since he didn't have an official duty related to the board meeting. That would free up some space.

For now, though, he got to work with the space he had. He checked his message queue and found a message from Shao with the details she'd dug up on the mind-control program. She wanted him to dig into it to see if there was a way to spot those under its influence. It included a link to the deep directory where it was hidden, so he opened it to start working.

He noticed it was in the directory he'd been about to start digging into when Special Projects had gone dark, and felt some small satisfaction that he'd been on the right trail. Finally, with something to do other than searching, he sank into the code behind the software that had cost Annica her trip with her husband.

It didn't take long for him to figure out that the base code was definitely German. There were comments in the code in German, which gave it away. The original author had also signed his work with his handle. Some quick research turned up that the handle belonged to a German hacker he knew also did side work for the German government as a way of staying out of jail.

"What did you do with it, Paula?" Sergey said to himself as he looked for modifications.

Any programmer worth their salt would put notes in where changes were made. It was beneficial for debugging, and not to mention, programmers were vain. They wanted anyone who looked at the code later to know who'd done what. For the next few hours, it was a matter of finding out what had changed.

The first adjustments he noticed were a set of new triggers. The initial software had had simple keywords as triggers, rarely used words that would trigger the programmed actions. It was nasty, and it could be used to turn an average person into an assassin if the right word was uttered or even read. Paula had added visual triggers, but they weren't just images. It was a complex sequence of colors that had to be shown at just the right speed, in just the right order, something that would never be mimicked in nature or by accident.

"By the gods," he muttered as he realized what she'd done.

The lights weren't just a trigger, they could also *be* the programming. All you had to do was program what you wanted, send it to someone, and as soon as they looked at it, they'd be programmed and activated at the same time. It was a combination of subliminal messages and shocking the mind into being receptive to suggestion.

He realized quickly that they'd need some kind of professional in brain manipulation to understand it, but the implications, based on Paula's comments in the code, were clear. It was a psychological weapon of mass destruction. It could completely take over someone's mind, as it had with Annica. Things like this typically wore off, but she'd covered that, too. Built in was a routine that would force the person to reprogram themselves every day, first thing in the morning. If they didn't, it would wear off.

Sergey heard the doors open and stood. To his relief, Anton walked in and waved. "Morning," he said.

"Yeah, it is. Look, I'm buried here in code; can you take over the surveillance? They haven't even gotten up for coffee yet."

"Sure. Um… where?"

"You can use Paula's station. Seems fitting to have it used for something good. Here," Sergey said, and led him to where Paula had sat.

Anton sat down and was able to log in with his usual method.

"Nice setup you geeks have down here."

"Yeah, it's not bad. There're drinks and snacks back there if you need anything. Here, I'll bring everything up."

Sergey leaned over Anton's shoulder and typed out a shortcut he'd created that brought up all the monitoring with one command.

"There you go. Have fun!" Sergey said and went back to his desk to continue working.

"You must be onto something."

"Yeah. I've got the software that was used to program Annica."

"Damn…"

"You have no idea. I'll fill you in with everyone else if you don't mind."

"No problem. Looks like our first rich asshole is awake."

* * *

Earth, Terran Space Project Campus, Annica's Apartment

Annica woke early and groaned. She tossed and turned for another hour, wanting to get more sleep, but it refused to come. Her mind decided to go through every nightmare scenario she could think of when she interacted with the board, so she got up and made coffee.

While she waited for it to brew, she considered the night before. The informal reception hadn't included her, which had felt somewhat odd. Checking the past, she found that was normal, but it still felt odd for the director of the organization not to be there to greet the board.

She reviewed the day's schedule in her mind again. The morning would start with a briefing from the CFO on the state of the finances, which seemed to be the most important thing, since it came first. Then, after lunch, Annica would make her presentation and answer questions. The session was expected to last all afternoon. The schedule for after dinner was open for her time with the board to continue, or for the board to adjourn for the day. The choice would be theirs by majority vote.

When the coffee was done, she prepared her first cup and sat down at the kitchen table with her tablet in front of her to review the notes she had for her presentation. It felt like she'd gone over them more times than she'd gone over the briefing for the *Traveler* mission. The stakes were pretty much the same, or so it felt. Her life.

The board was full of wealthy but intelligent people. They had to realize, as soon as she took control, that things were going to change, and that she'd investigate everything thoroughly. If she went public with the faked sighting and the fact that the board knew, not only would TSP suffer, but so would they. Public trust in anything they

298 | ALEX RATH

had their hands on would suffer. But she knew she couldn't do that without risking a follow-up mission that was still years away from being ready. She could, however, selectively reveal certain information that would erase trust in the board, while at the same time maintaining public trust in the organization now that she was in control. At least, that was her plan, but Annica was ready to change it, based on how they responded to what she had to say.

* * *

Earth, Terran Space Project Campus, Annica's Apartment

Annica spent the entire morning in her apartment preparing, not even wanting to go to her office. Finally, it was time. She couldn't even eat lunch, as she felt her stomach would rebel against anything but coffee, which it had become hardened to over the years. She dressed in her best business suit, grabbed a protein bar just in case, and headed out.

As soon as she opened the door to her apartment, she found Konda standing outside.

"What are you doing here?" she asked.

"My job," Konda responded. "I'm your bodyguard today, remember? That means I guard wherever you are. I was just about to knock to get you going."

"Well, no need for that. Let's go," Annica said and walked away after she closed and locked her door.

Konda fell into step beside her, rifle in hand at low ready.

Annica glanced to the side. "Is that really necessary?"

"Let's hope not."

"How reassuring."

"Look, the board, pretty much to a person, brought their own armed security. I don't know what their orders are, but I know what mine are. As far as I'm concerned, anyone who isn't MilForce is a threat."

"Well, that's a rather pessimistic view."

"You have other ideas?"

"Not really."

"Even Colonel Carey doesn't like that they're allowed to have armed guards. It's an insult to him and MilForce, because it seems to assume either we can't be trusted, or we're not good at our jobs. It's in the charter, though, so he has to allow it."

"Well, on that we can agree."

"You really don't trust him, huh?"

"I'm still not sure. The fact that he didn't let you investigate my state of mind bothers me. A lot."

"Yeah. Valid point."

"Anyway, we can decide later whether to bring him in or not. His reaction to what I have to say today, part of which is going to be released, will help."

"You're really going to go through with it?"

"The recording at least. Yes."

"You know I can't go into the room with you, right?" Konda asked as they entered the elevator to go to the boardroom area.

"I know. It'll be okay. It's probably the safest room on campus. It's still guarded by your folks, isn't it?"

"It is, and there's a concealed x-ray in the door frame. We'll know if anyone tries to get a weapon in."

"But they could protect against that."

"If they knew it was there," Konda said and glanced over with a grin. "It was Malmkvist's idea, from what I heard."

Annica nodded and mentally noted the obvious omission of his title of director.

As soon as they walked off the elevator, Konda nodded to Colonel Carey, who stood in the middle of the room. "Sir."

"Captain. Director. Good to see you both."

"I'm rather busy, as you might imagine, Colonel," Annica said, caught slightly off guard by his presence.

"I understand. I'm just here to wish you luck and offer again any assistance I can provide. In any way," he added, and she felt a subtext there.

"Captain Sanako is doing a perfect job, thank you. Now, if you'll excuse me…"

"Of course. The board is assembled and ready for you," he said and gestured toward the doors.

The guards on the door reached over, pulled the double doors open for her, and stood at attention.

Annica took a deep breath and walked into the chamber to find out what her fate would be.

* * *

Earth, Terran Space Project Campus, Board Room

Annica walked up to the dais and faced the board. This was the first time she'd seen all of them in person. Some she'd met during mission prep, but it was Max they'd come to see, so she'd been mostly the smiling wife and XO of the mission. Much less important.

"Ladies and gentlemen of the board, good afternoon. I have a lot of material to cover, so let's get right to it," she said, slotted her thumb drive with her presentation, and moved to hit a button to bring up the first graphic, which did nothing, because she hadn't actually hit the button.

"Seriously?" she asked, exasperated, and mocked hitting it again.

"Problem, Director?" one of the board members asked.

"It seems my presentation won't come up. Please bear with me while I bring in a tech to handle this."

"Is that really necessary?" another asked.

"It is, I'm afraid. I'll be right back," she said, and held up her phone to show why she had to go outside.

She pushed the doors open and walked outside, putting on the best annoyed director act she could muster.

"Keep the doors open, I'll just be a minute," she said, and dialed Sergey.

He answered immediately as he was expecting her call.

"Mister Yegorovich, you assured me everything was set, but my presentation will not load. Get up here *now* and fix it," she said loudly and hung up before he could respond.

She walked back in and resumed her position.

"My apologies. Perhaps I could take a few questions while we wait for a tech from Special Projects to arrive?"

"What happened to Gustav? Why did you shoot him?" a female voice asked.

"I'll be covering that in detail in my presentation."

"Well, that's likely to be your answer to everything, so why don't we just wait," another voice said.

A few minutes later, Sergey ran into the room, huffing and puffing, out of breath.

"Sorry, Director, let me see what's going on," he said.

Annica threw up her hands. "Please do, it's only a presentation to the board of directors."

"Yes, ma'am," he said, but didn't look up from the keyboard. He typed rapidly for a moment, then stabbed a button, and the TSP logo appeared on the screen.

"There you go. Should be good now. Should I wait outside just in case?"

"Please do," Annica said and shooed him away.

"Yes, ma'am," Sergey said and left the room quickly.

Once he was out, the guards once again closed the doors.

"Let's try this again, shall we?" she asked and went to the first slide of her presentation, which was an image of the fake probe supposedly in Alpha Centauri.

"First, we'll cover the fact that you authorized the faking of a probe sighting, which put my husband and hundreds of other people's lives at risk. We'll get to the fact that I was brainwashed, mind-controlled, and forced to stay here on Earth in a few minutes."

There was mumbling as some of the directors talked amongst themselves, but Annica didn't slow down.

"You already know this, but the video you're watching was faked. A well done movie created by the Special Projects team," she said as she played the video of the probe sighting.

"Exactly why is still a mystery to me, but I'm hoping you can shed some light on that, since it couldn't have possibly been done without your knowledge or approval."

"Now listen here—" one of the board members began.

"No. *You* listen now. I'll listen to you when I'm done!" Annica said, and her anger finally showed as she pounded her hand on the podium.

"The day before this fakery emerged, I was put under a mind-control program by Gustav Malmkvist, using a program developed by Paula Handley from Special Projects. We have her in custody to find out more. Shao Yating, our CIO, is also involved in investigating that, among other things. While under his control, I left my husband, missed the mission, and apparently moved in with Gustav, which makes me sicker than you can possibly imagine."

A gasp from one female in the audience told Annica that at least someone wasn't aware that had happened.

She tapped the display to bring up booking photos of Adel Ragnarsson, Empyre, and Courtni.

"These three people were also allowed onto the ship through manipulation and, I believe, murder of one of our investigators by Gustav Malmkvist. Exactly why, we're not sure, but we'll find that out, too, as time goes on, I have no doubt.

"There are still several facts we have yet to uncover. For example, Gustav mentioned 'friends from out of town' and we're still working on who they are. Again, I'm hoping you can shed some light on that. We're also not sure why this whole fake had to happen to begin with. Mostly, that's the core of it. Why? Why any of this?

"Now, you can talk," she said.

"I believe, Director Reeves, we may need a few moments to confer, if you don't mind?"

"Of course. Just know one thing before I go. You can get rid of me. That's your right, but I'd hate to see all this go public," she said and left the room before anyone could respond.

* * *

Earth, Terran Space Project Campus, Board Room

The guards pushed the doors closed behind her, nonplussed that she'd stormed out and nearly hit them by throwing the doors open unexpectedly.

Konda immediately hugged her, and Sergey looked up expectantly from one of the seats. She was surprised to see Colonel Carey still there, leaning against a wall with his arms crossed.

"I had a feeling I wouldn't want to miss this," Carey said.

"How'd it go?" Sergey asked as he got up.

"We'll find out in a few minutes. As soon as I was done, they asked me to step out."

"Deciding how to handle you. Wouldn't you love to be a fly on the wall?" Sergey asked with a grin.

"I would, indeed," Annica said and returned the grin, feeling a bit better knowing she had people here for her.

Sergey walked over and awkwardly hugged her, only to whisper in her ear, "I caught a burst transmission when you opened the door, so no matter what, we have your presentation recorded."

She nodded as he stepped back.

"So, what now?" Konda asked.

"We wait to see if they're going to fire me or answer my questions."

"Looks like we don't have to wait long," Sergey said and pointed at the opening door to the boardroom.

"We're ready for you, Director Reeves," a man she recognized as Eugene Watson said. She'd met him before.

"Good luck," Konda said as Annica turned and went back into the boardroom.

Annica walked up to the dais as Eugene sat down and the doors closed.

"I speak for everyone when we say we're sorry you had to come to this information the way you have," Eugene said. "If anything happened to Director Malmkvist, the next director was supposed to be completely briefed on the situation. However, we understand the transition was… less than normal. We've also reviewed the report that followed you killing Director Malmkvist and find that most of us would have reacted in a similar manner. Though, admittedly, most of us wouldn't have resorted to such drastic measures."

He paused a moment to let that sink in, then continued.

"I want you to know that we had no knowledge regarding you being held back from the mission. I recall meeting you once on a visit, and I felt you and Captain Reeves were absolutely perfect for the mission, as a team. The board officially, and on the record, condemns his actions in that regard. As for the rest—well, there's a lot you don't know, and need to know, to continue the mission."

Annica raised a hand for him to stop. "Mr. Watson. Thank you for all that, but honestly, I'm going to find anything you or anyone here tells me extremely hard to believe. With your permission, I'd like to bring in the team that's been handling most of the investigation. It'll save me having to repeat everything you say."

"I understand, but that's… difficult. No one but the director and the board is supposed to know the extent of this mission."

"I'm afraid I can't agree with that stance, and I can assure you that anything you tell me will be shared with my team, which consists of Shao Yating, two members of MilForce, and a Special Projects team member. They already know more than you'd probably like, so you might as well read them in, because if you don't, I will."

She'd had enough of the lights in her face, so she opened the control panel and changed the lighting to standard room lighting. That way she could see them as well as they could see her.

"And we might as well include Colonel Carey. So, what's it going to be?"

Eugene pursed his lips, then he shrugged. "If that's the way it'll be, that's the way it'll be. Bring them in."

* * * * *

Chapter Twenty-Six

Landing + 41 Days

Mythos, Eos City, Planetary Control Center

A few hours later, Max walked into the PCC to a warm reception. Kellie noticed him first and ran from his desk to jump into his arms. He steadied himself and hugged her tightly.

The rest of the PCC noticed when she shrieked, "Max!" as she was running and all stood and clapped.

"Okay, okay, it was just my hand. Everyone, back to work," he said as he set Kellie down. "How's everything going?"

"Pretty well," Kellie said as they walked back to his desk. "Rhonda and Sadie just finished the noise canceling and turned it on. According to Annie, it's working."

"So we could see the griffins again at any time. Any risk?"

"I think Hugh has everyone mostly calmed down. There are a few who went to take out their frustration on other local wildlife, but Bernadette will certainly see some benefit from that, so we're letting it go."

Max nodded as he took his seat.

"First load from the mine is in the air and will be processed as soon as it arrives. It depends on the purity, but we're thinking at least one satellite per load, at least while the veins are rich."

"Excellent news. Sounds like I can take a vacation; you've got this covered."

"Hardly. There's still plenty you need to dig into, but nothing urgent. Mostly, I've just let people do their jobs."

"One of the top lessons of leadership. Let the people who know what they're doing do what they do."

"They're back," said Casper Kracht, who was taking a shift monitoring the surveillance cameras.

"Could you be more specific, Sergeant?" Max asked.

"The griffins sir, they're hovering above the tree line like they're waiting for something."

"Waiting to be sure no one's going to kill them," Kellie suggested.

"Probably not far from the truth," Max agreed. "Do me a favor, find out in person if Leopold is up to coming out? I'd like to get this communication effort going ASAP, and he's the key to explaining it to them."

"You got it," Kellie said and left the PCC.

"Annie, notify the team that's been assigned to the communication with griffins to report to the park, please."

"*Of course, Max. Good to have you back in command. Kellie did well filling in, but you are the true leader.*"

"Um… thanks, Annie."

Max frowned slightly. That just didn't seem like Annie. She'd always acted a bit protective of Max, which had to be in the programming, but something didn't feel right about the slight against Kellie. The words were right, but the way Annie's voice had sounded said something different.

"Sir, one of the griffins is holding something in its talons. Can't get a good look, but it's definitely clutching something."

"Shit… okay. Sergeant, have Essena meet me out at the park, please. No emergency, but I'd like her handy."

"Yes, sir!"

* * *

Mythos, Eos City

Max stood and walked out of the PCC, hoping there was about to be another positive interaction for Eos and its people. On the way, several people stopped and greeted him, expressing their relief to see him out of the hospital. It was nice to be appreciated, but he had a singular focus, and that was making sure there wouldn't be a fight between humans and griffins right here in the city.

On instinct, he looked at the guns on *Traveler*, which were up and ready in case there was an attack by something they hadn't seen yet. Several of them were trained on the griffins hovering just outside what they considered the controlled zone.

"Annie, turn the guns up."

"*I am protecting your people, Max.*"

"They're not my people, I'm just in charge at the moment, and I don't feel they are in danger, so turn the guns away. Now."

"*As you wish,*" she said, sounding annoyed through the radio clipped to his belt.

It took longer than it should have, but the guns finally turned—marginally—away from the griffins. Max sighed and rolled his eyes, not wanting to deal with it at the moment. Instead, he stopped short of the park area and looked toward the hospital, where Kellie had emerged, accompanied by Leopold and Sergeant Jana Nováková. She seemed more like a mother hen than MilForce as she tried to support Leopold, apparently against his wishes.

A group of people carrying tablets walked toward him from *Traveler.*

"Captain Reeves, I'm Jaylee Conway. You probably don't remember, but—"

"One of our ufologists. You believe you found and decrypted alien markings on the Moon. I figured you'd be working on transcribing the book from the alien craft," Max said with a smile.

"You remember me? Wow. Um. Anyway, I'm working on that, but this was too good to pass up! I mean, books are great—who doesn't love books? But working with a real life griffin?"

"I understand completely," Max said, trying to hide his amusement.

"You think I'm silly."

"No, I think you're passionate, but you need to understand, these things can be dangerous."

"This whole mission is dangerous," she said and shrugged. "I heard what they did to your hand, and honestly, that was your fault."

Max raised an eyebrow. She wasn't wrong, but someone willing to actually say it was refreshing, to a point.

"You figured out something was bothering them, then shoved it in their face? I'd probably hit you, too."

He couldn't stop the grin from forming on his face.

"If you want me to leave, I understand. I have a tendency of saying what I think."

"No, Jaylee, I think you're in the right place. I remember reading your file before approving you for the mission. You were fairly critical of some of the policies we had in place, and some of them were actually changed a bit because of your ideas."

"Wow. Cool. When do we get started?"

"As soon as we convince them we're not going to kill them. Stand by, we'll let you know," Max said and walked over to meet Leopold as he approached.

"Leopold, good to see you up and moving around."

"Against doctor's recommendation, but I couldn't let you handle this on your own. Hopefully seeing me will let them know it's okay. Let's go to their preferred spot in the grass," he said and led the way, leaning on Jana a bit more than he'd like to, Max thought.

"We appreciate it, Leopold, and I want you back in the hospital as soon as this is handled," Max said. "We have a team on standby, ready to get started, but I want you to explain to the griffins that we want to learn to talk to them and help them communicate better with us."

"Gotcha. I reckon I can handle that."

Once they reached the spot where the griffins liked to lay down, Leopold waved to them.

Max and Kellie stayed back a bit to let Leopold do his thing, with Jana supporting him. Out of the corner of his eye, he saw Essena sitting on a park bench with a rifle in her lap. Apparently, she was learning that Max didn't like hovering, but he did want cover, so she was providing it from a distance. Then he realized the only reason she was doing that was that Jana was right there as well.

The griffin they thought of as the leader swooped down first and landed in front of Leopold, while the others remained where they were. Leopold pointed back at Max, then wiggled his fingers, probably explaining to the griffin that Max was fine. To support Leopold,

Max waved his right hand, then gave a thumbs up, which he felt silly for, because he was sure the griffin would have no idea what that meant. For now.

The griffin fixed Max in his gaze, then chattered at Leopold for a moment, then looked back to Max.

"I think he wants you up here, Max."

"Max... I don't know about this," Kellie said.

"It'll be fine, or Essena will put a bullet in all of them before they can blink," he said under his breath.

Feeling no small bit of trepidation, Max walked forward and pasted a smile on his face. He'd thought he'd be okay with it, but he could feel the nerves as he got closer to the griffin. When he got to Leopold's side, he held out his right hand, and the griffin leaned in to examine it.

Max fought the instinct to flinch back and held steady under the examination.

The griffin looked, confused—if anything—as it tilted its head and looked at Max.

After a moment, it seemed to accept that Max was indeed okay, and turned to screech toward the other griffins. Max thought it might be his imagination, but it seemed quieter than previous times he'd heard it. Maybe they'd realized that the sounds they made could hurt the humans. It seemed farfetched, but if it was true...

The other two griffins came in to land, and the one who'd injured Max was indeed carrying something in one talon. It slowly extended the talon and released what it was holding. Everyone's jaw dropped when they saw them.

"Are those..." Max began but couldn't finish.

"Weapons," Jana said, "and not ours."

"Some kind of apology?" Max asked.

"I reckon so, since he's the one who was carrying 'em. Maybe even some kind of symbol that he was carrying 'em in the talon he used to rake you. Could have been punishment, not being able to use it while he was carrying the things."

Max triggered his radio. "Essena, we're going to need you up here. Now. Something you need to see."

He knelt down to examine them without touching them. There were three rifles, one of them in pieces, but it appeared to be all there. The stocks were unusually long, far too long for a human to use.

"Son of a bitch… that's it," he said.

"Sorry?" Leopold asked.

"The weapons, I bet they belonged to the aliens from that ship. Maybe that's why they were stuck on the ship. The griffins cornered them. I wonder if there were more than those we found at some point. That never made sense to me, why they were on the ship. This could explain it."

"I reckon I'd be afraid to go out if they were pissed at me."

"Yeah, me, too," Max said. "Especially if they'd taken my weapons."

Essena walked up. She hadn't run, but it had been a near thing.

"Where did these come from?" she asked immediately as she knelt beside Max.

"They brought them in. I'm thinking the aliens."

"Dimensions make sense. Longer arms, longer stock. We will want to check these out. Carefully."

"Agreed. Let's get something to store and transport them in, but I don't want them on *Traveler*."

"Yes. Will set up out on edge of city," Essena said and got on her radio to get what she needed as she walked away.

"Well, if this was an apology, I accept," Max said and stood.

He nodded his head at the griffin who'd injured him. That was one bit of body language they apparently understood.

"Now, let's get the team to work on communication."

* * *

Mythos, Eos City, Planetary Control Center

With the team starting its work with the griffins, and Leopold safely back in the hospital, Max walked back into the PCC with Kellie.

"Well, I feel like we know why the aliens were on the ship now," Max said as he sat down.

"Maybe," she said and sat in the second chair that was always present now.

"Hopefully we can find out more if the communications team can make some progress."

"That would be nice. Can you imagine just carrying on a conversation with them? How much they could teach us about the planet?"

Max nodded. He could indeed imagine. Right now, though, his thoughts were on the weapons. It wasn't a shock that another race with the technology of space flight would have weapons, but why so few, and why hadn't they found any more on the ship? Of course, there were several compartments they hadn't been able to open yet, plus some they might not have found. Some of the doors were powered and couldn't be opened.

"How are we on the hoist, again?" he asked now that he was thinking about the ship.

"It's ready when you are."

"Captain, I'm getting a weak communication signal; I can't quite make it out."

"Problem at the mining site?" Max asked urgently.

"Um, no sir, it's not coming from the mining site. Actually, it's not coming from the *planet.*"

"Could you be more vague?" Kellie asked.

"It's coming from space."

"*The tone from the alien craft has stopped, Max,*" Annie said suddenly.

"Shit. There's more of them," Max said.

"And they're on the way. The signal's getting stronger by the minute."

* * * * *

Chapter Twenty-Seven

Earth, Terran Space Project Campus, Board Room

Konda, Anton, Sergey, and Colonel Carey were the first to arrive, as they'd all been standing in the ante-room, anyway. Konda and Anton fetched chairs from a storage room for everyone to sit, and a table meant for extra work-space was set up in an open corner of the room. Shao arrived a few moments later and took a seat as well.

"Well, we're all here," Annica said. "The floor is yours."

Eugene nodded. "For those of you who don't know, I'm Eugene Watson, president and CEO of Watson Aerospace. I was one of the first backers and founding members of the Terran Space Project and, to my knowledge, I'm still the primary backer."

"No one's taking that title away from you, Eugene," said a female Annica recognized as Elissa Gray, president and CEO of Gray Industries, an aerospace contractor.

There was some chuckling at that, though a few others seemed a bit put out.

"Anyway, with that being the case, I also probably know more of the whole picture from memory. We'll start with one thing you probably dismissed, but which is the root of most of what we're doing here. The 'friends from out of town' are more important than you alluded to. Put simply, they're aliens."

317

"Told you," Sergey said.

"You figured it out?" Eugene asked, interested.

"Aliens?" Annica asked.

"Well, I saw that movie, whatever it was," Sergey said with a shrug. "It was a shot in the dark."

Eugene grinned. "That's where I got the idea. Smart kid. Anyway, yes, aliens. Beings from another world. Another galaxy, as it happens. I won't go into the whole origin story, but let's just say, we've made contact. Several years ago, in fact."

"Wait. Hold on. How is that possible? The press would have gotten word of it. The military would have been given orders. *Nothing* is that good a secret," Colonel Shaw said.

"This is," Eugene said simply. "A few world leaders know; they tell those who take over from them, if someone does, and that's it. Everyone who knows understands the global panic that would ensue if word got out, especially considering the fact that they can come here, but we can't go there. Yet. *Traveler* is the first piece of that puzzle."

"So, basically, everything else was a smoke screen for this?" Annica asked.

"Yes. I can tell you, you were *supposed* to be on the mission. I can't tell you how pissed I was when I found out you were still here."

"And if I'd known what he'd done, I'd have killed him if you hadn't," Elissa added.

"And the criminals they sent on the ship?" Sergey asked.

Eugene shrugged. "We had nothing to do with that. This mission is vital to the future of the human race. There are literally *hundreds* of habitable planets out there, unclaimed and uninhabited, according to our friends. We wouldn't want anything to endanger that. From what you've told us, I believe Gustav had his own agenda, and it didn't completely jibe with ours."

"What *is* your agenda?" Annica asked. "The people here at TSP are good people. We're here for this mission and the ones to follow. Why not tell us? Why not tell those of us who were a part of the Wormhole Traversal Project?"

"That may have been a mistake. If all had gone to plan, Gustav left a message that would open automatically for Captain Reeves after wormhole transit that explained everything, as well as giving him the blueprint for a satellite that would allow communication with Earth through the wormhole. I assume no such communication has been received, based on your efforts."

"No, nothing," Annica said, deflated.

Eugene sighed and rubbed his eyes.

"This could be bad," said Kevin Walsh, another board member.

"That's an understatement," Elissa said.

"Once I'm out of this communication black hole of a room, I'll send you what you should've received when you took over, Director Reeves. It's a full download on the project, the aliens, and everything you need to know to facilitate communications. But unless they build that satellite…"

"They're isolated," Annica finished for him.

"Exactly, and that's bad. Our friends will expect *Traveler* to be expecting them."

"So do they have a name?" Shaw asked.

"They just refer to themselves as friends. And, by the way, they speak perfect English. They've been intercepting our communications for years, and English is the one they picked up on, though they speak others as well."

"But if they're in another galaxy, the waves wouldn't have had time to reach them," Sergey said.

"They would if our friends have more local satellites, placed through a wormhole," said Elizabeth Byrne Lodell, president and CEO of Found in Space Communication. "There are so many satellites in orbit, they've been able to place their own, and everyone just assumes they're someone else's. It was actually my people who found them and started digging, then we worked with Eugene's people when they had some special needs. One thing led to another and... here we are."

"So they weren't ready to make contact until we found them?" Annica asked.

"The way it was explained to me, it was something of a test," Eugene explained. "We passed, so we were chosen. We agreed to keep their secret. In exchange, they provided certain... technologies. They want to meet others, just like we do."

"What are their motivations?" Carey asked. "Obviously, they're far superior to us in tech, so what do they have to gain?"

"I'm still asking myself that, Colonel Carey," Eugene answered, "but I couldn't pass up the opportunity. The way they explain it, they're simply interested, and something they said struck true to me. Even in the vastness of space—especially in the vastness of space—it's good to have friends. Honestly, they aren't that far ahead of us, the way they tell it. They just happened to have an open wormhole near them they were able to study, so they learned about it. The one near us is basically a pinpoint, and very well hidden, so it was nearly impossible to study and learn from until it was pointed out to us."

"So now that we know about the wormhole, how are they getting in and out undetected?" Sergey asked.

"They aren't," Elizabeth said. "We simply aren't telling anyone. Found in Space owns all the satellites that monitor the wormhole, so it's easy to just filter out their signals."

"So it's a global, corporate conspiracy to hide the fact that there are aliens," Shao said to sum things up.

"Cynical, but accurate," Elissa said.

Annica leaned back in her chair, suddenly exhausted. She'd imagined all sorts of scenarios, but this one had never come up. Aliens. There were *aliens*. The cover-up explained everything, except Gustav's motivations for the moves he'd taken, apparently on his own.

"So, no one here knows why I was kept here, or why he put criminals on *Traveler* with my husband?" she asked, pleading.

Silence was her answer.

"I don't know, Director Reeves," Elizabeth said compassionately, "but I promise you, I'll help you find out."

"Agreed," Eugene said. "I'll reach out to our friends and find out if there was any extra communication we weren't aware of with Gustav."

"There wasn't," Elizabeth said without doubt. "I'd know."

"Still, it can't hurt to check," Eugene said. "Besides, I need to let them know there's a chance *Traveler* isn't expecting them. That could be... awkward."

"What if they found a different planet?" Elissa asked.

"Gods, I hadn't thought of that."

"Different planet?" Annica asked.

"Part of the download Captain Reeves should have received was directions to a planet to meet our friends. It's habitable, and frankly beautiful. There should have been a delegation there ready to receive them when they landed."

"So, Max could be in a different place? Or could have found them and thought they were dangerous? Or vice versa?"

"At this point, anything's possible, I'm afraid."

"What about Annie?" Elizabeth said. "She should have the data, as well."

"True. He was supposed to implant that just before *Traveler* departed."

"We know the core was sent to him," Konda said. "We got that out of one of the techs."

"Good," Eugene said. "Hopefully he at least did that right."

"All this could've been avoided if we'd been briefed before the mission departed," Annica said and stood. "Don't think coming clean now absolves you of anything. As far as I'm concerned, all this secret keeping has cost me, personally, quite a bit, and I don't forgive or forget easily."

"Director Reeves, I can't begin to understand what you've gone through. What you're *still* going through. But you must understand that we didn't—" Elissa began.

"I don't have to do a damn thing other than find my husband!" Annica said and stormed out of the boardroom.

* * *

Earth, Terran Space Project Campus, Board Room

"Is there anything else you can tell us that might help us?" Shao asked.

"We'll open everything to you… and we'll answer any questions you have. But honestly, I can't think of anything specific. We've told you everything except the technical details, which will take hours."

"I have the time," Shao said. "Sergey, I'd like you to remain as well. Colonel Carey, your choice, but you'll likely get bored. Captain Sanako, Sergeant Essen, please make sure Annica doesn't do anything... rash," she said and gave them a knowing look.

"Shit. Right," Konda said and dashed out of the room, with Anton on her heels.

"I think I'd better find out what the hell is going on," Carey said and followed them out of the room.

"What exactly *is* going on, Ms. Yating?" Eugene asked.

"I'm afraid I'll have to leave that to Director Reeves, Mr. Watson. We have some secrets of our own, you see. Now, you said technical details. Mr. Yegorovich here and I are techs, so we're all ears."

"What do you want to know?"

"I think we're in one of those 'we don't know what we don't know' situations, so let's focus on *Traveler* and what we can do to reach them."

# # # # #

About the Author

Alex Rath is a best-selling Military Science Fiction and Post-Apocalyptic author, currently residing in Columbia, South Carolina, with his wife and daughter.

With works published in the Four Horsemen Universe, This Fallen World, and the Salvage Title universe, Alex has now spread out with his own Colonization Science Fiction with the Terran Space Project, starting with "Seeds of Terra."

By day, Alex is an IT professional, and has been for 25+ years. He has worked as a programmer/developer, webmaster, information security specialist, and solutions design specialist. This background allows him to incorporate some technical savvy into his stories, while his experience interacting with non-technical customers allows him to do so in a way that isn't confusing, or 'too technical' for a layperson to understand.

* * * * *

Get the **free** Four Horsemen prelude story "**Shattered Crucible**"

and discover other titles by Theogony Books at:

http://chriskennedypublishing.com/

* * * * *

Meet the author and other CKP authors on the Factory Floor:

https://www.facebook.com/groups/461794864654198

* * * * *

Did you like this book?
Please write a review!

* * * * *

The following is an
Excerpt from Book One of the Lunar Free State:

The Moon and Beyond

John E. Siers

Available from Theogony Books

eBook, Audio, and Paperback

Excerpt from "The Moon and Beyond:"

"So, what have we got?" The chief had no patience for inter-agency squabbles.

The FBI man turned to him with a scowl. "We've got some abandoned buildings, a lot of abandoned stuff—none of which has anything to do with spaceships—and about a hundred and sixty scientists, maintenance people, and dependents left behind, all of whom claim they knew nothing at all about what was really going on until today. Oh, yeah, and we have some stripped computer hardware with all memory and processor sections removed. I mean physically taken out, not a chip left, nothing for the techies to work with. And not a scrap of paper around that will give us any more information...at least, not that we've found so far. My people are still looking."

"What about that underground complex on the other side of the hill?"

"That place is wiped out. It looks like somebody set off a *nuke* in there. The concrete walls are partly fused! The floor is still too hot to walk on. Our people say they aren't sure how you could even *do* something like that. They're working on it, but I doubt they're going to find anything."

"What about our man inside, the guy who set up the computer tap?"

"Not a trace, chief," one of the NSA men said. "Either he managed to keep his cover and stayed with them, or they're holding him prisoner, or else..." The agent shrugged.

"You think they terminated him?" The chief lifted an eyebrow. "A bunch of rocket scientists?"

"Wouldn't put it past them. Look at what Homeland Security ran into. Those motion-sensing chain guns are *nasty*, and the area between the inner and outer perimeter fence is mined! Of course, they posted warning signs, even marked the fire zones for the guns. Nobody would have gotten hurt if the troops had taken the signs seriously."

The Homeland Security colonel favored the NSA man with an icy look. "That's bullshit. How did we know they weren't bluffing? You'd feel pretty stupid if we'd played it safe and then found out there were no defenses, just a bunch of signs!"

"Forget it!" snarled the chief. "Their whole purpose was to delay us, and it worked. What about the Air Force?"

"It might as well have been a UFO sighting as far as they're concerned. Two of their F-25s went after that spaceship, or whatever it was we saw leaving. The damned thing went straight up, over eighty thousand meters per minute, they say. That's nearly Mach Two, in a *vertical climb*. No aircraft in *anybody's* arsenal can sustain a climb like that. Thirty seconds after they picked it up, it was well above their service ceiling and still accelerating. Ordinary ground radar couldn't find it, but NORAD *thinks* they might have caught a short glimpse with one of their satellite-watch systems, a hundred miles up and still going."

"So where did they go?"

"Well, chief, if we believe what those leftover scientists are telling us, I guess they went to the Moon."

* * * * *

Get "The Moon and Beyond" here:
https://www.amazon.com/dp/B097QMN7PJ.

Find out more about John E. Siers at:
https://chriskennedypublishing.com.

* * * * *

The following is an

Excerpt from Book One of The Combined Service:

The Magnetar

Jo Boone

Available from Theogony Books

eBook and Paperback

Excerpt from "The Magnetar:"

Chalk felt the inertial shift even through his suit. Every warning the *Magnetar* possessed went red, bright terrible red, on every display. They had minutes, maybe less, before the ship's structural integrity began to fail from the damaged areas outward, possibly in ways they could not stop. On the tactical display, Sasskiek's analysts had added acceleration arcs that showed when the scout ships would be able to engage their gravitic drives and another arc that showed the *Magnetar's* own projected course and location. Underneath that was the faint gray line that no spacer ever crossed, showing where the minimum safe distance would be for the *Magnetar* when the two scout ships engaged their drives.

They might make it.

If the remaining reactors held. If the *Magnetar* didn't go to pieces first.

If Gabbro didn't miss.

"How close?" Chalk said. Too far, and the scout ships could easily evade or counter the *Magnetar's* offensive barrage. Too close, and they risked doing themselves more harm—but that might be better than letting the scout ships engage their drives.

"Adjusting firing solutions now," Gabbro replied, battle-calm.

"Five more ships approaching," Sasskiek reported. The ships appeared as uncertain yellow diamonds on the tactical display. "Lead ship is Terran configuration, gaseous atmosphere, two-four-zero rotation two-one-zero, four hundred million kilometers. Four trailing ships have octopod configurations, seawater atmosphere, pursuit course."

Friend or foe? Chalk wondered, but he could not address it now. Two minutes from now, it might not matter anyway.

The *Magnetar* and the scout ships were closing on each other rapidly.

"Three hundred thousand kilometers," Sasskiek reported. "Two hundred fifty thousand kilometers."

He counted it down slowly, while Lieutenant Rose at the helm and St. Clair in engineering pushed the ship for all it could give; pushed for that green curve that represented safety—at least, from one of the hazards they faced.

Chalk sat on the edge of his chair. The orders were given. Nothing he could say now would change the outcome.

Was it enough?

He hated the helplessness; it came with a wave of despair, a preemptive surge of grief for the failure that had not yet come.

He would not be able to mourn afterward.

But he did not dare give in to it now.

His hands clenched around the arms of his chair.

"One hundred thousand kilometers," Sasskiek reported. Maximum effective weapons distance. "Fifty thousand. They're firing."

* * * * *

Get "The Magnetar" now at:
https://www.amazon.com/dp/B09QC78PLJ/.

Find out more about Jo Boone at:
https://chriskennedypublishing.com.

* * * * *

The following is an

Excerpt from Book One of This Fine Crew:

The Signal Out of Space

_____

Mike Jack Stoumbos

Now Available from Theogony Books

eBook and Paperback

Excerpt from "The Signal Out of Space:"

Day 4 of Training, Olympus Mons Academy

I want to make something clear from square one: we were winning.

More importantly, *I* was winning. Sure, the whole thing was meant to be a "team effort," and I'd never say this to an academy instructor, but the fact of the matter is this: it was a race and I was in the driver's seat. Like hell I was going to let any other team beat us, experimental squad or not.

At our velocity, even the low planetary grav didn't temper the impact of each ice mogul on the glistening red terrain. We rocketed up, plummeted down, and cut new trails in the geo-formations, spraying orange ice and surface rust in our wake. So much of the red planet was still like a fresh sheet of snow, and I was eager to carve every inch of it.

Checking on the rest of the crew, I thought our tactical cadet was going to lose her lunch. I had no idea how the rest of the group was managing, different species being what they are.

Of our complement of five souls, sans AI-assist or anything else that cadets should learn to live without, Shin and I were the only Humans. The communications cadet was a Teek—all exoskeleton and antennae, but the closest to familiar. He sat in the copilot seat, ready to take the controls if I had to tap out. His two primary arms were busy with the scanning equipment, but one of his secondary hands hovered over the E-brake, which made me more anxious than assured.

I could hear the reptile humming in the seat behind me, in what I registered as "thrill," each time I overcame a terrain obstacle with even greater speed, rather than erring on the side of caution.

Rushing along the ice hills of Mars on six beautifully balanced wheels was a giant step up from the simulator. The design of the Red Terrain Vehicle was pristine, but academy-contrived obstacles mixed with natural formations bumped up the challenge factor. The dummy fire sounds from our sensors and our mounted cannon only added to the sense of adventure. The whole thing was like fulfilling a fantasy, greater than my first jet around good ol' Luna. If the camera evidence had survived, I bet I would have been grinning like an idiot right up until the Teek got the bogey signal.

"Cadet Lidstrom," the Teek said, fast but formal through his clicking mandibles, "unidentified signal fifteen degrees right of heading." His large eyes pulsed with green luminescence, bright enough for me to see in the corner of my vision. It was an eerie way to express emotion, which I imagined would make them terrible at poker.

I hardly had a chance to look at the data while maintaining breakneck KPH, but in the distance, it appeared to be one of our surface vehicles, all six wheels turned up to the stars.

The lizard hummed a different note and spoke in strongly accented English, "Do we have time to check?"

The big furry one at the rear gruffed in reply, but not in any language I could understand.

"Maybe it's part of the test," I suggested. "Like a bonus. Paul, was it hard to find?"

The Teek, who went by Paul, clicked to himself and considered the question. His exoskeletal fingers worked furiously for maybe a second before he informed us, "It is obscured by interference."

"Sounds like a bonus to me," Shin said. Then she asked me just the right question: "Lidstrom, can you get us close without losing our lead?"

The Arteevee would have answered for me if it could, casting an arc of red debris as I swerved. I admit, I did not run any mental calculations, but a quick glance at my rear sensors assured me. "Hell yeah! I got this."

In the mirror, I saw our large, hairy squadmate, the P'rukktah, transitioning to the grappler interface, in case we needed to pick something up when we got there. Shin, on tactical, laid down some cannon fire behind us—tiny, non-lethal silicon scattershot—to kick up enough dust that even the closest pursuer would lose our visual heading for a few seconds at least. I did not get a chance to find out what the reptile was doing as we neared the overturned vehicle.

I had maybe another half-k to go when Paul's eyes suddenly shifted to shallow blue and his jaw clicked wildly. He only managed one English word: "Peculiar!"

Before I could ask, I was overcome with a sound, a voice, a shrill screech. I shut my eyes for an instant, then opened them to see where I was driving and the rest of my squad, but everything was awash in some kind of blue light. If I thought it would do any good, I might have tried to plug my ears.

Paul didn't have the luxury of closing his compound eyes, but his primary arms tried to block them. His hands instinctively guarded his antennae.

Shin half fell from the pivoting cannon rig, both palms cupping her ears, which told me the sound wasn't just in my head.

The reptile bared teeth in a manner too predatory to be a smile and a rattling hum escaped her throat, dissonant to the sound.

Only the P'rukktah weathered this unexpected cacophony with grace. She stretched out clearly muscled arms and grabbed anchor points on either side of the vehicle. In blocky computer-generated words, her translator pulsed out, "What—Is—That?"

Facing forward again, I was able to see the signs of wreckage ahead and of distressed ground. I think I was about to ask if I should turn away when the choice was taken from me.

An explosion beneath our vehicle heaved us upward, nose first. Though nearly bucked out of my seat, I was prepared to recover our heading or even to stop and assess what had felt like a bomb.

A second blast, larger than the first, pushed us from behind, probably just off my right rear wheel, spraying more particulates and lifting us again.

One screech was replaced with another. Where the first had been almost organic, this new one was clearly the sound of tearing metal.

The safety belt caught my collarbone hard as my body tried to torque out of the seat. Keeping my eyes open, I saw one of our tires—maybe two thirds of a tire—whip off into the distance on a strange trajectory, made even stranger by the fact that the horizon was spinning.

The red planet came at the windshield and the vehicle was wrenched enough to break a seal. I barely noticed the sudden escape of air; I was too busy trying, futilely, to drive the now upside-down craft…

* * * * *

Get "The Signal Out of Space" now at:
https://www.amazon.com/dp/B09N8VHGFP.

Find out more about Mike Jack Stoumbos and "The Signal Out of Space" at: https://chriskennedypublishing.com.

* * * * *